TRUSTING LUCK

A KIMBELL TEXAS SWEET ROMANCE
BOOK TWO

ANGEL S. VANE

BONZAIMOON BOOKS

BONZAI
MOON

BonzaiMoon Books LLC
Houston, Texas
www.bonzaimoonbooks.com

CHAPTER 1

R*ONAN*

~

"Please tell me you told them no," Connor, my twin brother, says, giving me a stern look as we reach the low white fence that marks the back entrance to Bell Park. His dark blue scrubs are wrinkled from working all night. Even though I know he wants to pass out, he never misses a chance to walk with me as I take his nephews to daycare on the days of my shift at the fire station. It's one of the few times we see each other with our busy schedules.

Wide oak trees with thick trunks and long branches dot the perimeter. Sunrise is about thirty minutes away and the brightening sky is a cool, dark blue. The lights of the gazebo cast a faint glow over us as we cross the lush, green lawn.

I glance down at my sons, deep asleep, as I carry one boy in each arm. The days of me doing this are numbered. In fact, if I was a smaller man, they'd already be too big for the task.

They'll have my size and strength when they get older. At four years old, they're almost four feet tall and weigh a healthy fifty pounds each.

They are the most beautiful boys in the world with olive skin, black hair and faces like their mother. But they have the slate-blue eyes that run in the O'Reilly family.

Like mine. Like my brother, Connor's.

Just hope that's all I passed on to them. I wouldn't wish my lousy luck in relationships on my worst enemy. Definitely not something I want the two people I love most in this world to deal with. I push those thoughts away. I'm decades from seeing how that plays out. No need to worry about that now.

Connor stares at me, waiting for a response.

I shake my head. "Have you met my sons, Finnegan and Declan? When do they take no for an answer? They badger and plead and beg and demand until they get their way. Of course, I let them watch the video."

The latest music video release of rising musical talent, Nikki Dart, had dropped this week. The song, Playground Love, was blazing up the Billboard charts and could hit the top ten.

The ladies at the daycare were careless enough to allow my boys to see a glimpse of it. The boys had begged me to watch it when they got home.

I gave in and my sons were up most of the night in tears. I kiss each of them, then try to ignore my brother and the lecture I know is coming.

"How many times do I need to tell you that limiting their interaction with their mother, if you can call her that, is what's best for them? It's bad enough every time you let them visit Georgia, she tries to manipulate them into thinking Nikki is misunderstood and actually loves them."

The only reason my sons know anything about their mother is because of their granny, Georgia. The woman practically has a shrine to Nikki in her house and does everything she can to stop my sons from forgetting her. To stop all of us from forgetting her, even though that's all I want to do.

"So, what happened?" Connor demands, walking next to me.

"Epic disaster. I tried to explain that a music video is make believe, but they weren't buying it," I say, as my chest tightens from the memories. How do you respond to your kids asking why their mommy looks so happy without them? When they asked what they'd done that made her not want to know them, I couldn't stop pure fury from pulsing through my body.

"Hard to watch Nikki singing and dancing with other kids in the park and not feel like she's happier without them," Connor says, shaking his head.

"When did you watch the video?" I raise an eyebrow at him.

"One nurse had it pulled up on the computer. Trust me, I wasn't out there searching for it," Connor says, then gives me the look again. "What did you think of it?"

"The video?"

"Yeah."

"Didn't watch it," I admit. "I sat the boys at the kitchen table, turned the laptop toward them and pressed play. The only thing that mattered to me was their reactions, not what Nikki was doing."

"Good," Connor says, venom dripping from his tone. He'd never been a fan of Nikki, going so far as to try to kidnap me the night before she and I snuck off to Vegas to elope. Sometimes I wish he'd have succeeded.

"Why is that good?"

"Because you're still not over her. Seeing that video would've hurt you just as much as it hurt your sons," Connor says, then grips the back of my neck.

"You seriously think I still have feelings for Nikki?" We trudge across the manicured lawn. A miniature windmill turns, creaking as a slight breeze blows. "You know me better than that."

"Exactly." Connor points a finger at me. "You're not sure how you feel about the mother of your sons after all this time. That's the problem."

I ignore my twin and increase my pace. I want to tell him he's dead wrong, but I can't. When Nikki walked out on our marriage, abandoning me with nine-month-old twin sons, I was furious, bitter and devastated.

She was the love of my life and I thought I was hers.

Truth was, I came a very distant second to her first love—music.

Everyone knew it and deep down, I guess I did, too.

It was just a matter of time before the muse came calling and Nikki was gone to make her dreams of becoming a pop singer a reality.

She wasn't satisfied with our family, the boys and me. She wanted to be the next Taylor Swift with adoring fans and a collection of music awards.

It didn't matter that she had a husband who adored her more than any stranger could. She wanted out. I just never expected that she'd move back to London.

As the months turned into years, my anger at Nikki grew. The last time she saw her sons, they could barely crawl. Now they are walking and talking with their own unique, and at times exasperating, personalities. She doesn't know the amazing little boys they've become.

Sending a courier to deliver divorce papers to me over a year ago was the last straw. She was a coward for walking out on her family in the middle of the night and a bigger one for not telling me to my face that she wanted a divorce. The document didn't ask for visitation rights to see the boys. It's like they didn't matter. Didn't exist.

And that's the reason that my brother is right.

I don't know if I'm still holding a torch for her or not because I can't feel anything but my rage at her for robbing my sons of having a mother. She's not here to see their longing gazes as the other kids are picked up from daycare by their moms. It breaks my heart every time.

"There's no problem," I insist. The muscles in my jaw clench. "What Nikki and I had is over. I want her to wake up and realize her sons are worth getting to know. This is only going to get harder for them if she doesn't."

"She lost the right to have a place in their lives. She doesn't deserve those little boys."

"Think about it, brother. My sons are getting older. They're going to find her on social media and on the covers of magazines. Watch her interviews on television. Hear her songs on the radio. I can't shield them from that. The best thing would be if Nikki tries to be a mother to them before then."

Connor would love nothing more than for me to turn Nikki into a villain for the boys. To make her a woman they never want to have a relationship with, but I can't do that.

"You're crazy if you think that's going to happen," Connor scoffs. "She's too selfish to think about anybody but herself."

"I'm only letting you talk like this because Finnegan and Declan are still sleeping," I say, a warning in my tone. "Don't say those things in front of them. Ever. You understand me?"

Connor raises his hands in mock surrender, but there's a challenge in his gaze and I don't like it. He stops at the entrance to the daycare and opens the door for us.

As I pass him, he says, "All three of you are better off without her. You need to remember that."

Before I can reprimand him, he pivots and walks back along the sidewalk toward the parking lot.

"Was that Uncle Connor?" Finnegan asks, rubbing his eyes with the back of a snot covered hand.

"Yes it was buddy," I say, then lower him to the ground.

"Why didn't you wake us up, Daddy? We want to talk to Uncle Connor," Declan whimpers as I place him next to his brother.

The twins are adorable in their matching Elmo pajamas. Identical frowns crease their foreheads as they show me their displeasure. Even though they are fraternal twins, like me and Connor, they have the dubious distinction of looking nearly identical, unlike me and my brother. The only way to tell them apart is to get them talking—

Declan's dimples mirror his mother's, while Finnegan doesn't have dimples at all.

"Hey Ronan," a soft, feminine voice floats from behind me.

I turn around to see Tiffany Stafford, the owner of the daycare, standing with her hands on her hips. She's wearing a t-shirt and leggings with her chestnut brown hair pulled into a high swinging ponytail. She smiles at my boys, then looks up at me with undisguised desire.

"Hey Tiff." I cringe, regretting the one time I succumbed to my loneliness and hooked up with her. She's been trying to rekindle that flame ever since, but the truth is she caught me in a moment of weakness a year ago. The day Nikki served me with divorce papers.

A twinge of guilt pricks me for not being interested in her. She's a sweet girl and cute, but in a forgettable way. When she admitted to having a crush on me for years, I should've taken that as a sign to steer clear of her, especially since I felt no spark between us. And it has nothing to do with Nikki like Connor and most people in this town think.

I'm not opposed to starting a relationship ... with the right woman. I have a long history of choosing the wrong ones. The next time I commit to someone, I won't make the same old mistakes. The stakes are too high now that I have my sons.

But when do I have time to date?

Being a father takes up every second of time I have when I'm not working or at the gym.

Tiffany stands next to me and asks, "Now, why are the two of you angry at your daddy?"

Instinctively, I cross my arms over my chest and try not to give her any attention that she could misread.

"Daddy didn't let us say bye-bye to Uncle Connor," the twins whine in unison. It still shocks me how they can do that with no prompting or planning. They are completely in sync.

"Well, there are donuts in the kitchen that might make y'all feel better," she says.

My sons' faces light up and they turn to me. Declan asks, "Can we get a donut, Daddy?"

"Please!" Finnegan adds.

"Just one," I say, then holler after them. "Don't run. Walk to the kitchen."

"They got over that pretty easy." She bumps her hip against my thigh.

"That's how they are." I ignore her subtle flirting and keep my tone even and professional.

"Will they be here overnight, or is Connor coming to pick them up?"

"Overnight." I slip the credit card out of my pocket and hand it to Tiffany. The cost of daycare for two boys is already expensive. Paying for overnight care for the nights I'm on the schedule is down right exorbitant.

But what other choice do I have?

Tiffany swipes the card. "Too bad. I was hoping we could grab dinner later."

"Not a good idea," I say slowly.

Her face falls, but she nods. "Anyway, I've gotten some new complaints from the other parents about the twins."

"More complaints?" I groan under my breath. I swear, some of these parents are too sensitive. Kids need to be allowed to be kids. Have fun and yes, make some mistakes.

"Seems that they've been practicing wrestling moves on other kids when we're not looking. One little boy claims they body slammed him."

I wince with a pang of guilt. This was one hundred percent my fault. "Any injuries?"

"Not this time."

"It won't happen again." I must do a better job of filtering what the boys watch. No more UFC and WWE. It'll be public television from now on.

"I hope not or I might have to take drastic action, even though I don't want to do that to them," Tiffany says. She rubs a hand down my arm. "Or you."

The last thing I need is for the boys to be kicked out, especially since this is the only place in Kimbell that provides overnight care. The boys come back from the kitchen with mouths full of donuts.

I scratch my head. Looks like they tried to eat the donut in one bite. Both boys have cheeks stuffed with food and they are struggling to chew.

I squat down and extend my arms toward them. They run to me and wrap their arms around my neck. I give them a tight hug back. "Be good today," I say, then kiss them each on the nose. "No wrestling. No fighting. Be respectful. Okay?"

"Yes, Daddy," they say, perfectly contrite, as bits of food fall from their mouths. I wish I could believe them. I reach down and pick up their mess and toss it in a nearby trash can.

"See you later, Tiff."

"I hope so, Ronan."

CHAPTER 2

M^{YA}

"IT'S OVER, JAMAL. I THINK WE BOTH KNOW THAT THIS relationship isn't working. The love between us is ... gone. But I believe we respect each other enough to end things ... amicably." I grip the steering wheel with white knuckles.

A low, strained whimper fills my car. I glance over at Jellybean, the red nose pit bull I rescued from an animal shelter a few years ago. He looks unconvinced.

"I know what that means." I reach over to rub his shiny coat. "Nice try, but I'm not ready."

Jellybean barks once, then twice. The military style dog tag engraved with my contact information bounces against his neck.

He agrees.

Breaking off a six-year relationship isn't simple. Our lives are intertwined. Finances. Friends. But luckily not family. I'm estranged from mine. He's not close to his. I'm grateful I resisted Jamal's pressure to have a child. I was fine with buying a house together without being married, but I drew the line at kids. His insistence that we take that next step was my wake up call. I knew in that moment I wasn't able to see a future for us anymore.

Sure, I could've pushed for a wedding. Jamal wouldn't have hesitated. He likes having a sugar mama, not that I'm rich by any stretch of the imagination. I just have more money than him. I would be Mrs. Jamal Evans, the most miserable and depressed wife on the planet. Thank God I was smart enough not to make that mistake.

I brake at the stop sign, then make the turn onto our street. I'm usually out of the house before Jamal wakes up on purpose. I've taken to avoiding him as much as possible, hoping he'll pick up on the distance and dump me.

Fat chance.

That's why getting to the gym and realizing I'd left my training binder had flooded me with dread. It's only been an hour since I left him snoring in bed, wearing his favorite Spiderman pajama bottoms.

By now, he's finished his customary bowl of Lucky Charms cereal and is in his gaming chair, entertaining a live audience. For a professional gamer, he barely makes enough money to cover a few of our bills. I can't figure out why he thought abandoning a lucrative career as a personal trainer to become a broke professional gamer was a good idea. The only thing he has going for him is his looks, which has gotten him the couple hundred followers who dutifully watch his channel. All female, of course.

Approaching our house, a groan escapes my lips.

"What is my boss doing here?" I mutter under my breath. I ease behind the car parked in our driveway. A shiny silver Mercedes coupe with license plate PMONEY.

This can't be a good sign. Things have been tense between Paige and me ever since Jamal quit training at the gym. He was her top trainer and brought in more than his fair share of clients. When he left, many of them didn't stick around. I know she blames me for Jamal abandoning his career, but I was as blindsided as everyone else.

Glancing down, I rub a finger along my grandma's face tattooed on my forearm. I need her strength right now for whatever awaits me inside. I don't know what I'll do if Paige convinces Jamal to return to work. Long days of training clients at the gym is my sanctuary. While the extra money would be nice, I don't think it's worth sacrificing the peace I feel from being away from him for ten or twelve hours a day.

As much as I want to avoid going into the house, I can't. My clients are waiting back at the gym. I exit the car and make my way past the oversized clay pots filled with dead hibiscus flowers and barge through the door.

Loud talking, almost screaming, stops me in my tracks.

My heart races as I try to make out the conversation.

"I can't believe this!" Jamal says. His footsteps pound against the tile floor. "Are you sure it's mine?"

"Don't start that crap with me, Jamal," Paige Malone retorts, her voice trembling with rage. "When do I have time to sleep with anyone but you! I'm here every day like clockwork after you send you little girlfriend to work. This baby is yours!"

"I don't want to be your baby's father."

"Too bad. In six months, that's what you'll be. I don't need your money, but this baby deserves to know you. To have you in its life."

"This is too much. I wasn't expecting any of this—"

"Neither was I," I say, my voice barely above a whisper, yet it stops both Jamal and Paige. They look at me standing in the foyer, eyes wide with shock.

"Mya, sweetie, I can explain," Jamal rushes toward me.

I hold up a hand, warning him not to come any closer.

I focus on Paige. "So, this is why you're never at the gym when I'm working. You're sneaking over here to have an affair with Jamal." I'm seething, but not for the reasons they think. If I'd known Jamal was cheating on me, I would've left him a long time ago. How much of my life did I waste sticking around? I have to know. "How long has this been going on?"

"Sweetie, that doesn't matter. The only thing that matters is I love you, not her," Jamal pleads.

Paige exhales loudly. "You don't seem so in love with her when you're ripping my clothes off—"

"Paige, shut up!" Jamal warns.

Paige ignores him. "It's no secret that Jamal and I dated before he met you. You're a nice girl and I wasn't trying to hurt you. About a year ago, I came over to check on him and one thing led to another and … now I'm pregnant."

I look down at the black lacquered polish on my fingernails and fight the urge to scratch Jamal's eyes out. "You've been cheating on me for a year."

"Don't listen to her," Jamal says. "Let's go outside where we can talk."

"I'll wait in here," Paige says, plopping down on the sofa.

"I have nothing to say to you." I say, looking at Jamal. The concern and shame etched on his face makes me feel … nothing. I wait for rage or sadness to overtake me, but it doesn't come. I feel … relieved. Relieved that life forced the outcome I hadn't had the courage to do myself. I won't let that happen again. I won't stay in a relationship that isn't good for me.

Lesson learned. The hard way.

"Move," I say, bumping Jamal as I storm into the kitchen. It doesn't take long for me to gather a handful of trash bags and stuff everything I own into them. I drag each bag to my run down Honda under the watchful gazes of Jamal and Paige. I move faster, stuffing bags until the backseat and trunk of the car are almost overflowing. There's just enough space for me and Jellybean in the front seats. With the last bag loaded, I run back into the house and slam the keys onto the table in the foyer.

Jamal crosses the room. "Please, hear me out." He rests his hand on my forearm. I look down at him touching me. It will be the last time.

"Fine." I turn to walk outside.

"Mya," Paige calls to me.

I stop, but don't look at her.

"Don't bother going back to the gym today. You're fired. You'll get your last check in two weeks."

I want to hit Paige in the face, but instead I walk out the door into the stagnant humidity of the Texas morning. Losing Jamal I can live with. Losing my career, the clients and the connections I've made in the personal training community in Round Rock is much harder to bear.

Facing Jamal, I say, "Start talking."

He crosses his arms over his chest and asks, "When was the last time you told me you loved me and meant it?"

The question rattles me.

"Months ago? Years? You think I couldn't tell you were going through the motions, Mya?"

I look away, pondering his question. I was only nineteen when we met. He was ten years older, sophisticated and sexy. He swept me off my feet. He made me feel wanted, supported, and loved. The family I'd been craving all wrapped up in one irresistible package. No wonder I went against my parents' wishes to be with him.

Remembering the exact moment we fell in love is easy.

Pinpointing when I fell out of love is much harder.

Was it watching my career as a personal trainer at the gym excel while Jamal's ambition and drive waned? Could it have been when he became content with playing games all day while barely earning minimum wage? Or was it realizing as we passed each other silently day after day and night after night that we had nothing in common?

What day was that? And does it matter now?

He knows the truth and so do I.

"Trust me, you don't want me to answer that question," I say. I feel a twinge of guilt at the pain and hurt in his dark eyes. Telling him the truth would hurt more than keeping quiet. That's the last gift I can give to him.

I give a quick whistle and Jellybean rushes from his spot, lounging under the tree. Opening the passenger door, the dog jumps inside as if he's been waiting his whole life to leave this place.

"So, this is it." He steps closer to me, a frown etched on his face.

I say the only thing I can at this moment. "Goodbye, Jamal."

Opening the car door, I get inside and start the engine. As I pull away from the curb, I steer the car toward the one town that might still feel like home—Kimbell, Texas. I hope I'm still welcomed there.

CHAPTER 3

If you're stupid enough to throw your life away over that thug, then we won't stop you. But don't come running back home when things blow up in your face, Mya. And trust us ... they will.

My parents' words ring in my ears.

I curse under my breath.

"Why, Jellybean? Why did they have to be right?" I slam my fist against the steering wheel, sending the car veering toward the ditch. I jerk in the opposite direction, trying to stop myself from crashing.

A scream escapes my lips as a loud bang rattles the Honda Civic. Startled, Jellybean barks.

I grip the steering wheel tighter.

The tires screech as my car fishtails across the asphalt into the opposite lane. I say a silent prayer that the road is deserted. There's no danger of crashing into another vehicle, but that doesn't stop my heartbeat from kicking in my chest.

The county road is littered with tar patches and potholes I avoided until now. My luck has run out when I hear the loud thump, thump, thump of a busted tire.

This day keeps getting better and better.

Jellybean grows quiet, searching my face for an explanation for our current predicament.

"It's okay, boy," I say, patting him on the head. "We got a flat tire. Should be easy enough to fix." My answer seems to satisfy him. He crouches low, resting his head against my thigh.

I steer the car toward the side of the road, past a sign that says 'Kimbell City Limit Pop. 3,089' and put it into Park. Letting the windows down to allow a breeze into the car for Jellybean, I press the button for the hazard lights, then get out. I stop to tuck the chin length strands of my hair behind my ears, then glance down at the back tire on the driver's side. It's a mess of shredded and split rubber. The metal frame of the wheel is exposed and bent from scraping against the asphalt. A rancid smell assaults my nose as a tinge of smoke snakes from the back wheel.

If my parents could see me now, there would be no limit to the depths of their utter disappointment. Not only would the 'I told you so's' roll off their tongues, but they wouldn't lift a finger to help me.

I suppose that's why I headed east to Kimbell instead of to Austin to seek refuge. Not that I'm sure there's anything left for me in the small town that makes up most of Lasso County. I only have fond memories of my grandma taking me here to my great-uncle Tony's house during the summers. I looked forward to getting away from the disapproval of my parents. Grandma let me be wild and run free, something my parents would have frowned upon. Didn't matter because they were too busy lobbying state senators and representatives for their clients than to raise the daughter they never wanted.

But grandma made me feel loved until the day she passed away, ten years ago. I still miss her dearly. I wonder if I'd have made different decisions if she was still alive. Probably. Jamal wouldn't have looked like a viable option if I still had my grandma's love and guidance.

I'm hoping that my great-uncle Tony will have a soft spot for me, even though I haven't kept in touch with him for years. It's a gamble showing up at his house unannounced, but I have no other place to go.

Groaning, I gaze up at the bright blue sky crowded with glorious popcorn clouds. The hazy sun casts blazing rays down onto the asphalt, ratcheting the temperature higher.

I mutter, "Alright Mya, this ain't your first rodeo. Changing a flat is no big deal." Grandma had graced me with a love of books and being outdoors, and an ability to handle common problems ... like a flat tire. I wish she'd taught me how to avoid getting stuck in a terrible relationship. She passed away when I was only fifteen. Much too young for her to share that wisdom.

I make my way to the trunk. Opening it, I let out a frustrated sigh as I look down at the trash bags filled with everything I own crammed into the space. Snatching the bags out and tossing them on the ground, I access the floorboard of the trunk. Lifting it high, I'm glad to see the spare tire looks in decent shape. Grabbing it from the compartment, I lay it on the ground then reach for the lug wrench and jack.

It takes a few minutes to loosen the lug nuts with the wrench, then I'm positioning the jack underneath the car near the flat tire. Sweat beads along my neck, coursing down my back and dripping onto the road. I lean forward and crank the handle, putting all my weight onto the metal. The car lifts higher from the ground, then the handle grinds to a halt. I try to turn it with all my strength, but it won't budge.

Yanking at the handle, I lean into it, hoping to get it to continue to turn.

I hear a low straining creak.

In the blink of an eye, the handle dislodges from the jack and flies toward my face. I raise my arm to protect myself and feel the painful sensation of sharp metal slicing against my skin. Falling backward onto the ground, I land with a hard thud onto my injured arm and let out a howl of pain. Jellybean scrambles toward the open window of the driver's door, barking down at me.

I turn over and give him a grimaced smile.

"It's okay, boy. I'll be fine," I say, but he doesn't look convinced and neither am I.

A car idles behind mine. Folks who care enough to stop and help are what I've always loved about Kimbell.

"Hey, you okay?" I glance over at the woman as she approaches me. Despite the scowl on her face, I can tell she's more than a little pretty and what the guys at the gym referred to as thick—overweight but with curves in all the right places that no man would mind the extra pounds.

She leans down next to me and lifts my arm.

Nausea races through me as I watch the gushing blood.

"What's your name?" she asks. Something about her tone worries me.

"Mya ... " I say, then add. "Young."

"Mya, I'm Jasmine, a doctor at St. Elizabeth's. This is a deep cut with a lot of dirt and grime contaminating it. But what worries me is the location and the amount of blood you're losing."

"Is it bad?"

"You've cut a major artery. Probably not completely severed, but I need to treat this immediately," Jasmine says, then jumps as Jellybean barks. She glares at my dog, then turns her attention back to me. With quick efficiency, she lifts my arm and wraps it with heavy gauze that appears like magic from one of her pockets. She then directs me like a drill sergeant to make several movements with my hand. I mirror positions she's demonstrating. It's painful but doable.

"Good. Doesn't seem like you have any nerve damage, but I'll need to clean out the wound to prevent infection. The cut may need to be repaired in the O.R."

I blink, not sure I heard her correctly. "The operating room?"

Jasmine nods. "Place your hand here." She raises my arm and

positions my hand against the wound. "I need you to apply pressure until I can get you to the hospital. Can you stand up, Mya?"

I nod, then ease myself from the ground. I lean against the car. "What about my dog?"

Jasmine looks at me like I have three heads. I would've laughed if the seriousness of the attention she's paying to my arm didn't have me scared out of my mind.

"I don't do animals," she says with no apology. "Your windows are down to give him air, and he's not at any risk of dying."

What she doesn't say, but I can read in her expression, is that the same can't be said for me.

"He'll have to stay here," Jasmine says matter-of-factly, and leads me to her car.

An hour later, I'm resting inside a cubicle in the emergency room of St. Elizabeth's hospital. My arm is bandaged and my head feels like it's in a fog.

Jasmine pokes her head inside and gives me a thumbs up.

"Guess it pays to have the Head of Emergency Medicine find me on the side of the road," I say, giving her a thankful smile.

"Who told you?" Jasmine crosses the small space and sits on a stool next to the bed.

"The nurses."

"Good thing is once I cleaned the wound, it wasn't as bad as I thought," Jasmine says, then scribbles onto a notepad. "I'm giving you a prescription for antibiotics and a mild pain killer—"

"Don't bother. I can't afford it. I don't have medical insurance," I admit, inhaling a shaky breath. "I'm not sure how I'm going to pay for what you've done already."

Jasmine rests a hand on mine and gives it a gentle squeeze. "No charge this time." She reaches into her pocket, pulls out a card and a twenty-dollar bill, and hands it to me. "Go to that website and sign-up, then take your member number to the pharmacy. Generic versions of these pills should only cost fifteen bucks." Jasmine finishes filling out the prescription, then tears the paper from the notepad.

"Thanks." I grab the paper and the cash, humbled by her generosity.

"Are you staying in Kimbell or passing through?"

"Not sure, yet."

My great-uncle has no clue I'll be on his doorstep soon. Although from what I remember, it's unlikely he'd turn me away. Still, I don't want to impose for very long out of common courtesy. A couple of weeks, maybe. A month tops. That shouldn't be too much to ask. I hope.

"Well, my cell number is right there," she points to the top of the prescription, then rattles off a series of symptoms. "If you experience any of those, I want you to call me. Got it?"

"Will do," I say as my cell phone rings.

"Your discharge papers are at the nurses' station. Take care of yourself, Mya."

Reaching for the phone in my pocket, I thank Jasmine again, then answer.

"Hello," I say, tucking the phone between my ear and shoulder.

"Is this Mya?" a man asks. His deep baritone voice sends flutters skittering across my skin.

"Yes, who is this?"

"Your dog got loose. I have him in Bell Park."

Panic slices through me. "I'll be right there."

CHAPTER 4

R *ONAN*

~

I GLANCE AT MY WATCH, TAPPING MY FINGERS AGAINST MY
thighs as I wait for the dog's owner to show up.

A couple of frantic calls into dispatch about a dangerous dog
stalking and threatening folks in the middle of Bell Park turned out to
be grossly exaggerated.

Which I figured.

I didn't bother asking any of the firefighters on my shift to come
along. As A-Shift Captain of the Kimbell Fire Station, I lead the most
unlikely of crews: a virtual cast of the haves, former NFL defensive
superstar Darren Manning and billionaire Nate Bell, and the have nots,
the playboy-geek Wiley Alexander and the goody-two-shoes Luke
Diamond. The rich boys are volunteers for reasons none of us have
been able to figure out. The others are full-time guys like me. Took us

awhile to gel, but we did, and now we're inseparable. Like family. A dysfunctional, but loyal family.

The crew could tell I was in a bad mood today and needed a little space to think. None of them reminded me of the proper protocol and process for responding to calls as I barged out of the station. They left me alone. I appreciate that.

Reaching forward, I rest a hand on the red-nosed pit bull's head and rub it gently. His mood matches mine. He lowers his head and rests against my feet.

I heard his low, pitiful moans as soon as I entered the park. He's the type of dog that usually inspires fear, with his athletic, stocky build, chiseled head and powerful jaws. But this dog had the opposite vibe of a fighter. He looked depressed, like he was missing his owner and searching to be reunited. He's well kept. More likely lost and not abandoned.

Quick discussions with the handful of people in the park this morning netted no information about who his owner could be.

It wasn't until I led him to the gazebo that I caught sight of the plain silver dog tag hanging from his thick neck. The name Mya and a phone number engraved onto the surface. 512 area code. Maybe someone passing through from Austin and headed to Houston. I'm guessing the owner stopped for a restroom break or maybe to grab some food from Gwen's Country Cafe, not realizing the dog had escaped from the car.

The dog glances up at me with sad, red eyes.

"Any minute now, fella. She's on her way," I say, scratching behind the dog's ears.

But taking her sweet time about it.

Forcing me to sit around while my thoughts wander to places they have no business being—thinking about Nikki.

I reach into my pocket and grab my cell phone. The mother of my boys had changed her phone number almost immediately after she abandoned us, but I could always send her a direct message through one of her social media accounts. Cross my fingers that she'd check the message. Or maybe one of the flunkies who works for her would.

Question is whether she'd care enough to respond?

Would knowing her twin sons cried their eyes out after seeing her music video spark any ounce of concern or love from her? Any desire to come back and see them? Or would she delete the message and ignore them like she's been doing for the past three years?

The answer to that question sours my stomach.

Wiley had stalked her social media and websites as a favor to me. A favor I'd never requested but appreciated all the same.

There's no mention of Nikki being a mother on any of her sites. It's like my sons don't exist. How she could turn her back on the most beautiful, rambunctious and playful little boys baffles my mind. Having kids had been unexpected, but I thought she'd love them as much as I did.

I was dead wrong.

A loud bark snaps me from my thoughts.

Before I can grab the dog, he's racing across the gazebo, making a beeline for a tall woman dressed in black leggings and a black halter top, showing off a body that could make a man lose his mind.

Instinctively, my eyes travel the full length of her. Starting with the impressive abs. She's got to be a fitness junky with muscular arms and legs that enhance her natural feminine curves. I lick my lips as my eyes settle on her face.

Stunning.

Like Meghan Markle, fresh and captivating.

Her jet black hair is shorter, though, in one of those trendy bob styles.

The dog leaps toward her. She braces herself, face lighting up with pure joy, as the dog jumps into her tattooed arms.

Heavily tattooed.

From shoulder to wrist.

Both arms.

Even more … intriguing.

She catches him as if he weighs six pounds instead of sixty, then twirls around as she holds him.

Everything fades away from my view as I stop my mouth from gaping open at the sight of her.

I push off the bench inside the gazebo and jump down the steps, walking toward them.

"Hi," she says, almost breathless. The sound tickles my ears. "Thanks for finding him. I don't know how he got out through the window of my car. I swear I only cracked it enough to give him a good breeze."

She lowers the dog to the ground. Obediently, he stands next to her panting happily and tail wagging.

"What happened?" I ask, noticing the bandage on her arm. "Why'd you leave him?"

She frowns, then relaxes her face. "I'm not in the habit of putting my dog in danger, if that's what you're implying."

"No, just wondering why you didn't leave him with someone. He was pacing across the park looking worried," I say, then point to her bandaged arm. "From the looks of that, seems like he had good reason to be."

My money is on her having a nasty gash that needed to be stitched up. Question is, how did she get cut? Or maybe who cut her?

I close the gap between us, lowering my voice. "Is everything okay? Are you in some kind of … trouble?"

"Back up, handsome," she says, pushing her hand against my chest.

My heart skips a beat from her touch.

"A girl can't handle all of this hotness early in the day, especially not after the morning I've had," she says, taking a step back. "Sorry. Can't believe I said that out loud. But it's true."

I bite my lower lip to stop the smile from spreading across my face. It's been a long time since a compliment from a woman has had this kind of effect on me. Now's not the time to focus on myself. I need to make sure she's not in danger. Make sure some crazy husband or lover didn't stab her and send her to the hospital.

"Tell me what happened," I say, more insistent.

Her lips turn up slightly as she tilts her head to the side, regarding me. She says, "I got a flat tire and tried to fix it myself. I've done it before, but today the handle slipped and stabbed me in the arm." She shrugs as if it's no big deal, but something about her expression tells me she was worried about the injury. With as much as it's clear she loves her dog, I bet that's the only reason she left him behind.

"You walked to St. Elizabeth's?"

"A doctor stopped to help me and drove me over," she says, then turns to look back toward Main Street.

"Where were you coming from?"

"Round Rock," she mutters under her breath.

"Alone?"

"Me and woman's best friend." She raises a hand to shield her eyes from the glare of the sun.

I step beside her and rest a hand on her shoulder, turning her toward the opposite direction. Pointing to where the county road intersects Main Street, I say, "That's the road that leads here from Round Rock. Remember anything about where you left the car?"

"A bunch of wildflowers and weeds in huge fields," she says, scratching her head. "Right past the Kimbell sign."

"That's a good four or five miles away. You shouldn't walk."

"I don't have any other choice."

My hand is still resting on her shoulder as if it's found a new home. "I could take you. Help you fix that flat so you can head on to wherever you're going."

I pause, hoping she'll fill in that missing detail. But she doesn't.

"How do I know you're not some crazy, bodybuilding, gorgeous ax murderer trying to make me your next victim? Why would I let you take me anywhere when Jellybean and I could run that in less than thirty minutes?"

"Jellybean?"

"Yeah, that's his name." She nods down at the dog.

"And you're Mya, right?"

"That's right." Her dark eyes sparkle as her eyes linger on my face.

"I'm Ronan. Not crazy. I thought about bodybuilding, then realized I didn't have the time or energy for it, and definitely not an ax murderer."

She laughs, no doubt noticing the other part of her description I failed to deny. Who am I to turn down a compliment?

"I'm a firefighter." I turn to allow her to read the back of my t-shirt —Kimbell Fire Department. "Helping people is in my job description."

"Protect and serve," Mya says, tapping a manicured black nail against her lips.

Pink glossy lips that are full and pouty, begging to be kissed.

I shake the thought away.

"That makes me feel a lot better about accepting help from you. Let me see your license."

"What?" I balk.

"Do you think I'm going to take your word for it? You could've bought that shirt from some costume store for all I know."

"Suspicious much?"

"Hand it over, or I'm running the four miles."

I roll my eyes, then reach into my pocket and take out my driver's license and firefighter ID card and hand them to her.

Her long dark lashes flutter as she scrutinizes them. Her light brown skin glows under the morning sun, making her more radiant.

"Ronan O'Reilly. A-Shift Captain," she says, then hands the cards back to me. I like the way my name sounds coming from her lips. "Where are you parked, handsome?"

CHAPTER 5

R*ONAN*

Ten minutes later, I'm pulling up behind Mya's Honda, which has seen better days. The inside is crammed with what looks like everything she owns. There's hardly enough room in the front seats for her and the dog to fit. The windows are completely lowered. The dog had free access to jump out of the car after she left to have her wound treated.

Mya opens the car and puts Jellybean inside, raising the windows enough that he can't squeeze out again. I glance away from her amazing body and focus my eyes on the discarded jack and lug wrench next to the flat tire.

"Starting a new life?" I grab the jack handle from the ground. The edge is coated in dried blood, evidence of the assault on her arm from earlier. I squat low and position the jack in place. As I crank, I wait for her to respond, but she says nothing. A quick glance up and I see her staring at me with a circumspect gaze.

Mya says, "Have you ever known something was inevitable, but when it happened, you still weren't ready for it? But you should've been."

My thoughts drift to the nights I'd come home and find that Nikki had left our babies with Georgia to drive to Austin for a singing gig. She didn't bother nursing, insisting they be fed by bottle. She barely held them. I'd go over to Georgia's house and wrangle my kids away from her, despite her protests. At home, I'd sit alone, changing diapers and rocking them to sleep, loving every single second of it. I couldn't understand why Nikki didn't. The day I woke up and found her 'Dear John' letter, I was stunned. But in hindsight, all the signs had been there.

"Yeah, I know how that feels," I say, wondering what pushed her to pack her belongings and take off on this road trip. "Let me guess ..."

"This should be interesting." Mya rests her hands on her hips and I take the moment to admire her physique for the hundredth time.

"You got fired, or you got dumped. Which is it?" I know the answer I'm hoping for, not that being attracted to a woman on the rebound is good. Connor would say it fits with my M.O. of making bad dating decisions.

The smile that lingers on her lips is like a sucker punch to my gut. This woman is sexy incarnate and I'm better off putting as much distance between the two of us as possible.

"Both. But I did the dumping."

A flush of warmth flows through me, pleased with that response. Not that I should be.

"Inevitable?" I ask, leaning onto the hood of her car. "Is that why you don't seem too broken up about it?"

"I should have had the courage to walk away from the guy years ago, but I didn't. The job is a different story. That's going to take a while to get over." She leans against the car next to me. Her closeness rattles me, makes me feel ... unsteady.

"Why didn't you leave the guy?" Another glance at her bandaged arm. Her tire was flat, but that doesn't mean her story about how her arm got hurt was true. A lot of women leaving abusive relationships never want to admit it. Still, something about Mya makes me think she wouldn't stay with a man who laid his hands on her. She seems frazzled, but there is an aura of confidence around her that is undeniable. I'm like a moth to a flame. Drawn to her.

"Aren't you the nosey one," she says, looking away. "Why don't you change the flat like you promised so I can get on over to Sterlingshire?"

"Sterlingshire?" I ask, thinking about the working class neighborhood on the opposite side of Kimbell from where the wealthy live. The same neighborhood where I met Nikki, playing a guitar and singing in Georgia's garage.

My cell phone buzzes in my back pocket. Probably the guys at the station wondering if something bad happened with the dog in the park. I glance at the screen and see the number to the daycare. I grunt and say a silent prayer that my sons haven't done something wrong.

I say, "Sorry, give me a sec."

Answering the phone, I'm relieved to hear Finn and Dec laughing on the line. "Alright fellas, did y'all ask for permission before you called Daddy?"

"Oops," Declan says.

"Sorry, Daddy," Finn says, then adds. "Are you fighting fires, Daddy?"

I hear Tiffany in the background sweetly scolding them and I can't help but feel a surge of pride. All my efforts to get them to memorize my phone number worked.

"No fires so far. But I am helping a nice lady who had car trouble," I say. Mya smiles at the mention. "Didn't the two of you promise to be good?"

"Yes, Daddy!" They say in unison.

"Okay, so make sure you ask Miss Tiffany before calling again."

"Okay, bye-bye." The boys say and with that, the call ends.

I slip the phone back into my pocket.

"Guess I should finish changing this flat."

Mya is quiet and nods at me.

I finish cranking the jack and easily lift the car. Sliding the mangled tire off, I put the spare on and tighten the lug nuts.

"So, you're a dad?" Mya asks after a long silence.

Her question lingers in the air. It's impossible to miss her not-so-subtle glance at my left hand. The one devoid of the wedding ring I used to wear. It's even more impossible to miss her smile when she notices it missing.

"Single dad," I say, emphasizing the word single. "Twin boys."

"Do your boys have a dog?"

I shake my head and wince. "No. My boys would kill a dog." I crank the jack, lowering the car back to the ground. Although if I had bought them a puppy, it would've given me an opening to suggest meeting up with Mya later. A way to see her again.

Her laugh pierces through the air. A pure, light fluttering sound that is like a warm caress against my skin. I stare at her, amazed by the joy on her face. She is absolutely gorgeous.

"Wait. You're not … joking," Mya says as her laughter falters.

"They're a rough pair. Not that they would do it on purpose. We've been watching a lot of wrestling lately. I can see them trying out the moves on the poor animal. Body slams. Choke holds. It wouldn't be pretty. That's why no matter how many times they beg me for a puppy, I still say no."

"Wow. How old are they?"

"Four."

Her eyes grow wide and I can't help but laugh.

"So, you are joking."

I scrunch up my nose. "No. Dead serious." I pick up the jack and wrench and return it to her trunk. Trash bags stuffed full of who knows what litter the ground behind the car. "Are these yours?"

"Starting a new life, remember?"

I grab the bags and put them back in the trunk, wondering how she got them to fit inside. After some careful wrangling and pointers from Mya, I close the trunk with all her contents inside.

"You're all set," I say, ignoring the disappointment coursing through me. My cell phone is buzzing out of control in my pocket again. This time it's Wiley. I know I need to get to the fire station before the guys strike out on a search party to find me.

"Thanks Ronan."

"Maybe I'll see you around, you know, since you'll be in Kimbell for a while?" It's a question, but she doesn't take it as one.

"Only if I'm lucky." Mya says, then gives me that sly sexy smile before getting into the car and driving away.

I blow out a long breath, then head to my SUV.

Luck hasn't shined on me in a long time. Somehow, I don't think it'll start today.

CHAPTER 6

~

"We're here." Rubbing Jellybean's back, I lean forward and glance through the front window at the house in front of me. It's been over ten years since I've seen this place. Time has not been kind to it.

The once vibrant red brick is now dull, covered with dirt and suffering from cracks. A walkway, uneven from tree roots growing underneath, leads to a front door with peeling paint. Overgrown hedges line the walkway. At least the grass has been cut.

Part of me wishes I'd forced Jamal to leave our house in Round Rock. But that wasn't an option. Even though I earned most of the money for the down payment and paid the mortgage, the house was only in Jamal's name. Another foolish decision I made out of what I thought was love.

I swallow my disappointment and get out of the car. I sigh heavily and lean against the hot metal as I see a sign in the front yard.

For Sale

Kincaid Real Estate

A phone number and website are listed for those interested.

The house looks deserted and I panic, thinking great-uncle Tony had passed away and my parents were cruel enough to not tell me. I shake away the thought. My second cousin would've texted at least to let me know his grandfather was gone. We spent a lot of time together in the summers growing up. He would've made sure I knew.

Jellybean crawls over the center console and exits through my open door.

"Stay." I tell him, then make my way up to the front door. He doesn't listen and follows me, glancing around from side-to-side ready to protect me at a moment's notice.

Just because the house is for sale doesn't mean my great-uncle isn't home. He could live here until someone places an offer. Standing in front of the door, I swipe at the cobwebs stretched across the frame, then ring the doorbell. I press it several more times, but I hear nothing. Not even a faint chime echoing from the inside.

Maybe the doorbell is broken.

I knock, hoping he comes to the door.

I don't know what I'm going to do if he's not here. I don't have anywhere else to go. All my friends back in Round Rock were Jamal's friends first. They're loyal to him. Sure, they'd give me a place to stay for as long as I needed, but would push hard for me to take Jamal back the whole time. I can't deal with that.

I knock again. Then jump as Jellybean barks loudly.

"Does he bite?" A voice calls from behind.

Turning around, I stare at a woman dressed in hot pink scrubs and matching Crocs. She's middle-aged, maybe forty. Her thick brown hair falls like waves around her shoulders. Her make-up is meticulously applied as if she'll be walking on set for a movie. A lollipop dangles out of her mouth.

"No, just overprotective of me, that's all." I say, shushing my dog. He gives me a stern look, then settles down. "I was looking for Tony Hayes."

"Mr. Tony moved to Mississippi to live with his son about a year ago. The house has been empty since then. I know he's trying to sell it, but nobody wants to live in Sterlingshire anymore. Not with the boom of houses coming up around Lake Lasso," she says, sucking on the candy. "You a … friend of his?"

"Family," I shrug. "I was hoping I could crash with him for a while until I get back on my feet."

Her eyes take me in from head to toe, then linger on my right arm.

"Oh goodness, are you Miss Marguerite's grand baby? The one she was taking care of in Austin?"

I smile brightly. "I am." I take a couple of steps toward her and extend my hand. "I'm Mya Young. Tony is my great-uncle."

"Wow. I remember you tagging along with your grandma at the library in the summers. You were a toddler back then, around my daughter's age. I used to go there to study for my nursing degree and see you with her," the woman says, shaking her head. "Grew up to be quite pretty, didn't you? Except for all that junk on your arms."

I laugh. "Not a fan of tattoos, I see."

"Nope," she shakes her head vigorously. "I hope my grandkids don't get any crazy ideas and want to have tattoos when they are older."

"You … have grandkids?" I sputter.

"Yes, I do. I got pregnant young, then my daughter got pregnant young. So, I'm a forty-five-year-old with grand babies I love to death. Not that I get to see them much," she says, rolling her eyes. "Where are my manners? I'm Georgia Knight. I live next door." She shakes a thumb over toward a red brick house next to great-uncle Tony's.

"I know this'll sound strange, but I haven't talked to my great-uncle in years. Would you mind giving me his number?" I ask. Driving to Mississippi hadn't been part of my plans, but it looks like I don't have any other options.

"I can do better than that," Georgia says, clapping her hands. "Let's call him. I have a spare key to the house and if he's okay with it, I can let you in so you can stay as long as you need."

"Seriously?"

"Yeah. Like I told you, that house isn't selling soon, so why shouldn't he let you crash there for a while?" Georgia pulls out her cell phone and dials the number, putting it on speaker.

"Hey old man, it's Georgia," she says.

"Now, what do I owe this pleasant surprise to?" Tony asks, chuckling. "Are you calling to let me know someone stopped by to check out my house? I'm going broke still paying the mortgage on that thing."

"Not exactly. But I have someone who stopped by thinking she would get a chance to see you."

"See me? Is she hot?"

I cover my hand to stop myself from bursting out laughing.

"She is, and she's also your great-niece." Georgia says, shaking her head.

"Mya? Is Mya there in Kimbell?" Tony asks.

I'm not his only great-niece, but some kind of way he knew it had to be me.

"Hi Uncle Tony," I say, voice shaking.

"Hey girl, did something happen between you and Jamal?" He asks.

Georgia raises an eyebrow. I cringe, but I'm not surprised my great-uncle has been keeping tabs on me this whole time. He knows the situation with my parents went from bad to nonexistent when I moved in with Jamal six years ago.

"Yeah, well, we kinda broke up."

"He dump you or you dumped him?" Tony asks, his voice gruff with emotion.

"I dumped him Uncle."

"Good for you, girl. I hate that I'm not in Kimbell to see you," he says, a wistfulness in his tone. "What else? I can tell you're holding something back because losing that knucklehead isn't enough to make you sound so sad."

"I lost my job at the gym. So, I need to find some work … eventually," I admit, although I'm in no mood to figure any of that out today or tomorrow, either.

"Mya stopped by because she needs a place to stay, old man. Her car is stuffed full with a bunch of bags. I'm guessing it's everything she owns," Georgia says.

I glare at her for being so blunt about my current circumstances.

"Georgia, you still got that key to the house?" Tony asks.

"You know, I do. Can I give it to Mya?"

"Please," he says. "And Mya, stay as long as you like."

"Thanks Uncle Tony." Relief floods through me. "I can help with the bills. My last check is coming from the gym soon, and I'm sure I can find some work around here to pay you back."

"Well, if you can, great. But it's not necessary. Marguerite would jump from the grave and take me out if I turned down her precious Mya. Mi casa es su casa."

"Thanks, Uncle Tony. Love you."

"Love you, girl."

Georgia ends the call and slips the cell phone back in her pocket.

"Did you have to make my situation sound so bad?" I ask, crossing my arms over my chest.

"You're lucky I didn't tell him about that bandage on your arm," Georgia says, concern in her eyes. "Did your ex beat you?"

"He wouldn't dare. No, I sliced my arm up, trying to change a flat tire. Long story," I say, taking a liking to the woman. There's something about the people in Kimbell that always makes me feel so welcomed and at home.

My thoughts linger on the handsome ginger man who changed my tire earlier. Talk about a pleasant surprise. Not that I should think about a man right now. I need to focus on my own life and how to get my career back on track.

"So, you dumped the jerk? What did he do? Cheat?" Georgia asks.

"With my boss, which is why I got fired."

"Ouch. Yeah, that's tough. But you're here now and this place has healed many a broken heart and wounded spirit. If there's one place you can come to feel better, it's Kimbell, Texas."

"My grandma used to say that exact thing."

"And she was right." Georgia walks over and loops an arm in mine as we head back up the driveway toward the door. "I am so proud of women who put their own needs first, even if no one approves. You know, my daughter had to do the same thing. She found herself in a marriage that never should've happened. Thank goodness she had the courage to end it before years of her life had been wasted."

"Wish I hadn't wasted so many years with Jamal." Pride had tricked me into staying with him for too long. I didn't want to face the fact that my parents were right, so I tried to convince myself things weren't as bad as they were. If I hadn't caught Paige with him this morning and found out about her pregnancy, who knows how many more years I would've suffered with Jamal before getting the courage to end things?

Georgia opens the door to the house, then turns toward me. "You don't have kids, do you?"

I shake my head. "Just my fur baby." I jerk a thumb at Jellybean, who is mesmerized watching a squirrel scamper up and down the trees in the front yard.

"Even better. That's the tough part of my daughter's situation. Her ex harasses her and then makes it extremely difficult for me to see my grandkids. He's still so bitter about the break up and doesn't realize he's using access to their kids to punish her family," Georgia shakes her head. "It's not right. One of these days, he'll regret all the hurdles he's put in place for us to see them."

"Well, hopefully things will work out so you can see your grandkids," I say, then glance down at the tattoo on my left arm. "My grandmother practically raised me and I don't know where I'd be now if she hadn't been such a positive presence in my life."

"That's all I want. A chance to be a positive influence in my grand babies' lives." She scowls. "Anyway, I'm guessing you don't have any furniture stuffed in that tiny car of yours."

"No, I don't ..." I peer into the empty house. All the furniture I remember is long gone. The living room is bare with dingy cream walls and worn tan carpet on the floor. "There's no furniture."

"There's no food in the refrigerator, either," Georgia says.

"It's okay. I'll figure something out. Right now, I need a shower." Sweat and grime cover my skin and I want nothing more than to stand under steamy, pelting water and forget this day ever happened.

Well, maybe not all of it.

A vision of that fire fighter comes to mind. I wrack my brain, trying to remember his first name ... something strong and burly. A great fit for the massive muscular man I met. Ronan. Yeah, that's right. Thinking about him will be the perfect distraction.

"How about this? I have an air mattress in the garage and an old television you can borrow until you figure out what you want to do for furniture," Georgia offers.

"You don't mind? I won't lie. That would help me out a lot."

"Of course not. And I'll toss a sandwich and some lemonade in with that."

I choke back an unexpected sob.

In one day, the people of Kimbell have shown me more kindness than I could've gotten from my own parents. Maybe I made the right choice coming here, after all.

"Thanks," I say, smiling.

CHAPTER 7

R *ONAN*

~

"WHO'S COMING FOR BREAKFAST?" WILEY ASKS, PUSHING the door to the Kimball Fire Station open with a loud bang.

"After last night, I have a date with my bed," Darren says, saluting us as he turns the opposite way and heads to the parking lot.

"Wuss!" Wiley screams at Darren, then turns to look at me. "You in, Ronan? A Gwen's Special is what your body is craving and you know it."

My stomach answers for me with a loud growl. Hunger wins the battle over exhaustion and I give him a nod.

"Luke, Nate?" Wiley asks.

"How in the world are you this energized after battling that blaze for seven hours? What are you? High?" Nate frowns, pushing Wiley out of the way.

"I'll take that as a no," Wiley says, then points at Luke.

"I'm in. As tough as that blaze was, it's nothing compared to putting out the fire at Elm Street Brewery a month ago," Luke says. "At least none of us spent the night in the hospital this time."

"Here here, brother," I say, giving him a fist bump.

"Enjoy yourselves, gentlemen," Nate says with a glum expression. "Got a voicemail from David. He insists I come in this morning to participate in a negotiation session for a company we're thinking about acquiring."

I can tell from the edge in Nate's tone he's annoyed. It's better to not tease him about the contentious relationship he has with his father, or the untimely demands the man places on Nate's life.

"Should we grab Santos?" Wiley asks.

I shake my head, knowing my best friend is going to have his hands full today working the Elm Street Brewery arson case. "Didn't you see who Gary had with him when he got to the station this morning?"

Wiley looks confused and shrugs.

Luke responds, "Yeah, that was Eric Watson, the forensic accountant. What do you think that means?"

"I think Eric has some evidence that's going to lead Santos to whoever torched the brewery. He's going to be busy for a while."

"My money is still on Joe Little," Wiley says.

"Your money needs to be on breakfast," I say, tired of the constant speculation about who set fire to one of Kimbell's most famous businesses and beloved landmarks. Gossip had dominated the town for over a month, as Santos led the investigation to find the culprit.

Luke says, "Let's go. I'm starving."

I shove my hands in my pockets as I round the corner and follow Luke and Wiley to Gwen's Country Cafe. After greeting Gwen Paul, the owner, and giving obligatory waves to the cops eating in the opposite corner of the restaurant, we slump down at our regular, reserved spot.

"Good morning, fellas," Ivy says, sauntering over to the table. Gwen's oldest daughter is the only one who took an interest in running the restaurant with her mother. She has a knack for customer service that rivals Gwen and with those voluptuous curves, it didn't take her long to become our favorite waitress.

"Morning Ivy," we say in rounds.

"Got something for you, Luke," Ivy says, giving him a sultry gaze that goes unnoticed. Poor Ivy has tried for years to get Luke's attention. She thought it was hard before. It's almost impossible now that Luke is enthralled with Channel 4 News for You Houston superstar reporter Ciara Thompson.

Wiley watches me as he struggles to maintain a straight face. We exchange a look, knowing Ivy doesn't stand a chance of snagging Luke anymore. But neither of us has the heart to tell her.

"What's that?" Luke asks.

"The latest copy of Hill Country Fitness, hot off the presses." Ivy again gives Luke her best flirty stare. He doesn't notice as he grabs the magazine from her. "The article on you was amazing."

"Thanks," Luke says, finally giving her a slow smile. "Really appreciate you grabbing a copy for me. I'd forgotten all about this."

Wiley kicks me under the table as we see Ivy almost melt into a puddle.

"So, we're kind of starving over here, Ivy," Wiley says, breaking her trance.

"Oh, of course. I'm sorry. What can I get for you?" Ivy asks, flushing red with embarrassment.

Wiley orders three rounds of Gwen's Special, then turns his blue gaze toward me as Ivy walks away. "Don't think we forgot about you taking forever to respond to that call about the dog in the park."

Luke adds, "And before you try to come up with a lie, just know that Mrs. Willliamson called to thank you for wrangling the animal … over an hour before you came back to the station. There's no reason you should've been so late. So what gives? Where were you?"

"Nice to know y'all care," I say, taking a sip of the rich, strong coffee Ivy placed in front of me a minute ago. "If you must know, I got caught pulling a Luke."

Wiley bursts into laughter.

Luke's head jerks up. "What's that supposed to mean?"

"It means he was off being a savior for somebody in need," Wiley says, his cackle growing louder. "You know, your favorite pastime."

Eyebrow raised, Luke looks from me to Wiley and back to me. "I don't get it."

Wiley says, "Luke, every time we see you, there's a new story about you swooping in to save some damsel in distress."

"Or elderly in distress," I chime in.

"Or kid in distress," Wiley adds.

"Or pet in distress," I pile on.

"You have a hero complex. Own it," Wiley says, snatching the magazine from Luke's hand. "Like this article they wrote about you in Hill Country Fitness. Most of it talks about your work with the community centers in Grimes County. Not the workout that keeps you in shape as a firefighter."

I fight back my laughter and try to keep a straight face since my comment started this little barrage against Luke.

"How is that a bad thing? We're firefighters. We're supposed to help people," Luke says, a seriousness in his tone that makes the situation more hilarious.

"It's not a bad thing at all," I say, trying to help Luke out.

"You're a magnet for the downtrodden," Wiley adds.

"So, what? Y'all sit around wondering who I'm going to help next?"

Wiley shrugs. "We don't have to wonder. News of Luke's great deeds spread like wildfire every week. You being selected for the Firefighters Alliance calendar is another sign that your reputation precedes you."

"Fine," Luke shrugs, snatching the magazine back from Wiley. "Since I was off my game, who did you swoop in to help, Ronan?"

Visions of Mya have dominated my thoughts ever since she drove off in her Honda yesterday morning. I should've come straight to the station, but found myself walking through the field of wildflowers, replaying our interaction in my mind. Something about Mya tilted my world off-kilter, and I'm not sure why or what to do about it. It would be easy enough to figure out who she knows in Sterlingshire and check on her, but I force myself to resist. Acting without thinking was how I got into a lot of bad relationships. I'm done making those old mistakes.

"Well, the owner of the lost dog in Bell Park—"

"Belonged to a beautiful fitness instructor," Ivy says, as she sits plates overflowing with four pancakes, three eggs and a heap of bacon in front of each of us. "I heard she got a flat tire and Ronan took it upon himself to take care of it … personally."

"Whoo hoo!" Wiley yelps, then high-five's Luke. He turns to me with his hand raised and I slap it down.

"Ouch," Wiley says. "That kinda hurt."

I turn to Ivy. "How do you know that?"

She raises an eyebrow. "Any of it not true?"

I don't respond as Ivy heads back to the kitchen.

"Look at you," Wiley taunts. "I'm happy for you, but I'm a little hurt that you didn't need my dating app to find your next love match."

"There is no love match between her and me," I say, more forcefully than I intended.

Wiley raises his hands in mock surrender and Luke gives me a look that makes me regret my outburst.

"None of this matters," I say, deciding I won't add any fuel to the fire of the gossip. "She's passing through town, stopping in Sterlingshire before she moves on."

"I'm looking to buy some property in Sterlingshire with the money coming in from my dating app," Wylie says with a sly grin. "Maybe I should head over there after breakfast and welcome her to town."

"Don't you dare," I say through gritted teeth. My fists clench and I feel tension clawing up the back of my neck. I try to force myself to relax. There's no reason for me to feel protective of a woman I only spent about half an hour with.

"Yep, you're interested," Luke says, then raises the magazine up to read it. "Tread lightly, Wiley. I've seen that look he's giving you before, and it's not a good thing."

My heart skips a beat as I see the woman gracing the cover this month.

"Wow, now that's a lady I wouldn't mind helping me keep in shape," Wiley says, gawking at the magazine.

"That's … her." I reach over and take the magazine from Luke's hand, laying it on the table as I stare at the glossy photo. She's stunning. Amazing body. Feisty expression that matches her bold personality. Intelligent, sharp eyes. Strong. Fearless.

Perfect.

Perfect?

What am I thinking?

"That's who?" Luke asks.

Wiley leans closer to me, drooling over the picture.

"The woman I helped with her flat tire," I say, still not comprehending how she could be on the cover of a local fitness magazine. "Mya."

"I understand why you were late. I'd forget all about work to help her any day," Wiley says, then adds. "You should send her the questionnaire from my dating app. I can let the AI tell you if y'all are compatible."

"He should not trust artificial intelligence for his love life," Luke says, shaking his head.

"Excuse me? Have you met Ronan? He has the worst luck with women. Always choosing the wrong girl. Trust me, I was around to see him fall for every chick this side of the Brazos River since we were in middle school and stood on the sidelines as every relationship crashed and burned. My app could help him not make another mistake," Wiley says.

"Tell me how you really feel," I grunt, displeased with their accurate assessment of my love life.

"What you want is to get her info so you can swoop in and try to take her from Ronan. Isn't that right, playboy?" Luke asks, tipping his cup toward Wiley before taking a long sip.

"Would I do that to one of my closest friends?" Wiley asks.

I scoff. "You have before."

"And that saved you from making a dreadful mistake with a woman who was no good for you," says Wiley.

Laughter escapes my lips as I roll my eyes at Wiley. I flip through the pages, looking for the article on Mya. There's no write up that tells me anything about her life. Only a two page spread with her in various poses demonstrating CrossFit moves. Near the bottom corner, there's a couple of sentences about her.

Mya Young is a certified CrossFit instructor and personal trainer at Malone's Gym in Round Rock, Texas. Her passion is helping women unlock their confidence and self worth through exercise.

I turn the page, but there's no other information about her.

No contact information.

"I bet she could kick your butt, Ronan," Wiley says, slapping a hand on my shoulder. "You sure you don't want me to get intel on her? Find out where she's staying in Sterlingshire and how long she plans to stick around?"

Stuffing pancakes into my mouth, I shake my head. There's no point in finding out more about Mya. Her life just imploded. She's dealing with the loss of a relationship and her job, but I don't share this with Wiley and Luke. The last thing she needs is someone coming onto her, no matter how much she flirted with me yesterday morning.

I can tell when a woman is on the rebound.

And Mya has a bright neon flashing sign telling me and my heart to stay far away.

CHAPTER 8

~

WHAT AM I DOING?

I stare at the ceiling fan, jerking as it turns and wonder if it's going to dislodge from the ceiling. Reaching a hand into my bag of Cheetos, I grab a bunch and stuff them in my mouth. Not the diet a personal trainer should be caught indulging in, but I'm not a personal trainer anymore. I have no clients. No income. I'm laying here waiting for the backstabbing cow who used to be my boss to email confirmation of the date my last check will be sent.

It's been five days since I arrived at my uncle's house in Kimbell. Days filled with nothing have passed in a blur. I've only left the house one time to grab toiletries and groceries, charging them on the only credit card I have left that isn't maxed out. Besides my great-uncle calling to check on me each morning, I haven't spoken to another soul. Malaise has crept into my bones and I haven't been able to shake it.

Jellybean squirms under my head. I raise up to give his stomach a reprieve from the pressure. He jumps up and trots to the patio door, panting as he looks at the backyard, then back at me.

"Fine, you can go outside and have fun. But I'm not coming with you," I say, then scramble up from the floor to open the patio door. Jellybean bolts into the backyard and begins his daily game of chasing the squirrels scampering around the yard. I plop back down on the sleeping bag and resume watching the ceiling fan turn.

I should be thinking about how to get my life on track, but more often than not, I find my thoughts lingering on the handsome ginger man who found my dog and changed my tire.

"Ronan O'Reilly," I whisper his name, triggering a surge of energy through my body. Those steel-blue eyes float to the surface of my mind, intense and kind. I could lose myself in staring into those blue pools. Not to mention he has one of the best bodies I've seen in a long time. And I've worked at a CrossFit gym for the past five years. I know what I'm talking about. The way his t-shirt fit him like a second skin, showcasing his bulging muscles, had me almost salivating.

But he isn't super model, man of your dreams cute.

Nor does he have the steroid-induced, jug head look of most gym rats.

Nope. His muscles are huge, but organic, like built from everyday labor as much as from hitting the weights. He has that kind of real man, rugged handsomeness that arrests all your senses and makes you wonder how his wife or girlfriend ever lets him out of the house to interact with other women.

Yet, Ronan had no wedding ring on his finger.

He made it clear he was single. A single dad. How honorable is that? Not shying away from his parental responsibility and taking the lead in raising his kids.

He's a small town catch.

And he went out of his way to make sure I knew.

I'm used to guys flirting with me. It was a common occurrence at Malone's Gym. What I'm not used to is initiating the flirting. Feeling that undeniable pull of attraction to a man so quickly. It wasn't like that when I met Jamal. More of a slow burn as I worked out at the gym for months before finally acknowledging his attempts to talk to me.

Still, shouldn't I be taking it easy right now?

Not ogling the first hot guy that crossed my path after ending my relationship.

My cell phone beeps and I grab it, click on the email app and see the new message from Paige Malone of Malone's Gym. I skim the contents, then do a quick calculation in my head to confirm the amount is correct. My gaze drifts to the payment date.

I bolt up.

Five days ago?

She sent the money the same day I caught her and Jamal together.

"No. No. This cannot be happening." I open the banking app and see what I feared.

Balance of $46.13.

Auto-deductions cleared my account yesterday to pay for the mortgage and utilities on the house in Round Rock.

"I've totally messed up," I say, dropping the phone onto the floor. I twist the strands of my short pig tails between my fingers and fight off the rising panic building in my chest.

I told Uncle Tony I would cover the expenses on the house while I stayed here. Even though he said it wasn't necessary, I wanted to show him how much I appreciated his help. With my last check from the gym, I would've had no problem paying all the bills this month. The house is old and Kimbell is a much cheaper place than Round Rock.

Except there's no money left in my account to pay for anything.

No money left to cover my living expenses—food for Jellybean and me, gas for the car, my cell phone …

Years ago, after Jamal had quit personal training at Malone's Gym, I'd set up the bills to auto pay so we wouldn't incur late fees or disconnections. He'd always been terrible with finances and paying bills on time. In hindsight, I don't understand why I agreed to the arrangement. Maybe I felt sorry for him as he struggled to earn money from online gaming. Or maybe it was a way to convince myself I was still committed to a relationship I felt disconnected from.

It doesn't matter now.

Twenty minutes later, the banking rep confirms what I suspected.

"I'm sorry, Ms. Young, but there's no way to recover those funds since they've been released." The rep says. "I've canceled the auto-deductions, so this won't happen again. Is there anything else I can do to help you today?"

"No," I say, then hurl the cell phone across the room. It lands with a loud thud on the carpet.

I'm so mad at myself for not pulling the plug on the relationship a long time ago. Deep down, I knew I didn't want a future with Jamal anymore. I'd stopped loving him, but I let the shame of knowing my parents were right about him stop me from doing what I needed to do.

Now, I'm paying for it in the worst way.

I need a plan and fast. Telling my uncle I can't cover the bills this month after all is not an option. He's the only person in my family who still supports me. I don't want to let him down. I don't want him to be disappointed in me like my parents.

Jamal comes to mind, but calling him would be a waste of time. He'll try to manipulate this situation to his advantage. Use it to convince me to go back to the house in Round Rock, since I've already made the mortgage payment. No, it's better for me not to call my ex.

I need a different plan.

Kimbell is small, but with my personal training experience and the publicity from being on the cover of Hill Country Fitness this month, I should be able to convince one of the local gyms to hire me. Convincing the owner to give me an advance on my paycheck so I can pay the mortgage is a different story.

But first things first.

It only takes two minutes to gather a whopping list of three gyms in all of Lasso County. I was hoping for better odds than this, but three is better than none.

A loud yelp, then frantic barking coming from the backyard grabs my attention. I scramble from the beanbag and race to the patio. Something's wrong with my dog.

CHAPTER 9

T HE BARKING CONTINUES, RAISING ALARM BELLS INSIDE me. I slide the glass door open, almost yanking it off its tracks, and step outside.

"What in the world?" My mouth gapes open as I stare ahead. Beyond the covered awning and near my uncle's abandoned garden, Jellybean squeals with glee as two of the most adorable little boys are hugging him and rubbing his belly. Writhing on the lush grass, Jellybean is on his back and loving all the attention he's getting from the kids.

Closing the door behind me, I glance at the gate. It's still shut and locked. The boys look too small to have jumped the five-foot high fence, but it wasn't impossible. Kids have been known to do strange things. I walk toward the boys and stop inches away from them.

"Looks like Jellybean has made some new friends." I put my hands on my hips as I stare down at the boys.

They stare back up at me with a hint of mischief and smile as they continue to pat Jellybean. Looking from one to the other, then back again. I suck in a deep breath. They are the most beautiful kids I've ever laid eyes on—thick dark brown hair in a buzz cut, olive skin tone and striking blue-gray eyes. They are twins. Identical. But maybe not quite. One has dimples and the other doesn't. If they don't smile, you'd never be able to tell the difference between them.

"Jellybean?" one boy says, then laughs. "I like that name."

"And I like that candy," the other boy says, then turns to look at me. "Why did you name him that?"

"Because he likes jellybeans more than you do," I say, then smile, thinking back on when I brought the red pit bull home for the first time. I had left him for only a few minutes and returned to see him devouring the jellybeans from the candy dish on the coffee table. "How did the two of you get back here?"

They look at each other as if communicating telepathically, then turn back to me and shrug.

"You don't know how you got into my backyard?" I ask, amused by their antics.

They shake their heads in a synchronized motion as if they can't help but be identical in every way.

"Well, I'm Mya. What are y'alls names?" I try a different tactic. Somebody is missing their kids and frantic right now. I've got to get these boys back where they belong.

"Hi Miss Mya, I'm Finnegan," one says, then extends a small palm toward me.

"Hello, Finnegan," I say and shake his hand.

"Whoa! Look at those tattoos! So cool!" The other boy yells. He jumps up from the ground and traces his little fingers along the edges of a unicorn etched into my forearm.

"And what's your name?" I ask, not pulling away from him.

"Declan," he says with pride, then glances up at me. "What

happened to your arm? Did you get hurt?" His eyes lock on my bandaged left arm.

I nod my head, touched by the concern creasing his brows. "I did, but the doctors were able to make it all better. I have to keep this bandage on for a little while."

"Did it hurt bad?" Declan asks.

"Not too bad," I respond, which seems to please them.

"You sure are pretty, Miss Mya," Finnegan says.

"Very pretty," Declan adds.

"Thank you both," I say, feeling like someone is punking me. I check around to see if a camera crew is going to pop out from the bushes, but we're all alone. "Where do the two of you live?"

"We like your dog. Do you have a ball so we can play fetch?" Declan asks, ignoring my question.

"Yeah, fetch," Finnegan adds, then scrambles to his feet to stand by Declan.

"You can play fetch with Jellybean if your mom says it's okay," I squat down to their eye level. "Let's go find your mom so we can ask her."

Finnegan shakes his head, then looks away. "Our mom is gone."

His words stun me and I ease onto the ground. The thought of them dealing with the loss of their mother at such a young age is terrible. They can't be much older than four or five.

"Finn cries about it," Declan says, matter-of-fact. "He's a cry baby."

"You cry, too!" Finnegan slaps Declan in the back. His little face growing red as tears prick his eyes.

"So what!" Declan screams back, glaring at him. "I don't cry as much as you do."

"I'm so sorry. How long ago did she … pass away?" I ask.

Declan blurts out, "She's not dead. She just doesn't want us."

His words stun me. Memories of my childhood pound in my head and I feel dizzy. Growing up, knowing you're not wanted is one of the most horrible feelings in the world. Trust me, I lived it. All the love and encouragement from my grandma wasn't enough to fill the hole left in my heart from parents who wished they'd never had me.

Finnegan nods in agreement. "She sings songs and makes a lot of money."

Hearing the pain in their voices breaks my heart.

"Maybe your mom needs to work through some things before she can come back to you. It doesn't mean she doesn't love you," I say, even though I have no clue if that's true.

Thinking about my own parents, they never settled into wanting me around. I suppose they love me in their own way. I can't imagine the shock my mom had, getting pregnant at forty-five after she and my dad had decided long ago to not have children. Me showing up would've put a wrinkle in everything they wanted for their lives, stealing their freedom to travel at a whim and taking time away from their lucrative lobbying firm. Lucky for me, my grandma made it her mission to move from Kimbell to Austin to ensure I was raised with love.

The boys look at me intently. I can see them weighing whether or not to believe me.

"That's what Granny says." Finnegan moves in closer to me and leans against my chest.

"We didn't believe her," Declan says, then steps closer to me. "But maybe it is true."

"I think you can trust your granny," I say.

"And we can trust you, Miss Mya," Declan adds, then wraps his arms around my neck.

"And we trust Jellybean, too," Finnegan adds, then wraps his arms around me.

I give both boys a tight hug, loving the feel of them in my arms. They have that sweet smell of childhood mingled with the heady scent of nature and grass.

"How about we go see your Granny? If she says it's okay, y'all can come back over here and play with Jellybean as much as you want. How does that sound?"

Their wide smiles and head nods are the only answer I need. All my money troubles and the wreck I made of my life fade into the background because of these two sweet little boys.

I ask, "Does your granny live close to me?"

Finnegan nods his head.

Declan points at Georgia's house.

Relief floods through me. These are Georgia's grandbabies. The ones she rarely gets to see. I hope she's not a wreck wondering where they've sneaked off to.

"Well, I had the pleasure of meeting your granny a few days ago. She was nice to me and helped me out."

"She's not always nice," Declan says.

"Yes, she is. I love granny," Finnegan interrupts.

Declan rolls his eyes. "I love granny, too."

"Okay, let's go see granny." I rise from the ground and extend a hand to both of them. They place their hands in mine and I grip them tight.

"We'll be back Jellybean!" The boys scream as I steer them into the house.

We spend all of five minutes getting Georgia's approval for the boys to play with Jellybean for the afternoon. She seems exhausted from her shift at the hospital and oblivious to the fact the boys had left her backyard and entered mine. Even though it's clear she loves her grandsons, I get the feeling she wasn't expecting to take care of them today. With everything she did to help me get settled into the house, I'm happy to return the favor.

Finnegan and Declan are the perfect distraction for my woes. They remind me that there is still some good in the world. A reason to smile and be thankful. As the boys and I play in the backyard with Jellybean, tossing a frisbee and watching my athletic dog deftly snatch it from the air without missing every single time, I can't help but hope that one day this could be my real life. That I would be playing in my backyard with my own sons and happy again.

And Jamal would be a distant and long-forgotten mistake of my past.

CHAPTER 10

~

"I'M GOING TO TELL YOU WHAT THE OTHER PLACES DIDN'T."
Wheeler Chesterton leans close to me. His hands fidget with the cap of
a water bottle.

I'm antsy enough, knowing this is my last chance. I don't need his
nervous energy making me more on edge. I'd already struck out at the
other two gyms despite my impeccable resume and client references.
Both claimed to not have enough membership or demand for another
trainer on staff.

I look beyond the five-foot-six inch former Olympic gymnast
toward the wall of windows overlooking the lake. The howls of wind
can be heard from outside, churning the waters and creating a choppy
surface for the boats bobbing on the water.

Chesterton's Gym is impressive for a town this small. The
architecture allows the beauty of nature around Lake Lasso inside.

Illuminated by bright sunlight streaming in through the wall of windows, the place is clean and welcoming. Faint aromatherapy pumps through the air conditioning, saving the place from the pungent smell of stagnant air and sweat. State-of-the-art gym equipment is arranged by function and traverse two floors. Outside on the lawn stretching toward the lake are two semi-covered spaces used for fitness classes.

Definitely the kind of place that could make me want to stay in Kimbell. If only he'd give me a chance. I take a deep breath, racking my brain for a way to convince him to give me a shot.

"I have more experience than anyone you've had walk in here asking about a job in a long time," I say, pleading my case.

"No question about it," Wheeler agrees, then points to the stack of magazines resting on the end of the counter. My face stares back at me on the cover of Hill Country Fitness. A booking I only got because Paige pulled some strings for me. She wanted a way to showcase her gym without it being obvious she'd bought her way into the magazine. I became her poster child. Another way my former boss had played me.

I smile, hoping his agreement is a good sign. My optimism fades as I see pity reflecting from his brown eyes.

Wheeler says, "The reason I can't hire you has nothing to do with your qualifications."

"*Can't* ... hire me?" I balk as tension claws up my neck.

"Paige Malone called me and dragged your name through the mud. Made it clear that I shouldn't hire you if you came into the gym looking for work." He shrugs. "I'm not sure what you did to make her mad, but she's gunning for you. Calling every gym in the Hill Country to bash you. I'm not in the mood to get in the middle of that."

"I can't believe this. You're joking." My voice is frail and distant as frustration wells inside my chest. I rake my hands through my dark tresses, squeezing the back of my throbbing head.

"I wish I was. Maybe in a couple of months, when things die down between the two of you, we can talk about bringing you on. Just not right now."

I don't have a couple of months. I need to prove I'm not a twenty-five-year-old epic failure. Helping my uncle with the bills on his house while he lets me stay there is the one thing that made me feel like I still had a grip on my life. Like I'm not the disappointment that my parents think I am. I let them down by being an average student, then not going to college, then dating a man they thought was beneath their status. Getting their acceptance after all of that is impossible.

But Uncle Tony accepts me. He loves me like grandma did. I know he wouldn't hesitate to tell me it's okay that I can't pay the bills. I don't want him to do that. I want to show him how much I appreciate his help. I'm just out of ideas on how I can get money before the bills are due.

"Okay, well, I guess," I pause, fumbling with my words. "Thanks for telling me. It's good to know what I'm up against."

Wheeler gives me a sympathetic smile, then walks over to help another guest check in. I maneuver out of the way and close my eyes, trying to figure out what to do next. What my options are now that I know Paige has enacted a smear campaign against me.

"Looks like you need to let off some steam."

I jump at the sound, stumble, then turn to face the towering, massive man standing behind me. My mouth goes dry as I look up at Ronan O'Reilly's ruggedly handsome face. In seconds, I devour the full sight of him. From the dark auburn hair styled in a slicked back quiff contrasting with the unruly full beard gracing the square jaws of his face. Broad frame and muscles are on display as he wears a sporty Under Armor sleeveless t-shirt and baggy shorts.

But it's the concern in his slate blue gaze that arrests me. I feel myself becoming emotional. Get yourself together, Mya. Don't fall apart in front of the hottest man you've ever met in your life.

"Hi," I say, injecting fake cheer into my voice. I wag a finger toward him. "Ronan, right?" As if I could've forgotten anything about this man.

"You don't have to do that for me," Ronan says, slipping his hands into the pockets of his shorts.

"Do what?"

"Pretend you're okay when you're obviously not." Ronan leans closer. The hint of his body wash intoxicates me. "You don't strike me as the kind of girl who wants to talk about it."

"I'm not."

"Didn't think so … Mya."

Butterflies race through my body from him remembering my name. I'm surprised, even though maybe I shouldn't be.

I look away, uncomfortable yet riveted by his scrutiny. "Well, not immediately. Maybe after I've calmed down a bit," I admit. I'm not sure why I'm being so open with him. Maybe it's easier to connect with a stranger. Someone who doesn't know my past and all the mistakes I've made. "What I really want to do is attack those heavy bags over there." I swivel around toward the boxing area. "Then run the stairs until my mind goes blank." I turn in the opposite direction and point to the stair master.

"Should you hit the bags with your arm like that?" He points to the heavy bandages on my arm.

"Nope. That's why I'll be doing a bit of kickboxing and not punching."

"Makes sense. So go for it."

"With everything I'm dealing with, splurging on a fifty-dollar day pass to work out at this gym is not wise."

"You don't need to splurge. I'll get you in with one of my buddy passes," Ronan offers.

Before I can protest, he raises a hand to stop me.

"Look, it costs me nothing. I get five a month for free and never use them because everyone I know is already a member of this gym," Ronan explains.

"Why are you so annoyingly helpful?"

"Why are you so annoyingly beautiful?" Ronan claps back, destroying any chance I have of a spunky retort. The smile that spreads across his face makes my legs turn to jelly.

"Wow, now you see how you made me feel last week," Ronan says, no doubt referring to my not-so-subtle ogling of him when we first met.

"This isn't fair, though," I say.

"Fair?"

"You found my dog, changed my flat tire and now you're going to give me a free pass to the gym," I say, finding my confidence again. "I'm wracking up debt to you, Ronan. You'll be asking for pay back soon."

He chuckles, then licks his lips slowly. "I promise anything I ask in return will be something that is … mutually enjoyable."

A gasp escapes my lips.

"But right now, you need to work off some steam." Ronan says, breaking the trance he put on me. "And so do I."

CHAPTER 11

~

"Bad day?" I ask.

Ronan nods, then hands his access card to the attendant and informs the guy that I'll be working out with him today on a buddy pass.

The guy takes his sweet time looking me up and down before handing me a card that will allow me to enter the women's locker room.

The glare Ronan gives him for the gesture sends my heart soaring, even though I know it shouldn't.

"Come on, the locker rooms are this way." Ronan leads me away from the check-in desk. I'm already dressed for a workout, but welcome a place to lock up my purse, so I don't have to carry it around the gym floor.

"Guess you're like me. Not much for talking about it," I say, although curiosity is getting the better of me. He's a firefighter, so I'm sure he sees more tragedy than I can imagine.

"I'm more of a talker than most would guess. Just didn't think you'd be interested—"

"You don't think I'm interested?" I interrupt, raising an eyebrow.

Ronan chuckles, a low timbered sound that tickles the back of my neck. He's definitely pushing all of my buttons in the best possible way.

"Okay, remember how I told you my boys are a bit rough?" Misery crosses his handsome face.

"What happened? Please don't tell me they actually killed somebody's dog." My hand flies to my chest.

"No, but what they did is almost as bad. The girls at the day care would play beauty shop. No big deal because the shampoo bottles were filled with water, except my little rascals decide to replace the water with … glue."

"What a disaster. I'm sure those little girls bawled their eyes out after it happened." The thought of my hair clumped and glued to my head makes me shudder. That has to be one of the worst things you can do to any female. Our hair is our crown and glory.

"Epic meltdown. The parents were livid. All I could do was stand there and take the verbal assault, apologizing for my kids. It wasn't the first prank they'd pulled, but the owner made sure it would be their last. She booted them from day care." Ronan shakes his head. "Now, I'm going to try the nanny route."

I'm struck speechless. "I'm sorry. Do you have any leads?"

"The day care owner connected me with a nanny service and I have a few interviews lined up this afternoon. Pressure is on because I need someone who can start in the morning. I have to go in for my shift tomorrow. Fingers crossed everything works out."

"But you're worried that none of them will be right for your boys?"

He nods. "Being a single dad is hard enough. Trusting my little monsters with a stranger is one of the hardest things I've ever had to do. Plus, nannies cost twice as much as daycare. Not something I'd planned for in my budget. That's why I'm here to work off all this pent up anger."

"Sounds like you need it as much as I do. What's your workout plan?" I ask, hoping to take his mind off his problems, which rival my own. Ronan rattles off a laundry list of exercises, all typical of what guys think they should be seen doing at the gym. Nothing inventive or that will push him to his limits, but I don't tell him that. I say, "You're going to be here for a while, even going heavy with low reps. That workout is going to last an hour and a half or more."

Ronan nods his head as if contemplating my assessment, then shrugs. "By that time, my head should be clear."

"Well, save your spots for the end and I'll come over and do that for you. I need to work off my debt." I give him a wink. Before I can lose myself any further in Ronan O'Reilly, I turn away from him and head into the women's locker room.

The next hour, I blast through one of the most intense workouts I've done in months. And all the while, I could feel Ronan's eyes watching me. No matter where I was in the gym, he was never too far away and always facing my direction.

I shouldn't have, but I found myself putting on a little show for him. Doing more than I normally would so he could see what a great trainer I am and all the things I could do that no one would expect of a woman.

As the stair master beeps and starts my cool down, I lift my gaze to the mirrors along the wall and meet Ronan's stare. He's doing bicep curls, but his focus is entirely on me. If my temperature wasn't already sky high, that look in his eyes would've sent it through the roof. I don't bother wiping the sweat from my face. It seems to add to the intensity of the attraction blazing between us.

Why, oh why did I have to meet him when my life is falling apart?

I don't have time to think about being attracted to a massive, muscle-bound ginger man. My focus should be on how I can find a job in the next week that will give me the money to pay the bills on my uncle's house.

The stairs slow to a stop and I jump off the machine, feeling refreshed. I never should've told Ronan to wait for me. The best thing for me is to put as much distance as I can between the two of us.

Too bad I have no plans to do what I should.

Grabbing a towel, I pat myself as I walk over to him.

"Looks like you're slacking. Switch to eighty-five pounds." I snatch one of the fifty pound barbells from his hands. "Heavy weights, low reps, remember."

"I already did a hundred. Four sets of five. I'm waiting for you to finish that beast of a workout you put yourself through," Ronan says, taking the barbell from my hand. He adds them to the rack, then turns back to me. "You're amazing, you know that?"

"So I've been told." I wonder if he meant my skills in the gym or something else entirely. "What's next on your list?"

"Chest press, which you promised to spot me," Ronan says, poking his finger in my side. I don't flinch as the touch sends a jolt through me.

"Let's do it," I say, then follow him to a flat bench.

I enjoy the view of his ripped muscles as he racks one hundred forty pounds worth of plates onto the barbell, then lays down on the bench. He positions himself under the bar with hands in a wide grip.

"How many reps are in your warm-up?"

"Fifteen."

"Then you're going to max?"

"You got it. I'll work my way up to two sixty."

My frown is involuntary.

"What's with that look?" Ronan asks.

"You can do a lot more than two sixty." I say, circling him on the bench. I love how his eyes follow my movements, as if he can't resist himself.

He raises up, confusion in his eyes. "I'm pretty sure I know my limits."

"No," I shake my head, pressing my hand against his rock-hard chest. I push him forcefully, causing him to lie back on the bench. "Let's start with your form. It needs some tweaks. Grip the bar."

Ronan follows my directions.

I walk behind him and lean over, resting my hands over his.

Our eyes lock on each other for a long moment and I feel as if he's seeing straight through into my soul. I lace my fingers within his, then nudge his hands into the correct position on the bar. I realize I'm clutching his hands tightly as I fight the wave of dizziness washing over me.

What is it about this guy?

His gaze never leaves mine and I have to force myself to let go and look away.

"Now scoot down about two inches," I say, putting some much needed space between me and the ginger giant.

A smile plays at the corners of his lips as he does as he's told.

I walk back around and nudge his legs into a better position to give him the stability he needs for the lift.

Stepping back, I ask, "How does that feel?"

"Like I've been schooled by a world class personal trainer," Ronan says, cracking a smile. "Much more comfortable than what I'd been doing."

"Okay, give me fifteen."

"You're not going to spot me?"

"Start lifting. You'll see you don't need a spot."

I watch as Ronan effortlessly lifts the barbell and executes the chest press with perfect form.

The amazement on Ronan's face is the only reward I need.

He says, "It's like night and day."

"Wait until you're lifting three hundred," I counter.

He scoffs. "Three hundred? By when?"

I glance at the clock on the wall, then say, "Twenty minutes from now."

"No way."

"I can't believe you're doubting me. Care to put a wager on it?"

His eyes are shrewd. "I feel like I'm walking into a trap," he says.

"No trap. If I can get you to lift three hundred today, then you buy my lunch."

"And if you can't, what do I get?"

"What do you want?" I ask.

Sizzling desire blazes in his eyes. The longer he hesitates, the more I find him utterly irresistible.

I throw up my hands. "Come on, handsome. It's not a trick question."

"A free personal training session," he says finally.

"That I can do." I say, resting my hands on my hips. I can't help but feel letdown he didn't use this opportunity to suggest a date. Could his flirting be meaningless? The realization is like cold water doused all over me.

Ronan raises up on his elbows. "How do you know I won't cheat to win?"

"Because you're a man and your ego won't let you do less than you're capable of," I say, easing down onto the bench next to him. The heat emanating from his body is mesmerizing. "Plus, deep down inside, you want me to win."

"Is that right?" Ronan asks, his eyes sparkling with the challenge. "Well, game on. Let's do this."

CHAPTER 12

R *ONAN*

~

THE SOUND OF MYA'S LAUGHTER TICKLES THE AIR. SHE'S acting like a kid in the candy store, her arms overflowing with the spoils of her victory—pre-made snacks, everything from sandwiches to muffins and croissants, bags of chips, bottled protein juices and a single cake pop.

Gripping the edges of the blanket, I shake it open, then lay it on the manicured sloping hillside that leads down to the lake. The area is picturesque, surrounded by towering pine trees and fields of wildflowers. Waves lap against knobby driftwood at the water's edge as a duck lazily swims by.

It's not lost on me that anyone passing by would think Mya and I were on a romantic date. The idea doesn't bother me, even though maybe it should.

"I knew you wanted me to win," Mya taunts. The afternoon

sunrays bathe her flawless skin in a warm golden glow. "But come on, Ronan! That was too easy. You went way past three hundred and lifted three twenty-five. Did you hustle me?"

"It wasn't easy. Plus, you came up with this idea and the bet, not me," I say, raising my hands.

"Right. Forgot that part. Okay, so turns out I was right about you. There's untapped strength in those massive muscles." Her hand slides down my biceps, then gives it a tight squeeze.

I close my eyes, enjoying her touch too much.

"If I'd known it was going to cost me sixty bucks at the coffee shop, I might have passed on the whole thing."

"An hour personal training session with me costs sixty bucks. That's what I would've given up if I'd lost. So, it makes sense that the value of my win should be the same. It could've been worse, you know."

"How so?"

"What if I had asked you to take me to that fancy restaurant?" Mya asks, pointing at Thorn on the opposite end of the dock. It's the only five-star restaurant in Lasso County and by far the most expensive.

"I'm sure that would've been a lot more than sixty bucks, so you got off cheap."

"Good point," I say, then lean back on my elbows and gaze at Mya. She studies a few sandwiches wrapped in plastic, reading the labels and the nutritional content before settling on turkey and Swiss on rye. She's relaxed and at-ease, all the tension and frustration from this morning gone.

"You never told me what had you so wound up earlier," I say, unable to fight my curiosity. She'd come to Kimbell after losing her job and her relationship. Had her ex come back into the picture? Was she struggling with wanting him back? Did I want to know the answer to that question?

Mya smiles at me. "I struck out on landing a job here. I found out my old boss who cheated with my boyfriend and got pregnant has also made phone calls to gyms all across the Hill Country bashing my name and reputation. No one is going to hire me here. I'll have to go to Houston or Dallas to get another job, which sucks because I hate, and I mean loathe, big cities."

"Wait a minute," I rise and turn toward her. "Back up. What did you say? Your ex cheated on you?"

"You heard me right," Mya says, suddenly riveted by the glossy black polish on her nails. "That morning when we first met, I'd caught them and the whole truth came out."

"Scumbag. I don't get why guys do that crap. If he stopped wanting you, he needed to man up, tell you and let you go!" I say, voice rising in anger.

Mya shrinks back a bit and I wonder if I've come on too strong. The last thing I want to do is freak her out … or scare her away.

"Well," she says, then takes a deep breath. "He claims that he never would've cheated if I hadn't fallen out of love with him. So, it's my fault that he slept with my boss and got her pregnant."

"Is that true?

"Is what true?"

"Did you fall out of love with your ex?"

Mya looks back at me, her eyes searching mine for something I can't read.

"Depends," she says.

"On what?"

"Will you think I'm a horrible person if I say yes?"

"No, of course not." I reach for her, wrapping an arm around her shoulders. I give her a gentle squeeze and caress her skin. She leans into my touch, relaxing more.

"I know what it's like to fall out of love with someone, especially when you'd been convinced that person was the love of your life. It's jarring," I admit, thinking back on the months after Nikki abandoned me and the boys to go back home to London. "You feel like—"

"A failure."

"Exactly. You spend half the time trying to convince yourself that you're still in love. That things are fine and that y'all can recapture what you used to have until you wake up one day …"

"And you can't ignore the truth anymore," Mya finishes my thought. "Is that how it was with you and your ex?"

"Yeah, but I had the luxury of being left behind by her. She claimed she still loved me and the boys, just needed space and time to pursue her career. But that was all a lie. I thought I'd wait for her, you know?" I drag a hand down my face. Mya nods at me, in sync with what I'm saying, because I can sense she's felt the same. I realize I've never talked about these feelings with anyone. Maybe talking to Mya is easy because she understands what I went through. It's so similar to what she's going through now.

Since I'm already baring my soul, might as well continue. I say, "As the months passed by, I realized that our relationship wasn't what I thought it had been. We weren't in a good place before she left. I can say it's a lot easier to move on when the person is long gone." I slip my arm from her shoulders, then grip her hands, holding them in mine. "You were in a tougher spot. Having to be the one to leave, even if it's the right thing to do, it's hard. Don't be upset with yourself for not leaving sooner."

"It's hard not to be upset. The life I had built for myself is gone now. If I had the courage to do this on my own terms, I could've salvaged things. My career wouldn't be in the toilet. I wouldn't be living off of my family struggling to figure out my next move."

"Hey, there's still time for you to do that."

"No, there isn't. I only have a few more days before I have to move on, even though I haven't figured things out," Mya says, pulling away from me. She takes a big bite of her turkey and swiss sandwich, chomping furiously in the cutest way. I drag my eyes away from her luscious lips and take another sip of my iced nitro brew. Not that I need a reason to be more amped up than I am.

"Then stick around. Kimbell's a great town. Friendly folks. Nature and plenty of places for you to hang out, meditate, do what you need to do to put a plan together." The urge to convince her to stay is impossible to stop. I'm not ready for her to go, but why do I want her to stay so bad? Isn't this how I always get myself in trouble? Falling for ladies too quick without getting to know them. But am I falling for Mya? Or am I trying to help someone who's going through what I've been through?

When Nikki left, the one thing that kept me grounded and able to figure things out was being here in Kimbell. Having the familiarity of the same surroundings and routines, even if people looked at me with pity in their eyes from being left by my wife. I couldn't imagine I would've gotten through all that pain if I was moving around, jumping from city to city.

"I don't have time for that," Mya shakes her head.

"Don't rush this. Now is the time for you to stay in one place, be still and listen to your heart."

"Listening to my heart won't pay the bills, Ronan. I can't survive without money. I need a job and there isn't one for me here. I'll spend the next few days making arrangements to crash at a friend's house in Austin, then I'm gone," Mya says.

The finality of her words is like a dagger in my chest. I look away from her, trying to wait for the sharp pangs to dissipate. I say, "Well, if you need anything while you're still here—"

My cell phone rings. I slip it out of my pocket and stare at the number. It's my house calling. A quick glance at the clock and I know why. I hold up a hand to Mya, then answer.

"I'm on my way."

"You better be," Connor yells into the phone, not bothering to hide his frustration. "Finn and Dec are fidgety and nervous, and they need you here. The first nanny is arriving in twenty minutes."

"I know, I know," I say, scrambling to my feet. "I won't be late." I put the phone back in my pocket.

"Everything okay?" Mya asks, looking up at me with concern.

"Time got away from me. The nanny interviews are starting soon. I gotta go." I say, but my body refuses to move.

Mya stands up. "This is my fault with my stupid wager."

"Don't. I enjoyed spending this time with you."

"Stop being so wonderful, Ronan. The last thing I need is to catch feelings for you before I leave town," Mya says, resting her hands on her hips.

"I won't see you again, will I?" I hold my breath, hoping for a sliver of a chance.

"Nope," Mya says.

"That's too bad. Take care of yourself, Mya."

"You, too. And thanks for the talk. It helped more than you know." Mya reaches for me.

Time stands still as I feel her arms slip around my neck. My arms enclose around her waist, pulling her into me. The feel of her body next to mine is like heaven. I press my nose into her hair, inhaling the flowery scent. We stand there for a long moment, holding onto each other. Neither one of us wanting to let go. I'm not sure what's happening or why, and I don't care. It's been a long time since I've felt this connected to anyone, and maybe I never have.

My cell phone rings again.

Mya pulls away, leaving me feeling empty and alone.

"You better go." She says, increasing the distance between us.

The look in her eyes tells me she felt it, too.

Just my stupid luck that the one woman I'd take a chance on is leaving town in a few days.

I don't bother saying bye.

With a quick wave, I turn and sprint toward the parking lot with visions of Mya dominating my thoughts.

CHAPTER 13

M^{YA}

~

Curling my legs onto the rickety bench under the awning of the patio, I watch Jellybean dashing back and forth along the fence as a crafty squirrel taunts him. Every few minutes, my dog jumps trying to knock the squirrel down, only to be thwarted each time. He looks back at me, as if asking for some assistance, but I don't budge.

Instead, I flip the card over and over in my hand as I put off doing what I know I should do right now. My latest procrastination tactic is the same as my old—thinking about the gorgeous ginger firefighter. Running into Ronan yesterday at the gym was unexpected, but definitely not regretted. The sweet memories of his tight, spectacular butt in those basketball shorts alone were worth it. It was like heaven watching him, watching me as we both worked out. That was nothing compared to how deep our conversation got over lunch. I opened up to him in a way I wasn't expecting.

It's uncanny how similar our past experiences are. I couldn't help bonding with him over escaping relationships that never should've happened. When he guessed that he wouldn't see me again, I felt more than a twinge of sadness to confirm that truth.

But that's not what kept me up half the night thinking about him when I was trying to come up with a Plan B or C or D to get the money for my uncle.

It was the goodbye hug that felt more like a hello. An opening or beginning of something neither one of us was expecting. The feel of his arms wrapped around my body as I leaned into the coarse strands of his bearded face had felt beyond intimate. If his phone hadn't rung again, I'm not sure when we would've let go of each other.

And that thought has lingered with me since the moment he rushed away.

I racked my brain all night trying to remember if that … feeling … is the same I felt for Jamal six years ago. Is this what it had been like? The answer came quick and decisive.

How can I feel something for Ronan in two brief interactions I've never felt for any man before? And what does that mean? Even though my relationship with Jamal was over a long time ago, could I still be on the rebound? Are these real feelings or am I clinging to some fantasy to avoid dealing with the grief of my last relationship being laid to rest?

I groan under my breath.

I don't want to think about this either.

Flipping the card in my hand again, I stare at the name and phone number scrawled in cursive handwriting on the front. Hendrix Jones. The man who stopped by earlier inquiring about renting the house.

He looked around, undeterred by the dingy tan carpet worn flat from forty-plus years of wear and tear and the gold peeling wallpaper. Hendrix can't purchase it, yet. He was hoping my uncle would rent it until he got his finances in order.

I promised I'd talk to my uncle about it and get back to him.

This is the best thing I can do for my uncle.

But I don't want to leave.

Being in this place is like being enveloped in memories of my grandma. She was relaxed and comfortable staying in this house with Uncle Tony in the summers in a way she never was in Austin. It made me love this town more. No worrying about letting my parents down again. No judgment. It was a place I could be carefree.

Uncle Tony's house, empty now, is still like a second home to me. I remember sitting between my grandma's legs as she braided my hair, listening to her and my uncle swapping story after story of their adventures growing up. My grandma's presence is all over this town.

Deep down, I guess I thought being here would help me tap into some wisdom from her. Reconnect with the sage advice she used to give me when I was growing up. I swear she had a way out of any situation. That's what I need right now. The answer to how I get my life together and find a way back on my feet after wasting years with Jamal.

Too bad I won't be here long enough to discern what advice Grandma would give. If I can't pay the bills, the least I can do is make sure I find a way for the bills to be covered for my uncle. It's the least I can do for the kindness he showed me after not hearing from me in years.

Resigned to do the right thing, I grab my phone from the end of the bench and scroll until I find my uncle's number in my contacts.

Loud banging on the door of Georgia's house stops my movement. Jellybean grows still, turning toward the sound, then to me. His muscles coiled and tensed, ready to pounce and protect me on my command.

The banging continues. Through the noise, I hear soft whimpers of cries. Jellybean howls, then races toward the gate, trying to get underneath.

"Hold on, boy," I say, running toward him. "Let me check it out."

He's having none of that as he howls more and scratches furiously to get underneath the wooden planks.

What in the world is going on out there?

Despite my better judgment, knowing Jellybean might pounce on some unsuspecting person, I don't waste time going through the house to get to the front yard. Flipping the latch, I swing the gate open and follow Jellybean along the narrow patch of grass until we reach Georgia's front yard.

"Miss Mya!" Finnegan wails through a tear-stained face and comes racing toward me. Declan is close behind him. I squat low and embrace Georgia's grandsons, rubbing their backs as I hold them. Jellybean paces around us in circles, obviously concerned about his new playmates.

In the distance, a thin woman wearing a blue sundress stops her pounding on the door and turns toward me with a scowl.

I pull back from the boys and search their sad eyes. Then instinct kicks in and I assess their arms and legs for any bruises or cuts, but find none.

"What happened? What are you two doing here? Who is she?" The questions tumble from my mouth.

"Our new nanny hates us," Declan says with a frown.

"We don't like her," Finnegan adds, then grips my neck tighter.

The woman steps off Georgia's porch and stomps over toward me. "Do you know where Georgia Knight is?"

"She got called in to the hospital for an emergency surgery this morning," I say, then stand to my full height, towering over the waif of a woman. "Who are you?"

"I'm Liesel, and I was hired to be the nanny for the O'Reilly twins." She runs a hand through her disheveled, blond curly tresses. "But I can't do it. They are the most horrible children I've ever had to take care of in my life."

Did she say O'Reilly twins?

Like Ronan O'Reilly?

I stare down at the little boys clinging to my legs. They look nothing like the handsome ginger man who's been dominating my dreams over the past few days. These cannot be his sons. Can they?

Liesel continues, "Do you know they found a snake and put it in my purse after breakfast? I almost had a heart attack. It was slimy and gross."

Finnegan says, "It was smaller than the one we found in your backyard, Miss Mya."

"You didn't scream or cry when we showed you the snake, Miss Mya," Declan adds, glaring at Liesel. "I don't know why she cried. It's just a snake."

Liesel flings her arms in the air, a disgusted look on her face. "And that was after I'd spent the past thirty minutes cleaning up the kitchen from their breakfast food fight. Instead of eating cheerios, they threw soggy cereal at each other and toss the milk onto the floor."

"Did y'all do that?" I ask, looking at Declan, then at Finnegan.

As if on cue, they turn on suitably remorseful expressions. In unison, they say, "We messed up."

"Yes, you did mess up. You messed up so bad that I'm not sticking around to take care of you any longer," Liesel tells them, then looks at me. "I called the fire station, but their father is working a fire in Burleson County. The receptionist didn't know when he'd be back and told me to bring the boys to their grandmother instead."

"Their father." I hesitate. The puzzle pieces are all coming together, but my mind is still refusing to believe what I know is true. "The firefighter."

"Yeah, Ronan." Liesel looks at me as if I've lost my mind. I know she's thinking that if I know Finnegan and Declan, then I must know their father. But the truth is, I don't. At least, I didn't realize I knew their father. Georgia never mentioned him by name when she complained about him limiting her interactions with the boys to punish her for what her daughter had done. The situation was painful for her, so I didn't pry.

Not once did it ever cross my mind that these two little guys were the same sons that Ronan talked about. Now that I look into their stormy blue-gray eyes that match Ronan's, I wonder how I could've missed it.

"He is struggling as a single father. These boys have not been taught any manners. They are rude. They don't listen to instructions and disrespected me at every turn. I don't have to put up with this." Liesel grips her purse.

Anger claws up my neck at her ignorant assumptions about Ronan. The behavior of the boys doesn't line up with how they were with me a couple of days ago. Her assessment of Ronan makes me want to slap her curly hair straight.

Liesel turns and stalks across the grass.

"Wait!" I call after her, pulling the boys along as I follow her to the Volkswagen parked in front of Georgia's house. "Where are you going?"

"Home to call my agency and let them know I need a new assignment."

"You need to wait until Ronan is back and talk to him about this," I say, growing increasingly frustrated with the woman. "You can't leave the boys here alone."

She gives me a flippant look as she opens her car door. "I'm not leaving them alone. I'm leaving them with you. You're a family friend and capable of watching them until Ronan is back."

As she gets in the car, cranks the engine and drives off, I stand there dumbfounded with Declan and Finnegan holding my hands.

CHAPTER 14

R*ONAN*

~

I SHIFT MY CELL PHONE AGAINST MY EAR, HEART POUNDING in my chest as I wait for the line to be answered. Battling a four-alarm warehouse blaze in Caldwell with fire fighters from three neighboring counties for the past five hours hadn't been enough to stop me from thinking about my boys and how their first day with Liesel, the nanny, is going.

After the fire had been subdued, I grabbed my cell phone from the fire truck and sent a quick text, expecting an immediate response like she'd done earlier this morning. After thirty minutes and a couple more unanswered text messages and several phone calls, I'm trying not to freak out as we get ready to make the hour long drive back to Kimbell.

"Still no word?" Darren asks, stopping next to me as he performs the last of the checks on the fire truck before we head back.

I shake my head. "I'm calling the nanny agency now."

Finally, the phone is answered. I ask for my call to be directed to Bert McNamara, the consultant assigned to me, and am placed on hold with irritating piano music blaring on the line.

Pacing the length of the fire truck, I open a bottle of water and pour it onto my sweat soaked chest. In my head, I know there's a reasonable explanation for the lack of response. Liesel could've taken the boys to the movies or something. If there had been an emergency, she would've called to let me know. Still, I can't shake the unease snaking through my veins.

I need answers.

Now.

"Hey … Ronan."

I freeze, arrested by the hesitation in Bert's tone. The guy was usually like a used car salesman, talking a mile a minute. The exact opposite of what I'm hearing right now.

"What happened?" I ask, steeling myself for what Bert will say next. Finnegan and Declan were notorious for being pranksters to new daycare workers and babysitters. I'd begged them this morning before leaving for work to be good for the new nanny and to make her like them. Everything had seemed well from all the check-in texts from Liesel. What could've changed?

The last text I got from her was brief.

Call me as soon as you can.

That came hours ago.

"I'm so sorry to tell you this, but Liesel quit."

"Let me guess, the boys terrorized her," I mumble under my breath, then glance at my watch. I guess I should be relieved that she could make it for ten hours today. I don't have enough fingers or toes to count how many babysitters didn't last that long. It was the one reason I'd been grateful things had worked out at Tiffany's daycare. But that came to an end.

Raking a hand through my wet hair, I stalk away from Wiley and

Darren as they secure the hose to the fire truck. Tendrils of white smoke billow into the sky from the burned warehouse ahead.

"In her message, she mentioned that the boys were mean to her and she couldn't take it anymore," Bert says, then clears his throat. "This kind of abandonment is not acceptable at our agency and we'll be giving you a full refund."

Shoulders slumped, I lean against the fire truck. "Alright, so we are in Burleson County, just finished fighting a blaze at the tire warehouse. It's going to take me an hour to get back to Kimbell. Can you ask her to hold on a little longer?"

If Connor isn't working, he can watch the boys for the night until my shift ends in the morning. My brother's going to be my next call.

Silence pierces the line.

The hair on the back of my neck stands on end.

"Bert," I say, trying to keep my voice calm. "Where is Liesel? Where are my boys?"

"I don't know, Ronan," Bert whispers.

"What did you say?" My voice rises as my blood boils.

"On the message she left, she was crying and distraught. I could barely understand what she was saying. She sounded spooked, and she said she left the boys."

"Left them where Bert? Where are Finn and Dec?" I scream, stomping back and forth in front of the fire truck.

Bert says, "I'm sorry, Ronan. I don't know. I'm doing everything I can to find them—"

I yank the phone from my ear as a string of expletives burst from my mouth.

Nate steps in front of me, stopping my progression. "What's going on? What happened to the twins?"

"The nanny quit and left my sons!" I say, jerking my hands toward the sky. "And this idiot doesn't have a clue where she abandoned them!"

Wiley comes over, followed by Luke and Darren.

"What do you mean, the nanny quit? Can nannies do that in the middle of a job?" Wiley asks.

"I guess so, since I found the one nanny who is unstable enough to leave four-year-old boys with no sign of where she left them," I growl in anger. Pressing the phone back to my ear, I say, "Bert, I swear if a single hair is hurt on their heads, I'm going to make you, Liesel, and your entire company pay! You hear me? Find my boys!"

Nate snatches the phone from my hands. "Let me see what I can find out from Bert."

Nate turns to Wiley. "Get Connor on the phone." Then he says to Luke, "You call Georgia." His last instructions to Darren. "Call Ronan's neighbors and see if she left the boys at his house." Nate looks at me, then grips my shoulder, giving me a reassuring shake. "We're going to find them."

I nod my head as each of them follows the instructions. My body trembles with rage and … fear. I sink to the ground, squatting low as I try to force myself to breathe. My hands shake and I feel like I'm going to vomit on the spot.

Darren squats down next to me, resting a hand on my shoulder. "Your neighbors said her car was gone by the time they got home from work. They used the emergency key to get inside, but the place is empty."

"Connor's not answering," Wiley says, sitting down on the grass next to me.

"I got Georgia's voice mail," Luke adds.

My heart sinks.

Darren says, "Call the hospital. Were Connor and Georgia working today?"

"Connor was, but he should be off work now," I say, swallowing past the lump in my throat. "No clue about Georgia. I haven't talked to her since a couple days ago when she watched the boys after they got kicked out of daycare." Something I never would've done if I hadn't been desperate that day.

"Almost ready to head out," Darren says. "If we have to go street by street and door to door, we're going to find them."

"Yeah," I say, letting out a shaky breath. Then focus on Wiley as he makes the call to the hospital.

"Hey, it's Wiley. Can you page Dr. Connor or Nurse Georgia for me? It's an emergency," Wiley says, drumming his fingers on his leg. "They are? Both of them? Okay, thanks." He looks at me, then says, "They both got called into an emergency surgery about three hours ago. Won't be done for another hour or two."

My vision blurs as I slump onto the ground, mind racing through possibilities of next steps to find my sons. The worse case scenario isn't one I want to dwell on. The situation where Liesel became so fed up with my boys that she did something to them. Something bad.

The veins in my neck jerk and throb as my back muscles tighten into knots.

No.

I force the gruesome thoughts from my mind.

"Bert is useless," Nate says, scrolling through my phone. "Who's number is this?" He turns the phone toward me.

I look at the digits, but don't recognize them. "I don't know."

"You have three missed calls from this number," Nate says. "Maybe it's Liesel telling you who she left the boys with."

"I had her number saved under her name." I scramble to my feet. "That's not her number." I take the phone from Nate, then put it on speaker as I dial my voice message service.

The automated tone declares, "You have one new message. Message one."

"Hi Ronan, it's Mya. I bet you're wondering how I got your number—"

Nate raises an eyebrow as I fumble the phone and take it off speaker. Wiley, Luke and Darren surround me, all with curious glances on their faces. Questions in their eyes I don't have time to deal with right now.

Mya's message continues, "Well, it took about an hour, but I got it from your two favorite people." In the background, I hear Finnegan and Declan squeal, "Hi Daddy!"

Mya continues, "Anyway, your nanny quit and was trying to drop them off with Georgia, but she got called into the hospital for an emergency surgery. So, your boys are with me. Guess I get to make it up to you after all. They're fine. Call me when you get done with the fire and I can bring them to the fire station. Okay. Talk to you soon. Bye."

I drop the phone to my side as her words sink in.

"They're fine. They're safe," I say, nodding my head as I exhale a shaky breath.

Luke steps forward, deep concern in his eyes. "Mya has your boys? You sure?"

"Mya? Hot Mya with the ripped abs and banging body has your little boys?" Wiley parrots Luke with his own special spin.

"Yes, that's what she says." I convey Mya's explanation, then put the phone back on speaker so they all can hear the message.

"Alright, let's go," Darren says. "We'll put the siren on and get back faster."

CHAPTER 15

~

FINNEGAN AND DECLAN PUSH THE TOY FIRE TRUCKS ACROSS the linoleum floor of the Kimbell Fire Station, barking orders at each other and making siren noises. Their voices echo in the room as I sit on the edge of the couch, feeling like I'm about to jump out of my skin.

I knew when I left the message for Ronan, he'd eventually call back. I have his sons, after all. The little boys he had no clue I'd watched for several hours a couple of days ago and kind of bonded with. I'm sure he's in a hurry to see for himself they are okay after being abandoned by the nanny he hired.

What I didn't expect were these pesky jitters racing through my body as I wait for his crew to arrive from fighting the fire in Caldwell. My stomach is doing flip-flops. I'm checking the digital clock hanging on the side wall every couple of minutes, wondering when he will arrive. Wondering what it's going to feel like to see him again after the moment we shared on the lawn outside Chesterton's Gym. Wondering if it was as special as I think or if I'm reading too much into things.

My cheeks flush at the memory of how his blue gaze arrested me. How his strong arms wrapped around me. The possessive hold he had on me as if he had no plans of letting go.

How I didn't want him to let go.

I push up from the couch and walk over to the boys, deciding it's better for me to get rid of some of this nervous energy by playing fire fighter with them than to continue to fantasize about their father. Again.

"Miss Mya, we're going to rescue a baby from the fire over there," Finnegan says, pointing to a chair in the corner where a Barbie doll and a baby sit on the edge of a potted plant.

"That's important work," I say, then glance at Declan, who is filling cups with water from the cooler. "What do you need me to do?"

"Daddy!" Declan yells, dropping the cups as he races to the glass windows looking out on Main Street.

My gaze goes from the water spreading across the floor to the fire truck slowing down in front of the station as it makes a turn into the garage. My breath catches in my throat and I know I'm not ready for this.

Finnegan and Declan race toward a side door, waiting impatiently for the firefighters to enter. I glance down at the oversized black cotton buttoned-down shirt and my gray leggings and wish I'd thought twice about what I had on before heading over to the fire station. I look like I'm wearing a muu muu. Not flattering at all to the assets I could display, but I spent the last several hours chasing two hyperactive little boys around the house and the yard. I try to smooth the wayward strands of my hair back into my ponytail, then fix my eyes on the door.

Minutes later, it opens and a sea of the hottest fire fighters I've ever seen in my life come barreling through. So much for the average fire fighter looking nothing like the men who portray them on television and stripper shows. These guys are the stuff drooling is made for. I have to force myself not to gape at them as they all take turns giving Finnegan and Declan hugs and high-fives.

Ronan is the last to enter.

I expect him to search the room for his sons first, but he looks directly at me. The relief and gratefulness in his gaze touches my heart. He gives me a slight smile, then reaches down to scoop up the boys, one in each arm.

Finnegan and Declan squeal with delight.

"Daddy, did you put out the fire?" Finnegan asks.

"Yes, we did," Ronan says, walking straight toward me.

Declan wiggles and squirms in his grasp. "Daddy, you stink like smoke. You need a bath!"

Ronan's laugh fills the space. I can't take my eyes off him with his sons. Seeing them together for the first time, I can pick up on the subtle similarities in their faces. But what strikes me the most is how the boys' mannerisms mirror Ronan's. They may not look a lot like him, but they are carbon copies of his characteristics and behaviors.

"You must be Mya." A deep voice interrupts my thoughts.

I turn to see a blonde haired, blue-eyed man smiling at me. My eyebrow raises involuntarily at the guy who, despite being covered in dirt and grime, looks like he walked straight off the pages of GQ.

I lick my lips, then respond. "Yes, I am."

"Good to meet you. I'm Wiley," the man says, then turns to the other firefighters and introduces them one by one. "That's Luke, Darren, and the one scowling back there is Nate."

"Nice to meet, y'all."

Nate gives the others a rough shove. "Let's hit the showers and give Ronan a bit of privacy."

I cross my arms over my chest and watch the sly glances passing between the four men as they head across the lobby and through a door on the other side. Even Erin, the fire station receptionist, seems to have vanished. I'm standing all alone in the room with Ronan and his sons.

Taking a deep breath, I turn to face him.

"Thank you," Ronan says, his voice low and full of emotion. "You don't know how hard that was for me, not knowing where these little monsters were."

"I can imagine," I say, then give him the play-by-play of how the nanny left the boys with me earlier in the day after they'd unnerved her with a small snake.

"Still, it's a lot to ask for you to take care of two little boys you'd never met before. I really appreciate it," Ronan says.

"We know Miss Mya, already," Declan says.

Finnegan nods his head. "We played at her house on Saturday."

"You did?" Ronan asks, then looks up at me with a slight frown on his handsome face. "Where? How?"

"She our neighbor," Finnegan says.

"No, silly. She Granny neighbor," Declan interrupts.

Finnegan says, "And Granny said it was okay that we play with Jellybean while she took a nap."

"Jellybean is a dog," Declan explains.

"I didn't know they were your sons," I say, shaking my head. "They don't look like you. Except for … the eyes."

"Yeah, they look more like their mom." The tension in those words is unmistakable. But the boys don't seem to notice.

I chime in to help connect the dots. "Anyway, I'm staying at my uncle's house, which is next door to Georgia's. That's how all of this kind of happened."

"Your uncle is Tony Hayes?"

"Technically, my great-uncle. He and my grandma were brother and sister."

Ronan bites his lower lip in the cutest way as he puts the pieces together. "I thought he was selling the place."

"He is. But he's also letting me stay there until I can figure out what to do about my … situation." I rub the back of my neck. The situation that was unresolved since I'd spent the day taking care of Finnegan and Declan and not calling my uncle to tell him about Hendrix Jones's offer to rent the house.

"Can Miss Mya be our new nanny?" Finnegan asks, tugging at Ronan's dingy yellow firefighter pants. "We like her."

"Please!" Declan adds, jumping around me in a circle.

"No," Ronan says. He grips their hands and leads them over to the couch. "Miss Mya isn't a nanny. Sit here and don't move."

"Why not?" Declan demands.

Ronan silences the boy with a stern glance. Declan looks down at his hands as Finnegan wraps an arm around his brother's shoulders.

"Do not move," he repeats, more sternly than before. "I need to talk to Miss Mya," Ronan says, then heads my way. We walk to the corner of the lobby out of earshot of the boys.

"Hey," I say, resting a hand on his arm. Ronan looks down at my hand against his skin for a long moment, then back at me. I swear the look in his eyes makes my knees wobble. I force myself to speak. "I don't mind keeping them until your shift is over. I mean, I know you don't know me that well, but I've watched them before. Plus, I spent most of my high school years babysitting kids for dozens of families on the weekends. It's no big deal."

"It is a big deal. They're a handful. But I can tell they like you, which means you must be able to handle them."

"Snakes don't scare me and they can't tire me out."

"I know your uncle well. He's good people and I can tell you are too. Still, it's a lot to ask."

I watch as he battles an inner tug-of-war on whether to take me up on my offer or shut it down. I wonder if his resistance to the idea is less about my babysitting skills and more about the embrace we shared yesterday. The closeness that seems to be building between us that neither of us can explain.

I give him a playful grin. "I get it. You don't want your boys being watched by a woman with tattoos." I push the sleeves of my shirt up and turn my arms in the light.

"I'm sure they think those are super cool."

"They do as a matter of fact," I say, then grip his hands. "Look, you helped me out when I first got into town. Then again at the gym yesterday when I found out there's no way I'll be able to get a job in Kimbell. Now let me help you. I promise you I can handle those two. Plus, I'm unemployed, remember?"

Ronan's eyes light up. "I could pay you. That would help us both and not make me feel like I'm setting you up with those two rascals over there."

"No, Ronan. No. Then I wouldn't be repaying my debt to you."

"Stop it. If you can do what the nanny couldn't, then you deserve to get her pay. It's only fair, and it's the only way I'll agree to this."

I don't have the sense to resist his suggestion. This could solve my money problems and give me a reason to stick around Kimbell longer. A reason to see Ronan again.

"You might be on to something," I say, tapping my fingers on the taut muscles of his forearm. He steps closer to me.

"What's going on in that beautiful head of yours?"

"You told me I need time to figure out my next move, and I know you need time to find a suitable nanny for your boys. How much was the nanny going to cost you for a month?"

Ronan rattles off the figure and my eyes go wide.

"You're joking?"

"Kids aren't cheap."

"I'll take care of them for half that for one month," I say, knowing that's still more than enough to cover the rent and utilities at Uncle Tony's house. "But I need the money in advance. What do you say?"

"I say you're insane," Ronan says with a deep chuckle that sends waves of excitement through me.

"Is that a yes?"

He pulls out his phone and asks, "Where should I send the cash?"

CHAPTER 16

~

I WON'T LIE.

I was expecting Ronan to call me this morning and call off our deal. Over the past few days, it was obvious he wasn't convinced that allowing me to take care of his boys today was the best thing.

He'd waffled back and forth, coming up with dozens of reasons I didn't know what I was getting myself into. Each time, I tried to reassure him I may not be a full-time nanny, but I wasn't a rookie at taking care of kids. It was how I spent every weekend in high school. The escape I needed from my parent's disapproving eyes. Showing I was responsible enough to care for our neighbors' kids had gotten me a smidgen of respect from them. Not a minor feat.

As I stood in his massive living room this morning, he rattled through a litany of information I needed to know about how to care for the boys. Then texted me a list of emergency contact numbers and the order in which to call them if the worse were to happen. After triple checking that my CPR certification was up to date, he finally left for work. Then I got a text from him right as the boys and I were headed out that he'd arranged for his brother to take care of them overnight to ease me into the role.

That didn't bother me much. I couldn't help but be impressed by how he vetted me after his initial quick acceptance of my offer to care for the boys. My uncle told me how he'd called him, and Georgia, too, to ask if taking care of the twins was too much for me. Of course, Uncle Tony sang my praises. I'm not sure what Georgia told him, since I haven't seen her in days, but whatever she said didn't change his mind.

His willingness to trust me with the two people he loved most in this world isn't lost on me. It means a lot and I don't want him to regret that decision. Plus, this temporary job also gives me a good excuse to be around Ronan. I swear my intentions were good when I offered him the deal. It wasn't some sleazy way of using his kids to get close to him. I would never try to manipulate him in that way.

But ... I can't deny that Ronan and I have started to get to know each other better over the past few days. I won't pretend to be upset or oblivious to that.

"Miss Mya, what are we doing next?" Declan asks.

I glance down at Declan on my left and Finnegan on my right, both of them clutching my hands as we skip along the sidewalk in downtown Kimbell. The area is overflowing with locals and tourists as the first day of Founder's Weekend kicks off with activities, games and enough food to feed a third world country. The annual celebration of Kimberly Bell founding the town is the biggest event of the year. The town center is transformed into a fairground with live music, booths for food and merchandise, and lots of games for kids.

A group of clowns wander over toward us, honking their noses and ruffling the boys' hair before squirting them with water from flowers pinned to their jackets.

The sound of the boys' laughter fills the air. Handsome little faces with broad smiles. Getting the chance to hang out with Ronan's twin boys has been the best day I've had since leaving Round Rock.

We explored all the interactive displays that highlighted the major events in the founding of the town and how it prospered in the years that followed. Then we were off to the train museum where the boys peppered the volunteers with dozens of questions and walked away with complementary miniature trains. Next up was story time at the library where the boys were captivated by the reading of Larry Llama Loves Lasagna, a children's book written by the local librarian Odalis Cruz. Purchases of four Larry Llama books later, I took the boys to Bell Park where a play land had been erected for kids. Two hours of nonstop play on the inflatable jungle gyms, monkey bars, swings, slides and see-saw had slowed them down enough to want lunch—sandwiches and juice from Gwen's Country Cafe booth near the edge of the park.

I think it should be nap time, but they don't look tired.

"Well, it's almost time for me to take you to the hospital to meet up with your Uncle Connor," I explain.

"No, we want to stay with you, Miss Mya," Finn whines as Declan stares up at me with sad eyes. Why do I feel as disappointed as they look?

"You'll see me again in a couple of days, I promise. How about we wrap up our day with a treat? What's a good place to get one?" I ask, trying to distract them from being upset.

Declan and Finnegan look at each other, and I can almost see the telepathic communication racing back and forth between them. After several seconds, they look at me and smile.

"Well?" I ask, not sure what I'm getting myself into.

"Elevation," they say at the same time, then point at a shop across the street. I look at the awning and see "Elevation Cupcakes" written in a cursive font.

"Good choice, fellas," I say, not minding the extra carbs after the day we've had. I open the door and watch the boys rush inside. The smell of decadent sugary sweets lingers in the air, making me almost as giddy as the boys. My gaze settles on a large red velvet cupcake with a swirl of white frosting topped with red sprinkles.

"What can I get for y'all?" the worker behind the counter asks. She's dressed in a bright yellow t-shirt and hat emblazoned with the cartoon cupcake logo of the shop. A name tag hanging around her neck reads Brianna.

"I want a red velvet cupcake," I say, pointing toward the case.

"No, Miss Mya!" Declan says, shaking his head.

Finnegan makes a gagging face. "Yuck!"

"I like red velvet cupcakes," I insist.

"Not from here," Declan says, a seriousness in his gaze.

Finnegan tugs at my arm, wiggling his finger for me to come closer. I bend down to stare into his slate-blue eyes, full of concern.

"Miss Mya," Finnegan says, "No one gets cupcakes from Elevation. They're nasty. You need to get something else."

I frown, then glance up at Brianna, hoping that she's not offended. I'm surprised to see her nodding at me.

"We're still working out the kinks of our cupcake recipe. It's … not quite there, yet," she says.

"Seriously?"

"Told you," Declan responds.

"But it looks so good." I walk closer to the scrumptious dessert underneath the soft lights inside the glass counter.

Brianna says, "Yes, ma'am. But that's for show. I couldn't sell it to you in good conscience. You wouldn't come back here if I did."

I exhale, unable to reconcile how a place called Elevation Cupcakes doesn't make tasty cupcakes. I scan the other contents of the case and see a variety of amazing looking desserts.

"What would you recommend, then?" I ask.

"Anything but a cupcake," Brianna says with a bright white smile.

"Got it," I say, resisting the urge to roll my eyes. I turn my attention back to the boys. "What do y'all want?"

"Ice cream!" They say in unison.

"Ice cream," I repeat, still flummoxed by this situation.

"Dec wants chocolate ice cream," Finn says.

"And Finn wants strawberry ice cream," Declan says.

"And for you?" Brianna asks.

"How are the pecan myrtles?" I glance over at the gooey mass of caramel and pecans covered in thick chocolate.

"Divine." Brianna's eyes light up.

Relieved, I say, "I'll take one of those and three bottles of water."

"Coming right up," Brianna beams as she turns toward the waffle maker and pours batter inside.

I follow the boys as they race to the only empty table in the place, a low round one with a cupcake made of mosaic tiles on the surface. As usual, Dec beats Finn, but Finn doesn't seem to mind.

I ease onto the stool between them and put my elbows on the table, resting my head in my hands to mimic them.

"Miss Mya, can I ask you a question?" Finnegan asks.

"You just did," I say, then squeeze his little nose.

Declan snickers under his breath.

"Go ahead," I say.

"Do you have any kids?"

"No, I don't." I run a hand along the side of his face as a twinge pierces my heart.

"You should," Declan says. "You would be a great mommy. You're smart and fun and nice."

"And really pretty," Finnegan adds.

"Thank you." It's the only thing I can think to respond.

"Wonder if our mommy is as smart and fun and nice as you," Declan says, resting his head on the table. His eyes search mine as if he expects me to have the answer to all the world's mysteries.

"You don't remember your mom?" Curiosity gets the better of me and I wonder how Ronan found himself a single father of two.

"No," Finn says. "Granny shows us videos on her phone of our mommy holding us when we were little."

"She sang to us. She sang really good," Declan says.

"But we don't remember it." Finnegan says.

The sad looks on their usual vibrant faces are like a gut punch. They're too young to understand or comprehend the complex emotions they feel about being raised by only one parent. I imagine it's easier for kids raised by a single mom since that's more prevalent in society. But what must it be like for Dec and Finn to hear most, if not all, of their friends talking about moms when theirs is no where around?

"What does your daddy tell you about your mommy?" I ask.

Declan flings a hand dismissively and shrugs. "Nothing."

Finnegan nods in agreement. "Daddy don't talk about Mommy at all. So don't ask him about her."

Declan jerks up from the table. "Don't tell Daddy we talk about this, okay?"

"I won't," I say, my heart breaking for the adorable little boys even more.

"You pinky swear, Miss Mya?" Finnegan extends his little pinky finger toward me.

I loop my right pinky with his and my left toward Declan, who grips it with his own. "Yes, I pinky swear."

Brianna walks to our table and hands the boys their ice cream, then places a small plate in front of me with the pecan myrtle along with a stack of wet wipes. I make the boys pause from devouring their ice cream to thank her before she walks away. A quietness settles on the table as they become consumed with who will finish the ice cream the fastest. All the melancholy and tension from the earlier talk about their mom vanishes as if it had never occurred.

I can't help but wonder why did the boys' mom walk away from them? Didn't she realize what a gift they were? One that shouldn't be taken for granted.

My phone vibrates in my pocket. I slip a hand inside and grab it with one hand as my other hand is busy handing wet wipes to Declan and Finnegan, the winner of this latest competition between the two. Gooey ice cream coats their hands and drips down their arms.

A quick glance at the screen and I see Ronan's name.

My heart leaps into my throat, pounding out of control. I need to get a grip. There's no way he can know about the conversation the twins and I had. I feel guilty keeping it from him, but I gave the boys my word.

Answering the phone, I say, "Hey."

"Hey. So, I heard from Connor." Ronan's deep voice sends a blaze of heat against my skin. I fan myself as I lean back in the chair. A vision of the sexy firefighter floods my mind and I almost forget he's on the other line. "St. Elizabeth's is short on pediatricians in the E.R. There's been a lot of heat-related illnesses and injuries from the activities today. They need him to work tonight. Not sure how long."

"Can't say I'm surprised. I heard some people saying this is a record crowd for the first day of Founder's Day Weekend."

The silence on the line extends for a few moments too long. I rise from the table and put a little distance between me and the boys so they can't hear the conversation.

"Ronan, what's wrong?"

"I was wondering if you wouldn't mind staying over my place with them tonight," Ronan says, his words coming quicker. "Hear me out. The guest bedroom already has everything you need. I had it stocked and ready for the other nanny to use. You could bring Jellybean over to the house. That wouldn't be a problem at all. The boys have a strict bedtime of seven-thirty. They can barely stay awake past seven. I mean, I know it's a lot to ask after I told you that you wouldn't have to do overnight duties."

"I'd love to." The words rush out of my mouth before I can stop them.

"You're sure you don't mind?" Ronan asks.

"I'm positive," I say, a flutter dancing through my heart. "I can do this for you."

CHAPTER 17

R ONAN

~

"Heard you had a rough night." Santos Estrada, my old college roommate and closest friend, strolls toward me on the sidewalk leading to the fire station.

It's after nine in the morning as my shift at the station is ending. Reluctantly, I tear my gaze away from the photos on my cell and stop in front of him.

"Rough. That's putting it lightly, brother," I say, then give him a half-hug.

"False alarms are the worst, especially when bonehead teenagers think their little pranks are funny," Santos says with a wry grin. He clasps a hand on my shoulder and gives me a hard shake. "You look like crap."

I roll my eyes. It's the kind of night we loathe as firefighters. Not that we want tragedy to strike. Managing the adrenaline spikes over and over with no release wreaks havoc on the body and mind. "I feel like it, too. It's always bad on Founder's Weekend, but this year is the worst. Four separate calls, strategically timed to have us racing back and forth across Lasso County for nothing."

"Can't take a chance that one of them isn't the real deal. A downside of the job," Santos acknowledges.

"What are you doing here, anyway?" I ask, pushing my hand against his chest to stop his movement. "Didn't you get booted off the Elm Street Brewery arson case?"

Santos rubs a hand through his dark curls and looks away from me. He knows what's coming next.

"Way to keep a secret from your so-called best friend. You owe me answers and you know it," I say, giving him a stern shake.

"Yeah, yeah, I know," Santos says, a sheepish grin crossing his face. "Let's say it was all worth it in the end. Plus, the perp is in jail and the evidence is sound. No way he'll avoid being convicted. There's some paperwork I need to sign off on before heading over to Bell Park to volunteer."

"Guess I don't have to ask which booth you'll be working at." Even at this hour in the morning, the crowds are building and the festivities of Founder's Weekend are already hitting a fever pitch.

"Nope," Santos says, ignoring my not-so-subtle ribbing.

"I don't understand how you pulled it off, but being in love looks good on you. Don't mess it up."

"I'll try not to," Santos says. A hint of worry crosses his face then disappears. "Are you going to bring the boys out today? I'm sure they'd love to go crazy in the Kid's Play area they constructed. It's twice as big as before."

"I'm too tired and, luckily, Mya already took care of that for me. She took the boys around all day yesterday," I say, then hand Santos my phone. He scrolls through the series of pictures, then stops on a selfie of Mya with the boys smiling.

A whistle escapes his lips. "You never mentioned that your

temporary nanny looks like ... this. Now I see why you gave her a chance."

"Don't start that crap," Irritation crawls up my neck. "The boys don't like any babysitter or nanny, but they like her. They are the ones that insisted that I give this arrangement a shot."

Santos's laugh is like nails on a chalkboard. "You trying to push this decision on my nephews? Come on, man. I'm not blind. This chick is your type, one hundred percent. Are y'all dating?"

"No." I pinch the bridge of my nose, then look down at a crack in the sidewalk. "And she's not exactly my type."

"Why? Because she's black?" Santos asks, chuckling under his breath.

"That's not what I mean."

"Straight talk, I could describe her and I could describe Nikki and use almost the same words. Light tanned skin, dark black hair, gorgeous face and one of the best smiles." He shrugs. "Makes no difference that one is black and the other is white. Look at this picture. If we didn't know that Nikki was the twins' mom, people could think these boys are Mya's and you know it. You have a type, brother, and this is it."

"You think I'm looking for a substitute for Nikki? Really?" I shove Santos harder. "No part of me wants anything to do with that woman ever again! A woman who treats my sons like they are nothing is dead to me. Forever. I'll never forgive her for the pain she puts my boys through almost every day. Forget the similarities in looks. Mya is nothing like Nikki."

"Oh, she's not?"

"No. Nikki is selfish and self-centered. She says all the things she thinks you want to hear when, deep down, she doesn't mean any of it. She lies about what she wants, then goes off and does the opposite," I say, raking my hands through my hair as I stalk away from Santos. I turn around and add, "Mya is one of the most honest people I've met in my life." I point a finger at Santos. "She says what's on her mind with no apologies. She's confident in who she is and she's not worried about pretending to be someone she's not. That's refreshing."

"Is it now?" Santos asks, a sneaky smile playing on his lips.

I inhale sharply.

"Go on. Tell me more about how great Mya is," Santos says, clasping a hand on my shoulder. "You got it bad for this chick and you can't see it, yet."

"Why can't two adults of the opposite sex develop a friendship? Why does it have to be anything more? I literally met her last week and have only had a few conversations with her over the past few days."

"Yet you've learned enough about her to trust her to keep your little boys. The ones you protect like a fierce papa bear. And they like her, too. All of this is adding up, brother. I don't care how much you try to deny it. I want you to finally find someone who is worthy of you. Mya could be that woman—"

"Shut up," my voice is low and full of warning.

"And I get you were desperate, but dude, the twins are going to kill any chance you have of dating that woman."

"Not so sure about that. Did you see those pictures? She enjoys being with them as much as they love being around her."

"Aha! So, are you ready to admit that you're interested in her?" Santos asks, as he hands the cell phone back to me.

"What I'm interested in is not important right now. Mya is dealing with a lot of things that she needs to work through. I won't add the stress of dating a single father," I say. There's no point to lie to Santos. He knows me too well. "Plus, I'm not sure I'm ready to carve out time away from my sons to date someone. Am I attracted to her? Yes. Have I thought about trying to date her? Yes. But it's not good timing for me and definitely not for her. So, drop it."

"Maybe luck would have it that the two of you are ready for more than you realize," Santos says, then taps a finger on the phone. "She sent you dozens of photos of the boys yesterday. She wanted you to live the experience with them through those pictures. I know how much you hate missing out on their lives when you're at work. Getting these photos must have made your day."

It did more than that.

Mya's thoughtfulness had touched me.

Being a firefighter with my 24-48 schedule gives me a lot of time to be a hands-on single dad, but it doesn't stop the guilt that gorges me every time I have to leave them to go to work. Ever since the boys were abandoned by their mother, I try to do everything I can to show my sons they are loved unconditionally. That their mother may have left them, but I never will. They'll always have me, no matter what.

At four now, they understand my job and look up to me as a hero. They love that Daddy saves people and places from bad fires. I can feel how proud they are of me. Still, I miss them terribly when I'm not with them. Getting the pictures and seeing them enjoying their time with Mya was exactly what I needed to put any concerns at bay.

My cell phone beeps and another text comes through.

"Whoa," Santos says, then fake fans himself. "This one is going to cause a blaze, if you know what I mean."

I jerk the phone from his hand and stare down at the photos coming through in a rapid succession of texts. No doubt, Declan, not Finnegan, has gotten his hands on her phone and some kind of way sent me a bunch of selfies of Mya from her camera app. Mya hasn't been shy in her flirting with me, but she wouldn't go so far to send so many pics with no message attached. Would she?

I scroll through the snapshots—gorgeous pictures that Mya took of herself around the grounds of the Founder's Weekend activities. I try to look away, but can't. It's bad enough that memories of the moment we shared outside of Chesterton's Gym still haunt me. Now I have pictures of Mya on my phone.

It's the sweetest torture.

I fumble with the phone as I put it in my pocket. "I need to get over to the house. I'm sure she doesn't realize the boys are playing with her phone."

"Maybe ... let me give you some advice."

"Please ... don't." I give Santos another warning as he responds with an annoying grin.

"I'm gonna keep it P.G. You need to find a real nanny to take care of those kids so you can give Mya the attention she deserves." Santos tips his head at me, then enters the fire station.

I can't say the thought hadn't crossed my mind.

I wouldn't mind giving Mya a reason to stick around Kimbell a little longer.

CHAPTER 18

R*ONAN*

~

T WENTY MINUTES AND A DOUBLE ESPRESSO SHOT LATER, I pull my Denali SUV next to Mya's Honda. My heartbeat kicks up a notch as I anticipate seeing her again. Something inside me craves the way she looks at me, the bold, sensual way she flirts without apology, the irresistible vibe that radiates between us whenever we're together.

Slamming the truck door, I force myself to get over this. I'm not some love-struck teenager. I'm a thirty-three-year-old man with kids. Too old to be feeling like this over a woman.

Or maybe I'm too stunned that any woman has made me feel like this again. It's not something I want to think about. Not now. Maybe not ever.

Stomping up the driveway to the front door, I let myself inside, then pause. The house is eerily quiet. Jellybean lies on the floor near the back of the couch, asleep next to Mya's strappy sandals. I drop my keys in the bowl on the table next to the door, then head down the hallway to where the bedrooms are located. I pass the closed door of my bedroom and cross over to the master bedroom, which I converted into a dual playroom and bedroom for the boys after Nikki left. Easing the door open, I walk inside, expecting them to be awake. But they're not.

I'm not surprised they are sleeping in after everything they'd done with Mya yesterday. No nanny before had the energy to outlast them, but Mya was too fit to let them wear her out.

I stare down at Finnegan, sleeping soundly on his side with his stuffed snake wrapped in his arms. Leaning over, I place a kiss on his forehead. I turn and shake my head at Declan. He's asleep on his back with his arms and legs splayed open wide. The covers are half on his body and half on the floor. I don't fix them since he'll kick them off again. I give him a kiss as I look around to see if Mya's cell phone is in the room. When I don't find it, I wonder if Mya had sent the pictures to me.

Maybe …

I lean against the dresser and watch the boys sleep for a while.

Despite their differences, Finnegan and Declan are a lot more alike than they are different, and that goes well beyond looking identical. Their thoughts and feelings tend to line up exactly, even if they choose to act on them in different ways. Discovering all these little things about my sons is the highlight of being their father. All the little things Nikki chose to walk out on. I push the thoughts away before they ruin the tranquility of my sleeping boys.

I'm guessing they'll be up in a couple hours.

Closing the door, I glance toward the end of the hall at the door of the guest bedroom. Part of me wants to check on Mya, but I'm not sure that's a good idea. Instead, I text her to let her know I'm home. I don't mention the ten or so photos of her someone sent to me earlier from her phone. I type quickly and ask that she wake me up when she and the boys get up. Part of me hopes she's already up and will respond. I waste time by heading to the laundry room. Easing out of my t-shirt and cargo pants, I toss them in the hamper and grab some clothes from the dryer to put on.

Another glance at my cell phone for a response from Mya. But there isn't one. I want to go into the guest bedroom. I want to see her. Talk to her. But I don't. Instead, I turn toward the kitchen and grab an ice-cold bottle of water to cool myself off.

I should take a shower, but I need a couple more hours of sleep.

Ignoring the disappointment of not hearing Mya stirring down the hallway or getting a response to my text, I head back across the living room to my bedroom. I gulp water as I push the door open and step inside.

The bottle slips from my hand and crashes to the floor. Water gushes into the carpet, but I don't care.

Nothing matters except the vision of Mya ... snuggled in my king-sized bed.

She jolts up from my pillows, giving me the most delightful view of her muscular, toned body. She has on a skimpy tank top and pajama shorts that leave hardly anything to the imagination. My mouth gapes open as I lose myself in the sight of her stunning body. Her hair is wrapped in some kind of turban looking contraption and her face is devoid of all make-up, allowing her natural beauty to shine.

"What's wrong? Are the boys okay?" Mya's eyes are full of concern as she searches mine. Her chest rises and falls, accentuating the softness of her curves.

I drag a hand down my face and avert my gaze. But that doesn't last long. My stomach has tied itself into knots as I stare at her.

"Nothing. They're fine. Still sleeping."

"Then what is it? Why did you come into my room?" She asks, easing back onto her elbows. Now it's her turn to stare at me. Her eyes traveling the full length of my body and back up again. My eyes are glued to her mouth as her tongue caresses her bottom lip.

"Your … room?" I frown, glancing around my bedroom, which she fits perfectly within. "Mya, this isn't the guest bedroom."

"It's not?" Her eyes grow wide as realization strikes. The cutest flush of panic spreads across her face. "Oh, no."

"You're in my bed," I say, then lean against the door frame. "And you look real good there."

MYA

I FREEZE MID-MOTION, MY HAND GRIPPING THE EDGE OF the covers, and stare at Ronan. Hundreds of thoughts are jumbled in my mind. How in the world could I've mistaken Ronan's bedroom for the guest bedroom? I glance around the space, which looks more like a hotel room than someone's private sanctuary. I was expecting his room to be crowded with the twin's toys, lots of family photos and firefighter gear, but none of that was in this room. It was neat and nondescript. Comfortable but not personal. The debate about how I ended up in this situation is drowned out by the realization of the words Ronan just said to me.

You're in my bed, and you look real good there.

His eyes are locked on my body and for the first time, I feel shy and unsure around him. I'm dressed in my most unflattering set of pajamas with my hair wrapped around my head. Not a good look and it's made worse by the fact Ronan is breathtaking. Standing in the doorway, he leans against the door frame with his rippling, defined chest and six-pack abs flexing, then relaxing. A pair of basketball shorts sit low on his hips. Everything about him oozes sensuality, but nothing more than the desire in his slate-blue eyes. The look that is ravishing me. I realize I'm holding my breath and I force myself to exhale. I've got to get control of this situation.

"I'm sure I'm not the only one who's looked good in this bed," I say, feeling under the covers for my robe, which is frustratingly out of reach.

"Actually, you're the … first."

I pause my search for the wayward robe. "What about … ?"

A flash of surprise crosses his face. "Tossed that bed after she left me. I'm the only one who's slept there … until now." He raises an eyebrow as a slow smile plays on his lips.

"Come here." I pat the opposite side of the bed as I swing my legs over the edge.

"No, stay. I can crash in the guest bedroom." Ronan retreats a step backward.

"Ronan, I don't bite … unless you ask me nicely … and I'm not going to jump your bones. Yet."

"Are you always like this?"

"Like what?"

"Flirty and irresistible and amazing."

"Yes, and no and no."

"I think what you meant to say is just yes," he says, crossing his arms over his chest.

"Seriously, you come lay down. This is your bedroom. I'll get up and go where I was supposed to be. You must be exhausted."

"Not anymore."

I laugh. "That's called the Mya Effect. It'll wear off as soon as I put some distance between us."

"What if I … don't want distance?" Ronan drops his arms and walks into the room. He stops halfway between the door and the bed.

"What do you want?"

"To find out more about you."

"Why?"

"You're so difficult."

"And you so like it."

"I do." He comes closer and eases down onto the mattress, careful to keep a full body width between us. A hint of his cologne drifts my way, causing heat to dance across my skin.

Now I have a decision to make. I can do the prudent thing and leave the man in peace to sleep, especially after I mistakenly intruded on his bedroom and slept in his bed like some modern day Goldilocks.

Or I can indulge my heart and stick around for a little longer. Give myself a chance to learn more about this man who's dominated my fantasies since the day I came to Kimbell.

I grab a pillow and hold it against my chest as I lay down facing him. "Okay, what do you want to know?"

He reaches a strong hand toward my arm and squeezes my biceps. A whistle escapes his lips. "How much can you bench press?"

Best question ever. I relax and smile at him. He grins back at me.

"About half of what you did last weekend," I say.

"One sixty or so. Not bad." He nods, then releases his grip on my arm. "Staying in shape is definitely a requirement in your line of work, like mine."

"Yeah, but I would, even if I wasn't a personal trainer. I always loved working out. My parents never understood that."

"What did they want you to do?"

"Go to college. Get some bland, generic office job where I work in a cubicle all day while dreaming about strangling my co-workers and boss."

He laughs. "Kind of like the show, The Office."

"Never watched it."

"Seriously?"

"I'm not much into television. I'd rather be in the gym or reading books. My grandma was an assistant to the librarian at the Kimbell

Library for most of her life before she moved to Austin to raise me. Because of her, I have this insatiable love of reading any and everything," I say, then tap my cell phone. "Thank God for e-books."

"What are you reading right now?"

I hesitate, then decide to come clean. "The Effect of Cross Fit Training on Severely Obese Children. I had a new client, a teenage girl, who I was trying to help before I got … fired. I'm a Cross Fit certified trainer and I tend to think that it is the be all and end all of training for everyone. But when a child came in, barely thirteen, I knew I needed to do my homework before taking her on as a client. I didn't want to do more damage than good, you know."

"Shows how much you care," Ronan says, his eyes softening as he shifts on the bed. "I can tell you a lot of trainers would've taken her money without a second thought on checking the effects of applying an adult training program to children. Were you chubby as a kid?"

"No, just not focused. Training gave me a purpose. A goal. Something to work toward and a lot of confidence."

"Doubt you need any more of that." Ronan taps my nose, then laughs under his breath.

"Shut up!" I squeal, then swat at his massive biceps. "Anyway, that's the reason I became a trainer. To help give women who lack confidence a way to find it again."

"Did you see that a lot with your clients?"

"I did. The gym I worked at catered to everyone, but I focused on women who were very heavy. Some were clinically obese. Others were slightly overweight but suffered from low self-esteem. They were all intimidated to come into a gym setting and only did it because they'd hit rock bottom with their weight gain. I wanted to help free them of that. Help them see that their value and worth have nothing to do with the number on the scale. Do you know how empowering it is for a woman to do a single push-up after she's been training to do that for over a year? Imagine what that does for her psyche when she finally accomplishes what seems like such a simple goal."

"I'm sure she feels like she can take on the world. Nothing is out of reach any more."

"Exactly. That's what I worked to give my clients. Some of them lost weight, others didn't, but they all left being transformed internally more than externally. It's very rewarding. I love helping people tap into their potential."

"Seems like you make a habit of doing that," Ronan says, grabbing his pillow and mirroring my position, gripping it in front of his chest. "The boys looked so happy in the pictures you sent me yesterday. You looked pretty happy, too."

A nervous laugh escapes my lips. I'd been dreaming about Ronan. When I woke up for a few minutes to check my phone, I got the bright idea to send him pictures of me, too. Maybe not my best move, but no reason to deny I'd done it. "Was that horrible that I sent you my selfies? Seemed like a good idea when I was checking my phone this morning, but not so sure—"

"Trust me, it was a great idea." The look in Ronan's eyes says a lot more than his words. Butterflies ripple through me and I blush.

Thankfully, Ronan changes the subject. "So, how did you tire the little rascals out so much that they're still asleep at past nine in the morning?"

"You know how they have that seven-thirty bedtime ..." I say, deciding to come clean.

Ronan gives me a shrewd look.

"I kinda broke that last night. We had a Disney movie marathon to make up for me refusing to let them watch UFC. It ended around midnight."

He shakes his head, but he doesn't look upset.

"That explains it," Ronan says, then yawns loudly.

"You're sleepy and I'm keeping you up," I say, feeling the need to put some distance between us. The relaxed vibe and attraction is becoming too strong the longer we talk.

Ronan is about to respond, but another yawn overtakes him.

"I can stick around a little longer. Watch the boys so you can get some sleep," I say, not ready to leave this wonderful man or his adorable little boys. I feel the edge of my robe and pull it from underneath the covers. Slipping into it, I ease off the bed and toss the pillow at him.

Ronan catches it with one hand, then stuffs it behind his head. The look in his eyes sends flutters through my body.

"You don't mind?" He asks as his eyes close.

"I wouldn't offer if I did," I say, but he's not awake to hear my response.

CHAPTER 20

R*ONAN*

~

WATER CASCADES DOWN MY FACE AS I RUN MY HANDS under the faucet. I splash more on my skin, avoiding my reflection in the foggy mirror. The truth of this situation is written all over my face, and it's not something I'm ready to see.

Mya's under my skin and I can't deny it anymore.

It would be different if I wanted a hook-up. A casual fling, something I could do and then forget all about after she was long gone from town. But that's not what I want. None of this makes any sense because we haven't spent much time with each other. But I'm drawn to her. I don't really know her. But I want to. I want to know so much more about Mya—what makes her tick, the thoughts behind her sassy quips, the experiences that cause her to expose brief moments of vulnerability.

But should I bother trying?

I have responsibilities now. It's not only me who will be impacted if I want to start a relationship, a real relationship, with a woman. I have my boys to think about. They've suffered too much loss in their young lives. I can't and I won't subject them to the risk of getting attached to a woman in my life only for things to crash and burn in the end.

Isn't that how all my relationships turn out?

From my high school sweethearts to the intense college connections to all the women eager to date a hero firefighter, I could never make any of them work. In fact, they all ended spectacularly bad.

And my marriage to Nikki was the biggest disaster of them all.

Why would anything with Mya be different?

"It won't," I say, pointing a finger at my reflection.

Resignation settles within me. I turn the water off and dry my hands and face. Inhaling, I open the bathroom door and walk out into my bedroom. The vision of Mya clutching my pillow, wrapped in my sheets, sears into my memories. I turn away from the bed and exit to the hallway.

The boys are squealing and laughing as Jellybean barks. I glance toward the living room windows and watch them as they play catch with the pitbull in the backyard.

"And you thought they'd kill a dog," Mya's voice wafts from behind me.

She's close. So close that the scent of her jasmine and spice perfume floats in the air, intoxicating me. I turn and feel like I've been sucker punched.

Mya is stunning in a black maxi dress with spaghetti straps. The soft fabric hugs every curve of her body. Her toned, muscular, tattooed arms have a shimmering glow. As usual, her face is fresh and devoid of make-up. Only a shimmering pink gloss on her lips. I could look at this woman all day.

I glance down at the glass of lemonade she's holding. Grabbing it, I feel the heat radiating between us as our hands brush each other.

She meets my eyes and I know she feels it too.

Mya says, "I can't cook, but I can order takeout. The boys said you usually order one supreme and one cheese pizza, so that's what I got. It should be here in about …" She pauses and turns back to glance at the clock in the kitchen. My eyes drift along her body, enjoying the view.

"Fifteen minutes," Mya says.

I regain my ability to speak. "The least I can do is feed you for staying so long."

"It was my pleasure." That smile almost knocks me down. Mya continues, "I want to apologize for getting mixed up with the rooms. I feel bad about sleeping in your bed. I can't imagine how it feels to find a stranger—"

"Are we?" I ask, then take a sip of the lemonade. "Strangers, I mean?"

"Good question," she eases past me, hips swaying and toying with all my resolve. I follow her into the kitchen. "I'm not a stranger to Finnegan and Declan anymore after the whirlwind day we had yesterday. Their granny and I have had more conversations than I can count since I came to town. I know her pretty well. I'm practically a close family friend," Mya says, leaning against the kitchen counter.

I lean against the counter across from her. "But you and I haven't had the same opportunities."

"No, we haven't, and that's a shame."

"Think we should do something about that?"

"Depends."

"On."

"What you had in mind." The seduction in her voice teases me. She narrows her eyes, daring me to say what we both know I want to say. She doesn't think I will. That I'll find an excuse to back away from this moment. And I should for my own good.

Too bad I won't.

The crappy luck in relationships fades from my mind as I focus on the advice from my best friend. Santos would tell me to seize this moment.

I say, "Dinner. Just the two of us."

Mya's eyes grow wide as saucers and her eyelashes flutter. She places her glass of lemonade onto the counter with a shaky hand, then pushes the strands of her jet black hair behind her ears. Her gaze drops to the floor as she takes a couple of deep breaths.

Shocking Mya is more rewarding than I thought it would be.

She arches a brow as she looks back up at me. Her voice is low as she asks, "Like a date?"

"Yes, a date."

"So no more harmless, flirting, and teasing. You want to go out. Why?"

"Why not?" I step closer to her. Her face is flushed a slight pink and her breaths speed up. "You're beautiful, intelligent, intriguing and someone I can't stop myself from wanting to know better."

Mya slides away from me and paces across the tight space of the kitchen. I watch her moving, not used to seeing this side of her. She's obviously contemplating my question and my response to hers, debating how she'll respond. It's fascinating to watch and does nothing to make me regret my choice. I want to know her more now.

Finally, she stops moving and faces me. "I'd like to go out with you."

"Okay."

She raises a hand. "Let me finish."

I nod.

"But I can't. I'm too complicated. My life is a mess. I'm still trying to figure out what I should do after losing my job. I don't know how long I'm going to be in Kimbell after this month. I'll probably have to go groveling back to my parents and waste a year or more trying to re-establish myself as a trainer in a new area. You need someone who has her life together, not someone like me. It's not a good idea."

And like that, everything inside me deflates. I never thought she'd say no. All her reasons make sense. They are rational, but they do nothing to stifle the weight of disappointment settling on me.

We face off against each other, neither of us flinching.

"Daddy! Daddy! Pizza here! Daddy!" The boys yell. Finnegan and

Declan come racing through the house from the backyard and rush past us to the front door. I turn my back on Mya and follow the boys.

Minutes later, I pay the delivery guy and bring the pizzas inside.

"Miss Mya, can we eat on our Elmo plates?" Finnegan asks.

"I'm sure you can. Where are they?" Mya asks.

Finnegan points at the cabinet as I place the boxes on the table and open the lids. The rich aroma causes my stomach to growl.

"You hungry, Daddy?" Declan asks. He climbs into his chair next to Finnegan as Mya places an Elmo plate in front of each of them.

"A little bit, buddy," I say, picking up a couple of slices of cheese pizza. I place one on each of their plates. They are at the age where they are incredibly picky about what they eat. Seeing any other toppings stuck to the cheese on their pizza grosses them out, so they will only eat it plain.

I turn toward Mya. "You want supreme or cheese?"

"I think I should go home now," Mya says, rubbing her hands over Finnegan and Declan's heads. "It was fun hanging out with y'all."

"No! Miss Mya, don't go," Finnegan says, gripping a greasy hand on her wrist.

"You have to eat dinner with us," Declan adds.

"Please," Finnegan piles on.

I can see Mya crumbling under the assault. I know better than anyone how hard they are to resist when they gang up on you.

"You're welcome to stay. There's more than enough pizza." Being turned down by her and having her still around enticing me is a tough pill to swallow, but I'll do it for my boys.

"You don't mind?" Her eyes conveying her real question.

"I wouldn't offer if I did."

She rolls her eyes, then smiles. "Okay, I'll stay."

A couple of hours later, I'm full of regrets.

Conversation between us over dinner was easy and effortless. There was barely a pause and no moments of uncomfortable silence as we drifted through a broad range of topics. Mya downplays her opinions because she didn't go to college, but there's no denying how smart she is. I was riveted by our discussion, as the boys did more playing with their pizza than eating. I try to remember the last time I had such a smooth conversation with a woman.

The answer shocks me.

Never.

No one has captured my attention and held it like Mya did tonight. I wasn't focused on how gorgeous she is or how amazing her body looks in that tight black dress. I was engaged in our talk and enjoying every minute.

She fits right in with me and the boys, like she's always known us and we've always known her. I suspected it would be like this, which is why I asked her out. I contemplate trying again, but I know she won't go for that. Her reasons are valid and in my best interest, too. Still, I can't deny that this evening has exponentially increased my interest in her.

"Okay, fellas. Time for you to get ready for your baths. Mya needs to get home. It's late." I say, even though Mya doesn't look like she's ready to go. She looks relaxed and at ease with us. I grab the boys' plates. Finnegan's filled with crust and no cheese. Declan's filled with clumps of cheese and no crust. Antics they employed to get a reaction out of Mya.

Declan and Finnegan scurry down from their chairs and walk over to Mya, wrapping her in big bear hugs.

"We see you when Daddy goes to work next time, Miss Mya," Declan says.

"Yes, see you in a couple of days," Mya says, hugging them back.

I point them in the hallway's direction. "Now go to the bathroom and start the bath water, but don't get inside until I come in there. Okay?"

"Yes, Daddy," Declan says, then wraps an arm around Finnegan's shoulders as they walk away and out of our sight.

"You're great with them. They love being around you," I state the obvious. The only person who enjoys being around Mya more than my sons is me.

Mya frowns as she looks at me.

"If you're worried about earlier, don't be. I won't make things weird and I won't ask you out again." My eyes never leave her face. I'm searching for some reaction. Any reaction. But she gives me none. "We can keep things professional."

She stands and closes the distance between us, a hint of worry lingering in her eyes. She places her hands on her slim hips and looks up at the ceiling. Her dark tresses brush the edges of her chin as she takes a deep breath. "Yes, I think that's best."

And with those last words, my string of bad luck in love continues.

CHAPTER 21

EVERY SECOND I SPEND WITH RONAN IS ANOTHER CHANCE for me to remember what a big mistake I made. I've taken care of the boys twice since the first time Ronan asked me out and I turned him down flat. Each time has been better than the last.

The days when it's the boys and me are perfect. They are so funny and manipulative when they want to be. Watching them grow more comfortable with me as they let down their guard has been more than I could've imagined. The pranks have died down and they are content with being regular four-year-olds.

But the days when Ronan's shift ends are another story.

Not that they aren't perfect as well.

And that's the problem.

I continue to take care of the boys until around five in the afternoon after Ronan has either caught up on his sleep or finished errands he doesn't have time to do when I'm not taking on nanny duties. I'm supposed to go home, but that doesn't happen. Instead, I sit around the dining room table with Ronan and his boys as if we're some happy, blended family.

I feel like I'm living in a utopian twilight zone.

I thought I'd need a lot more time to get past my break-up with Jamal, but turns out that's a long forgotten chapter of my life.

Forgotten because of Ronan O'Reilly.

I saw all of this coming the moment he rescued Jellybean in the park, and I still did nothing to avoid it. Now, I'm stuck with out-of-control feelings for a man I shut down.

He told me he would never bring up us dating again and he has kept his word. Not once has he come close to the topic. And while I can't say we're keeping things professional, I've noticed the flirting has ceased. He ignores any compliments I throw his way and treats me like … a friend.

"Ugh!" I scream as I pound on the air mattress. "I hate the friend zone!" I kick my feet against the plastic, bouncing erratically against the wiggly bed.

My phone rings.

I tumble over the side of the mattress and scramble across the worn, threadbare carpet to where I hurled my cell phone late last night. I hope it's Ronan, but part of me knows it's probably Uncle Tony calling to check on me.

"Hello," I manage, out of breath.

"Hi, is this Mya?"

"Yes, who is this?"

"It's Jas. I mean, Jasmine Jones. The doctor who took you to the hospital a couple of weeks ago and stitched up your arm."

"Oh," I say, laying against the carpet. "Hi, Dr. Jones."

"Girl, please. Call me Jasmine. I wanted to check on you. See how your arm is healing. I figured you wouldn't come back to the hospital for that."

I glance down at my forearm, impressed with the results. "It's looking good to me. I took all the antibiotics and followed the instructions on how to clean it and bandage it."

"I'm glad. I still want to see it, though," Jasmine says. "Want to meet me for dinner at Baker Bros. I can check you out real quick and then we can … catch up."

My stomach growls at the thought of barbecue. It would be a lot of fun to have a night out and escape from my miserable life with a potential new friend. Then I'm reminded of the dismal state of my bank account. "I can't afford to eat out right now, but thanks for the offer."

"My treat. Want to meet me in like an hour?"

"Why are you doing this?"

"I don't know," Jasmine says. "You seemed like a real nice person who has hit a rough patch. I know how it is to need a friend and not have one around."

Something about her tone tells me she might need a friend as much as I do. It would be good to get another perspective on my situation with Ronan.

"Jasmine, are you sure about this? I don't want to take advantage. You've already been so sweet and kind, waiving the cost of my E.R. visit and paying for my prescription meds."

"Sweet? Kind? Ha!" Jasmine says with a hearty laugh. "Wait until you get to know me better. See you in an hour?"

I give in. "Sure. I'll be there."

An hour later, I'm cleaned up and showered, dressed in skinny jeans and a tank top and sitting across from Jasmine at Baker Bros BBQ. It's rare to meet someone you feel that instant friendship connection with, but I've got that with Jasmine.

Makes me think there's something special about Kimbell.

Grandma is looking out for me, after all.

Jasmine asks, "So, you're the new nanny. I get that. But what in the world could those boys have done to get kicked out of Tiff's daycare? She's been trying to get her hooks in Ronan since Nikki left, so I'm shocked she booted them."

My neck tightens, and I massage the knot threatening to build away. Of course, other women are interested in Ronan. Am I surprised by that?

"Well, they have fake shampoo bottles filled with water for the kids to play beauty shop. Finn and Dec poured the water out and replaced it with glue," I say, holding my side as I double over with laughter.

"Stop!" Jasmine says, cackling. "I shouldn't laugh, but maybe my mom got some business from their little prank."

"She owns a beauty salon?"

Jasmine nods as the smell of intense, smoky meat floats in the air. The place is overflowing on this Saturday night. Jas had to pull a lot of strings to get us a table in the downstairs seating. The place is loud and rowdy, which is what I need. A great distraction from my constant thoughts about Ronan.

"Good to know," I say, smoothing down my edges and flipping a hand through my hair. "It takes a regular regimen of relaxers to keep my hair this bone straight."

"Creamy crack!" Jasmine says, then gives me a high-five. "Keeps my mom in business."

I grab a menu and lean back against the wooden bench seat. There's not much on the one-pager. A list of about every type of barbecue meat you can think of served along with three sides: jalapeño baked beans, potato salad and white bread. If you want different sides, a note at the bottom of the menu directs you to walk three blocks to Gwen's Country Café. If you want dessert, another note directs you to walk two blocks to Elevation Cupcake Shop.

"You're going to focus on that menu when half the men in this restaurant are salivating over you?" Jasmine asks, snatching the menu from my hand. "Plus, there's only one thing you need to order when you come to Baker Bros. Double brisket plate with potato salad. It made the place famous."

"Sounds good to me," I say, then glance around the restaurant. Jasmine wasn't joking. Our table has gotten the attention of most of the men in the place. Some are more subtle, while others crane their necks to look at us. "What makes you think they're looking at me and not you, hottie?"

"Because you're hotter and your body is banging. Most of these dudes don't go for thick chicks like me," Jasmine says, then waves a hand at a passing waitress.

"Dr. Jones," the waitress slams two twelve-ounce plastic beer mugs down on the table, then leans over and gives Jasmine a hug. She's dressed in cut-off shorts and a midriff tank top that leaves nothing to the imagination. Her bright red lipstick and dark lashes try to hide the fact that her face is the least impressive part of her body.

"Who's your friend?" She asks.

"This is Mya. She's new in town and will be here for ..." Jasmine glances over at me with a quizzical look.

"A while," I say, not sure how to respond.

"Nice to meet you, Mya. I'm Isabella, but everybody calls me Izzie," she says, giving me a bright smile. "Did you explain to her how this works?"

I ask, "How what works?"

Jasmine wiggles in her seat and claps. "No, I did not. You tell her."

Izzie claps her hands above her head, then says, "At Baker, the first round of beers is always on the house. But you have to follow our two rules. If you don't, you'll see the cost of two rounds on your bill at the end of the night. Got it?"

"What are the rules?" I ask, not sure I want to take part in whatever has Jasmine looking like the cat who ate the canary.

Izzie raises one finger in the air. "First, you must come up with a toast for the drinks and scream it out loud so the rest of the restaurant can hear."

"I guess that's what all the yelling was about," I say, putting the pieces together.

"That's right. And two," she raises a second finger in the air. "You have to chug the beer without stopping. You up for the challenge."

"Free beer and I don't have to waste time sipping it? Count me in," I say.

"I had a feeling you'd love this," Jasmine says.

"Great, you want your usual, Jas?" Izzie asks.

"Make it two."

Izzie gives us a wink, then saunters away from the table.

"What do you want to drink to?" Jasmine asks, cradling her mug.

"How about girls' night out? You don't know how much I needed this," I say, feeling a twinge emotional.

"You and me both," Jasmine says, her expression matching how I feel. "Let's do it on the count of three. One. Two. Three."

I scream at the top of my lungs, my words mingling with Jasmine's. Pressing the mug to my lips, I chug until the cold, crisp brew is all gone as the guys in the restaurant stand up and applaud us, hooting and hollering.

Jasmine erupts into laughter, pointing her fingers at me. "This is all for you, not me."

I shrug off the attention and swipe the liquid from above my lip, then study Jas for a moment. She's been fun and carefree all night, but I'm sensing she had a different reason for suggesting we meet up.

"Did you have a rough day at work?" I ask. I can't imagine how stressful her life must be, leading the emergency medicine department at St. Elizabeth's hospital. The thought of all the crises she deals with makes all my problems pale in comparison.

"Nope."

"So this is about a man," I say, guessing the next obvious reason.

"Yep." Jasmine nods. "Normally, I'd talk to my best friend about this, but he's part of the problem."

"Your best friend is a guy?" I raise an eyebrow.

She nods. "And I'm finding out that he's not a fan of the guy who's swooped back into my life unexpectedly, so I can't talk to him about it," Jasmine explains. "Then I realized I don't want to talk to anyone about it. I want a night out of fun so I can stop thinking about it for a few hours, you know?"

"Trust me, I know. I'm in the opposite situation. Finally ended a relationship that had long since expired, but it's still wreaking havoc on my life now. I don't want to think about that jerk," I admit.

"The best way to stop thinking about him is to move on to someone new. There are a lot of guys in here who I'm sure would love to take your mind off of the dude you left behind."

"As much as I'm tempted, a rebound relationship is not the right prescription, doctor."

"I'm sorry. When did you get your medical degree?"

I laugh out loud.

"I'm the only one at this table qualified to assess ailments and prescribe treatment. But now I feel the need to dig a little deeper. You act like you're over that relationship, but maybe that's not true. Do you have lingering feelings for the guy?"

"Absolutely not," I say with no hesitation.

Jas looks impressed. "I actually believe you. What made you stick around for so long?"

"Stupidity."

"Seriously?"

"My parents warned me I was wasting my time with him. They gave me an ultimatum. I could walk away from the relationship and they would cover my college tuition or I could stay with him and be cut off forever. Guess what I chose."

"And that's why you stuck it out when you knew it was over. You didn't want to admit to yourself that your parents were right and you should've listened to them."

"Who knows what my life would be like now if I had?" A storm of anger rages within me.

"Maybe you're focused on the wrong things, though."

"What do you mean?"

"You're only talking about what you lost out on, but what about the things you gained from being independent and making your own choices? The lessons you learned that have made you so much stronger now than you would've been," Jasmine says.

"You think so?"

She nods her head. "I was a nerdy kid, graduated at sixteen, and got accepted into Princeton. I was scared to death of moving thousands of miles away from my family to go to school alone in New Jersey. But my dad pushed me to do it. He told me I'd never know the real me until I was all I had to rely on. That was the greatest lesson he wanted me to learn."

"Wow, that's ... deep," I say.

"What are the good things that you know about Mya now that you didn't know before?"

I shrug, then look down at my black lacquered nails.

"That's your prescription," Jasmine says, slamming her hands on the table. "You need to figure out the answer to that question and stop worrying about what you missed out on."

I grow quiet, wondering if Jasmine is right. Maybe that's what I need to do with my time here in Kimbell before I barrel head first into trying to resurrect my career.

Izzie comes back to the table with two plates piled high with meat and places them in front of us, then refills our mugs of beer before heading to the next table.

Jasmine rolls a piece of brisket between her fingers, then pops it in her mouth. "Now, back to the remedy. Don't you see you were trapped in a loveless situation? You're craving the opportunity to try again with someone worthy of you, especially with all the lessons you learned from that last relationship."

"But would that be fair to him if I'm not sure I'm ready?" I ask, hoping Jasmine can give me some insight.

"Him who?" Jas says, leaning across the table. "Have you met someone already that you want to explore a relationship with?"

I bite down on my lower lip hard, kicking myself for letting that slip. "I meant the universal him—"

"Liar! And there's only one man who you could've fallen for so fast," Jas says.

I feel my appetite wane as I pick at the potato salad. "Don't say it."

"Of course, I'm going to say it. You want Ronan O'Reilly and I think you should go for it!"

CHAPTER 22

R*ONAN*

~

"You convinced Connor to sign up for your dating app?" I shake my head, not believing Wiley's claim. Raising a hand toward Gwen Paul, the owner of Gwen's Country Cafe, I wait as she heads over to our table.

"Where's the rest of your team?" Gwen asks, placing her hands on her plump hips.

"The rich boys headed out to Galveston and took Darren's yacht to Lake Charles for some gambling," Wiley explains. As soon as our shift ended this morning, they'd left skid marks on their way out of the fire station.

"Well, I know why you didn't go," Gwen says, nodding at me.

I tug at my earlobe, knowing what Gwen is thinking. She's got it all wrong. No doubt it would've taken a lot of arm twisting to get me to take off with Nate, Luke and Darren to Louisiana and leave my sons behind, but it's not like I haven't done that before. Our trips to Lake Charles are legendary for high-stakes gambling and picking up women for the weekend.

There's only one reason I declined the invite this time.

I can't stop thinking about Mya.

There's not a day that goes by I don't want to spend all my time with her. On her days off, I'm distracted wondering what she's doing and who she's doing it with. While I hope she's bored out of her mind thinking of me when we're apart, I don't fool myself. She's gotten the attention of plenty of guys around town. Guys she might be more willing to date than she was me.

I'm not kidding myself. I know Mya turned me down for one reason —I'm a single father.

She doesn't think a guy like me should date an unemployed woman with no kids and an uncertain future. That's how she sees herself.

But it's not how I see her at all.

For a moment, I wish she could see herself like I see her. If she did, maybe she wouldn't be so adamant that we shouldn't date.

There's nothing I can do to make that happen, though.

Instead, I allow myself to indulge in memories of her when we're apart. Even though I know I shouldn't.

Gwen gives Wiley a playful slap on the arm. "But I can't believe you passed on the chance to party at the casinos. I thought that was one of your favorite places to pick up ladies."

"Now why would I need to travel all the way to Louisiana to find a beautiful woman to pursue when I have you standing right in front of me?" Wiley asks, pouring on the charm. Gwen responds on cue, flushing bright red as she fans her face.

"Oh you, stop it, Wiley Alexander," Gwen says, grinning from ear-to-ear. "What can I get you, Ronan?"

"Just wondered if you could muster up some of your strawberry syrup?" I say, adopting as serious a tone as I can.

Gwen's mouth drops open. "You are worse than those adorable boys of yours."

"Is that a no?" I ask.

"Give me a few minutes," Gwen says, her eyes growing wide. "I'll make you up some."

"Thank you, Miss Gwen," I say, mimicking my boys.

Gwen bursts into laughter, then turns to Wiley. "You need anything, playboy?"

"Just you on—"

"Alright, that's enough," I say, cutting Wiley off before he says something inappropriate.

Gwen giggles, then dismisses us with a wave before turning to head back to the kitchen.

"Like I was saying, your esteemed brother, Dr. Connor O'Reilly, is the latest joiner on my app." Wiley picks up a piece of bacon and points at me. "He's popular from what my metrics show. City women love the idea of a down-home country boy who loves kids enough to become a pediatrician. Since you're his twin, I'm betting you'd be popular, too."

"We don't look alike," I say, not following Wiley's logic. "Fraternal twins, you know."

Wiley shrugs. "Doesn't matter. The two of you would be good advertising for the Ladies Love Country Boys app. We could do a photo shoot at Bell Park. Wouldn't take long. An hour tops. I'd get the pics I need to craft an ad campaign. Women already swoon over both of you. He's preppy and white collar. You're rugged and blue collar. It would show the diversity of men available on the app. What do you say?"

"No way, brother," I wince. "My luck in dating has always been bad. I wouldn't wish that on anyone trying out your dating app."

"At least you got two sons out of one of those disasters," Wiley says, raising his coffee mug toward me.

I pick up my mug and tap his. "That I did. So, how did you convince Connor to join?"

"You know those scientific types." Wiley rolls his eyes. "He scoffed at the idea that an A.I. could match him with the future love of his life."

"You challenged him to try it and my brother fell for it hook, line and sinker."

"Basically," Wiley says, leaning back in his chair. "It was the only way I could convince him to get back out there and try dating again. His drought has gone on long enough."

"True," I say, though I understand why my brother has sworn off dating and love in general.

"And I have a feeling your bad luck is coming to an end," Wiley says, stuffing his mouth full of omelet.

The waitress stops by the table and places a small bottle of freshly made strawberry syrup next to my towering plate of jumbo pancakes. I smear them with butter, then pour syrup over the stack until they are drenched in the reddish brown sticky deliciousness.

"What makes you think that?" I ask, but I already know what Wiley is going to say. He knows all about my attraction to Mya, but I didn't tell him I took a swing and struck out.

My ego is still bruised, but not so bruised that I've avoided Mya. Quite the contrary. Over the past week, I've spent more time with her than anyone else other than the boys. I promised her I wouldn't make things weird and I've stuck to my word. As hard as that's been.

I'm doing something I've never done in the past—get to know a woman as a friend. Problem is, the more I get to know Mya, the more I'm convinced my initial attraction to her was spot on. I fight the urge almost daily to ask her to change her mind about going out with me. The only thing that stops me is knowing in a couple of weeks, our arrangement will be over and Mya will leave Kimbell.

My boys are going to have a fit when she leaves, but I have a feeling I'll be the one in the house having the hardest time getting over her being gone.

"Don't think I haven't noticed you bailing on hanging out with us ever since Mya started taking care of the twins," Wiley says, raising an eyebrow. "You race home after our shift ends and we don't hear from you until the beginning of our next shift. That can only mean one thing—"

"Yeah, he's headed for another heartbreak."

I glance up and stare at Connor.

"What are you doing here?" I ask, in no mood to endure another lecture from him. "Shouldn't you be sticking a kid with a needle and giving them a lollipop right about now?"

Connor plops down into an empty seat at our table. He leans over and grabs a plate and utensils from a table next to ours. I slide my plate over toward him and watch as he slices into my pancakes and takes half of them.

Licking his fingers, Connor asks, "Is this strawberry syrup? I thought Gwen only makes this for Finn and Dec."

"She made an exception for me. You're welcome," I say, then stuff a few squares of the fluffy pancakes into my mouth.

"Tell me why the nanny service hasn't received any more requests for interviews from you since Liesel quit?" Connor demands.

"How do you know that? You spying on me?"

"Don't deflect. Answer my question."

"Things are working out with Mya and the boys. They love having her for a nanny, and she's good at the job."

"But she's a fitness instructor, not a nanny," Connor says, glaring at me. "And your little arrangement is only supposed to be for one month. But some kind of way, you've convinced yourself that she'll stick around and you won't need a new nanny because you're falling for her. Hard."

"What he said," Wylie says.

I glare at him.

"Ronan, she's emotionally unavailable. I'm all for you finding someone again, but Mya's not the one. She's on the rebound from a relationship that ended less than a month ago," Connor adds.

"You don't know what you're talking about. Mya's not emotionally unavailable or on the rebound. She stopped having feelings for her ex a long time ago. He cheated, and it was the final straw she needed to walk away."

"Okay, well, that changes things. Sounds like there's nothing stopping the two of you from seeing where things could go," Wiley says. "You need to give it a try."

"Shut up, Wiley," Connor snaps. "If it's one thing my brother does too quickly, that's fall in love. He has sons now that depend on him for everything. He can't go chasing after every hot chick that comes into town."

"You think Mya's hot?" I ask, muscles tensing.

"Dude, you know she's smoking," Wiley says.

I cut my eyes over at Wiley and watch his grin fade from his face.

"That's beside the point," Connor says, sighing loudly. "Here are the facts. She came to town after a failed relationship. She's passing through with no plans to stick around. But you find a way to convince her to stay in Kimbell, at least for now. Sound familiar?"

I cross my arms over my chest and lean back in my chair.

"Whoa. Sounds like Nikki 2.0. She kinda looks like Nikki, too," Wiley shakes his head. "Ronan, have y'all already booked flights to Vegas to get hitched this weekend?"

"No!" I slam a fist on the table. "Are you crazy? Look, Mya is nothing like Nikki," I say, louder than I expected. I push the plate of pancakes away. "She's open and honest about her feelings. Doesn't sugar coat anything and keeps it real. I know who I'm dealing with when we're together. She's not pretending to be who she thinks I want her to be. Hell, Mya wouldn't bother to pretend to be anyone other than herself. That's how comfortable she is in her own skin. When we talk, it's effortless and interesting and fun. Sometimes we agree, other times we debate, but in the end we learn more about how the other thinks ..." I notice the looks passing from Wiley to Connor and back, then drag a hand down my face.

"Does she know you're this into her?" Wiley asks.

"Yes, and we already decided that it's not wise for us to explore any kind of relationship," I say as misery seeps through my body.

Connor pushes my plate of pancakes back toward me. "That's the best thing I've heard you say. Still, you need to get another nanny lined up. Mya is leaving in two weeks. You're going to have to help Finn and Dec get over losing her. It's better if you're not struggling with getting over feelings for her, too."

CHAPTER 23

YA

"CAN YOU CALL DADDY AGAIN?" DECLAN ASKS, TUGGING AT the fabric of my leggings.

I glance down at those beautiful, worried slate-blue eyes, a replica of his father's, and try to calm my own fears. It's almost five o'clock and Ronan would normally wake up from his nap around now. Instead, he hasn't come home, and he hasn't responded to my texts to check on him.

"Sweetie, your daddy will be home soon," I say, not sure if I'm trying to convince him or me. A myriad of worse case scenarios have played through my mind, growing more and more tragic as the hours passed by. The lack of any response from Ronan made my imagination go to dark places.

Around lunch time, when he hadn't come home, I called the receptionist at the fire station. She confirmed his shift ended without any incident. It was a quiet night and the last she saw Ronan, he was headed to Gwen's Country Cafe to grab breakfast with Wiley.

I busy myself lining up the ingredients for the lasagna on the counter. My plans to make the dish last night had been thwarted when the twins begged me to wait and make it when their dad could be here and eat it with us. Saying no to those two is not a skill I've mastered, so now I have the added pressure of trying to cook dinner for the boys and their irresistibly handsome father.

That is, if he isn't dying after crashing his truck into some ditch on a county road.

"Don't start cooking. We don't want Daddy to miss lasagna," Finnegan adds, then turns his attention back to the action hero coloring book spread across the kitchen table.

For once, Finnegan seems less worried than Declan. I don't know if that's a good sign or a bad omen.

"Declan, why don't you go finish coloring with your brother? You both need something to give Daddy when he gets home."

"Okay, but call him one more time. Please!" Declan pleads.

Making another call that goes unanswered is going to send my blood pressure through the roof, but I indulge Declan and grab my phone. Scrolling through my call log, my phone rings as I'm about to tap Ronan's number. I don't recognize the phone number illuminated on the screen, which makes me more antsy.

I answer the call. "Hello."

"Hey, it's Ronan."

"Where are you?" I ask, lowering my voice so the boys can't hear. "I've been trying to call you all day. Is everything alright?"

"I'm sorry. I should've checked in with you earlier," Ronan says, sounding appropriately contrite. "Connor and I got sucked into taking some marketing photos for Wiley's dating app. Let's say one hour of our time turned into five. My battery died, so I'm using Wiley's phone."

"Dating app?" I feel my blood run cold. "Is it the Ladies Love Country Boys one?"

"Yeah," Ronan says, then pauses. "Are you on it?"

"No, I don't waste time on dating apps."

"Didn't think you'd need the help." A playful hint lingers in his tone, sending a flurry of butterflies skittering through me.

"I'm surprised you do."

"I'm not on the app. Just going to be the face in some advertisements," Ronan clarifies. I hate that his response relieves me.

"I'm headed home," he says. "Need me to pick up anything?"

"Is that Daddy?" Declan and Finnegan ask in unison.

I turn toward them and nod, covering the phone with my hand. "Yes, he's on the way home. Do you want him to pick up something on the way?"

"Ice cream?" Finnegan whispers to Declan.

Declan shakes his head and whispers back, "Cookies?"

Finnegan scrunches up his nose. "Brownies?"

"Yeah," Declan shouts.

They look up at me and say, "Brownies!"

I salute them, then turn my attention back to the phone. "Your sons have requested brownies."

"Got it. And what do you request?"

My breath catches in my throat. There are too many options for how I can answer that question. None of them should be said with two four-year-olds within hearing distance. I clear my throat, then say, "I don't need anything."

"Hazelnut dark chocolate truffle it is," Ronan says.

I can't stop the smile from spreading across my face. How does he remember the most obscure details about things I've shared with him?

"See you soon, Mya."

Slipping the cell phone into my back pocket, I turn toward the boys. "Okay, put the crayons and coloring books away. It's time to make lasagna."

Declan and Finnegan erupt in cheers. They throw the items into the play bin and race each other into the kitchen.

An hour later, Ronan is home and I follow the recipe Jasmine gave me for lasagna with the twins' help. The way Ronan watches me cook with his sons has goosebumps peppering my skin. He doesn't interrupt or interject, just seems to enjoy the view. Now, as the timer buzzes, I move past the boys with smiling faces smudged with tomato sauce and cottage cheese and pull the bubbling lasagna from the oven.

"Smell so good, Miss Mya," Finnegan says.

"You need help with that?" Ronan asks from behind me.

"No, I got it," I say, pleased with the finished product.

"Alright, we need to set the table and make the salad," Ronan announces. The boys leap around his legs, eager to help.

I glance over at them moving around the table in perfect synchronicity. Seeing how loving and caring Ronan is with his sons reminds me of everything I missed out on growing up. Grandma made me feel loved, but it never filled the gaping hole in my heart from having parents who were ambivalent toward me. After grandma died, I had no one. A family in name only, not the genuine kind I see between the twins and their father.

My heart aches at the sight as I imagine what it would be like if this was my life. If Ronan and his boys were my family. The idea should scare the crap out of me, but it feels oddly comfortable and right. I groan under my breath, then open a drawer to get a spatula. For the millionth time, regret oozes through me at turning Ronan down when he asked me out.

The ball is firmly in my court and I can't decide if I should take the shot or not. I don't believe for one minute that Ronan would turn me down if I brought the idea of us dating back up, so why am I hesitating? I never hesitate about anything.

And that's how I ended up wasting six years of my life with Jamal.

But do I think being with Ronan could be a waste of time?

Of course not. A relationship with him seems like the most logical progression in the friendship we've developed.

Still, there's no guarantee that we would end up together.

We could start dating and he could realize he's not that interested in me after all. The compatibility I feel for him might not be reciprocated if we open the door for something more intimate. Do I want to get rejected by him? Could it be better to leave things at the meaningless flirting stage?

"You okay?" I can feel Ronan's presence closing in on me.

I lick my lips and inhale sharply. Placing the spatula on top of the lasagna, I grab the edges of the pan.

"Of course, I'm fine," I say, my voice an octave too high. I turn around and slam into his rock hard abs.

"Ouch," Ronan yelps, then jumps back.

The pan of lasagna tumbles out of my hands and crashes to the floor.

"No!" I hear the boys cry as they scramble into the kitchen.

All my attention is on Ronan. I rush to grab a towel and some ice, then race over toward him as he lifts his shirt. A dark red line crosses his eight-pack abs where the edge of the pan burned his skin.

"I am so sorry," I say, pressing the ice filled towel against him. He rests a hand against my waist as he lets out a shaky breath.

"You should tell the lasagna that, not me."

I laugh. With his free hand, Ronan tucks a strand of my hair behind my ear.

"It's not my first kitchen burn. It'll be fine. Don't look so upset," he says, concern etched on his face.

"I got distracted and I should've paid closer attention to what I was doing. Now I've ruined dinner."

Ronan's hand covers mine as I press the towel on his abdomen.

"Daddy, our dinner is on the floor," Declan says in amazement, as if it's the coolest thing ever.

"Don't touch it and don't eat it." Ronan calls down to them.

"Let me clean it up," I say, pulling away from him. His hand grips mine, not letting me go.

"Is everything alright?"

I nod my head, then blurt out, "No, it's not."

Ronan cocks his brow, his blue eyes trained on me as he speaks to his sons. "Alright buds, I need the two of you to go into the living room and come up with another plan for dinner. You have five minutes. Go."

"Got it, Daddy!" Finnegan yells, then grabs Declan's hand as they race into the living room.

"What's wrong? Did I do something?"

"I spent all day worrying like crazy about you when you didn't call. I didn't know if you were dying in some ditch or what had happened to you. Then you call and you tell me you're going to bring my favorite dessert, which I don't remember when we talked about that. You've been perfect all night and I'm struggling with ..." I inhale a deep breath, then let it out. "How you make me feel. And now, I've burned you. That's how messed up my life is."

Ronan's face relaxes as I watch him fighting back a smile. His hand caresses my face, then cups the bottom of my chin.

"Daddy! Daddy! We want hot dog!" Declan yells, racing around the corner and into the kitchen, with Finnegan on his heels.

"How about we finish this conversation after the boys go to bed?" Ronan asks, his voice low.

"Sure." I look down at the boys and say, "Stay back. Don't step in the lasagna."

"You mind taking the boys to pick up the hot dogs?" Ronan asks. "I'll have all this cleaned up by the time you get back."

"Sure ..." I say, then take a much needed step backward away from his intoxicating presence. Grabbing my keys from the counter, I step over the blob of lasagna on the floor and grab Declan's and Finnegan's hands. "We'll be back."

CHAPTER 24

R*ONAN*

~

THE LIVING ROOM IS DARK, ILLUMINATED ONLY BY ONE
lamp, casting a golden glow across Mya's face. I lean against the wall
and indulge in the luxury of watching her lay across the leather sofa.
Legs on full display, barely covered by her cargo shorts. A tight black t-
shirt stretches across her chest, which heaves and falls with every
breath. Her eyes are closed, robbing me of the sight of those gorgeous
dark brown irises. Flawless skin framed by jet black hair arrest me.

She's under my skin, taking root and taking hold of me. I couldn't
shake these feelings if I wanted to. My heart races in anticipation of
resuming our conversation from earlier. Her admission of her interest
in me isn't a surprise. What catches me off guard is the subtle hint
that she's changed her mind about us. Giving us a chance to explore a
relationship had been a door she shut almost immediately, but now
that door has opened a tiny sliver. I plan to burst it wide open even if

there's a hundred and one reasons I shouldn't. But when have I ever done the safe thing?

I take big risks because I want big rewards.

Mya could be the biggest, yet.

But am I ready for this? Am I ready to risk my heart again?

I drag a hand down my face and take a deep breath.

Not knowing the answer to those questions won't stop me from trying. Mya has dominated my thoughts for weeks and the only remedy for this ailment is to spend more time with her. Find out if there is something to this, like a genuine connection, or if it's a superficial attraction.

Abandoning my post against the wall, I cross the living room and ease down next to her.

"Boys asleep?" Mya asks, without opening her eyes.

"Yeah," I say, leaning back. "I really appreciate what you did. I know making a second lasagna wasn't in the plans."

"It's so hard to say no to them. They acted out the entire Larry Llama Loves Lasagna story on the way to pick up the hot dogs in the car," she says, opening her eyes. Long lashes flutter at me, sending a jolt through my heart.

Mya says, "I knew they had their heart set on eating lasagna."

"Turned out to be a lot of fun," I say, thinking back on Declan and Finnegan crowded in the kitchen next to Mya and me as we made the dish. We were a tangle of arms criss-crossing past each other as we followed the recipe perfectly.

"And the lasagna tasted amazing."

"Old family recipe?" I ask.

"Got it from a new friend."

"The tomato sauce was key."

"She told me that was the most important ingredient. I was instructed to get a very specific brand of sauce that had garlic and basil included."

"Never took you as a rule follower."

"Only when I'm out of my element," Mya says, then laughs. "Don't think I didn't pick up on your culinary skills. You're no stranger to cooking."

"I do well enough to not starve myself or the boys." I lean over and stroke a finger along her hairline. She turns toward me, a sweet expression on her face. "You should let me make you dinner one night."

"Just us?" She asks.

"If that's okay," I say, hoping she doesn't turn me down again.

Her quietness alarms me, but I don't rush to fill the silence. I can almost read her need to process this situation and get comfortable with what she wants to say and do next. Until now, our flirting has been between imaginary lines we'd erected. Now, I'm asking her to cross those lines again. Take a chance to get to know me, not as Declan and Finnegan's dad or as a friend, but as something more.

"I guess now is the time for us to talk about what I said earlier."

"Only if you want to."

"I don't want to, but I need to."

"Why?"

"Because I don't normally hesitate like this."

"You think that's a sign that you shouldn't go out with me?" I ask, dreading her answer.

"I think it's a sign that you could be the man I've been looking for all along."

A smile spreads across my face. "Explain."

"I have only had one real relationship. I jumped into it so fast when I was only nineteen, thinking that I'd found the love of my life. But it was a complete disappointment."

"I know a thing or two, or three or four, about jumping too fast into relationships." I shake my head. It's as if we've had the same experience that brought us to this point of meeting each other.

Mya narrows her eyes as she stares into mine. "Now I'm intrigued. Tell me your story, then I'll tell you mine."

"There's only one relationship you need to hear about. The rest follow the same pattern, with one very important difference."

"And that is?"

"I only eloped one time."

"The twins' mom?"

I nod, then force her name from my lips. "Nikki Dart."

Mya inhales a deep, long breath, then exhales noisily. "Was she the love of your life?"

"I thought she was, but in hindsight, we never gave ourselves a chance to get to know each other on a deeper level. Everything was all passion and superficial and on the surface."

"How did y'all meet?"

"She came to Kimbell after a bad breakup with her boyfriend, determined to meet her biological mother for the first time. Her dad and stepmom raised her in England after her mom gave up her parental rights. It was an emotional time for her."

"I can hear the warning bells."

"Too bad I couldn't. She was vulnerable and wanted to connect with her mom, which she did. I gave her a convenient reason to stay in Texas that wouldn't hurt the parents who raised her," I say, thinking back on Nikki's desperate need to stay in Kimbell and build a relationship with Georgia. Falling for me was the perfect excuse to stick around, even though neither of us realized it at that time.

Mya shifts closer to me, her head resting on my arm. I'm drawn to her, making it that much easier to bare my soul. Tell her things that I had told no one. "We both knew she wanted to have a singing career, but some kind of way I convinced myself that she wanted me more than that."

"Since she's gone and you're raising the twins by yourself, I'm guessing you were wrong. How long were y'all married?"

"Not quite two years. The marriage was strained almost from the beginning. I wanted kids. She thought they'd derail any chance she had of getting her career off the ground. The pregnancy was an accident. Happened faster than even I was ready for—we'd been married for six weeks. She became despondent and detached. After the boys were born, she was desperate to get her singing career back on track. She booked a bunch of gigs, all out of town. She was never around and then, when they were nine months old, she left us for good."

Tears spring to Mya's eyes, and she sits up. I reach for her, resting a hand on hers.

"What is it?" I ask.

She shakes her head. "I don't understand how a parent can feel nothing for their own child. How could she walk away from them like that? Did she ever explain?"

I'm struck by the emotion in Mya's voice. I wonder what triggered this reaction.

"No, she didn't. Sometimes I wish she would have given me some reason that made sense, but in the end—"

"You know it wouldn't have satisfied you." Mya swipes at a tear before it can streak down her face. "Sorry, I don't mean to get all emotional. It's just I know how it feels to grow up with parents that don't want you. It was my life. It's the reason I got sucked in by Jamal, thinking he could be the family that I always wanted."

"What happened with your parents?" I ask, then hesitate. "Only if you want to talk about it. It's okay if you don't."

Mya turns toward me, chewing on her bottom lip. "My parents never wanted to have kids. My mom got pregnant with me at forty-five. She and my dad were convinced having a kid would ruin their lives. I was the one that would stall their careers and stop them from being able to travel and enjoy the life they wanted."

"Mya, I'm so sorry." Pulling her into my arms, I hug her tight to me as I feel her trembling against my chest. "Nobody should ever grow up feeling unwanted or like a burden. I can't believe they did that to you."

Maybe that's why she'd connected so quickly with my sons. She knows how they feel and how to help them because she has first-hand experience with what they are going through. She understands my sons in a way I'm not able to, which draws them to her.

"Horrible, isn't it? Thank God for my grandma. She moved from Kimbell to Austin and raised me. That was a relief to my parents because they didn't have to deal with me. They didn't hide their lack of interest," Mya says, letting out a shaky breath. "The thought that your sons could experience a fraction of how I grew up tears me up inside. They are such awesome little boys. No child should have to go through that. But I don't know your ex. Maybe it's not fair for me to judge her based on my own crappy childhood. I'm sorry."

"Don't be." I rock her in my arms.

Mya can't judge Nikki, but I definitely can.

I was there to witness my ex's selfish behavior. Seeing my boys struggle with not having a mom has made it that much harder for me to understand Nikki's actions.

Mya asks, "How were you able to deal with her abandoning her own flesh and blood?"

"I put it behind me. I had two little lives that depended on me. They were all that mattered," I say, remembering the difficulties of those early days without Nikki. "It hurt. I won't lie. But as the days turned into weeks and months, I felt relieved. It was so much harder being with her than being without her. I guess I loved her, but it wasn't the kind of love that stands the test of time. I'm thankful that she gave me the two most important people in my life. I'll always be grateful for that, no matter how things ended between us."

"You're sure you don't still love her?" Mya asks, worry clouding her beautiful eyes.

I shouldn't hesitate to answer her question, but I do. I'm pretty sure all those feelings are gone, but I wonder what would happen if I saw Nikki again. Would old feelings bubble up, or would I be indifferent toward her?

I lean my head against the sofa. "How can I love someone else when I can't stop thinking about you?"

"Is that right?" Mya bites her bottom lip. Her skin blushes a light pink under my intense stare.

"Now it's time for me to turn the tables on you. Do you still have feelings for your ex? Your breakup is a lot more recent than mine."

Mya rolls her eyes. A cute frown etches between her eyebrows. "Trust me, Jamal lost my love long before he cheated on me."

"How long were y'all together?"

"Six years too long," Mya says, chuckling under her breath.

"Couldn't have been all bad if you stuck around."

"It's not that simple."

"I know a thing or two about complicated. Why did you stay with him?" I ask, feeling an insatiable pull to know the answer. To understand how some other man could have Mya for all that time.

She shifts in my arms and looks up at me. "I guess I have to back up and talk about when my grandma died. She was the only person who loved me unconditionally. I was fifteen when it happened and I immediately felt so alone."

"Your parents didn't step up? They had to know you'd need them after that happened."

"They tried, but they didn't know how to be parents. They had all these expectations of what their daughter should do and be. I didn't live up to any of them. So, I stayed away as much as I could and found solace in a local gym where Jamal was a trainer," Mya says, curling up next to me. "I had no clue he was attracted to me at first. He would speak and we'd have decent conversations every time I came to the gym. He seemed to like me as a person, just the way I was. It was what I was longing for and I stopped feeling so lonely."

"He was older than you, wasn't he?" I guess, feeling possessive. I'd seen the type over the years—older guys preying on the maturity differences and vulnerability of younger women to lure them into relationships.

She nods. "Ten years older. When he asked me out, I thought he could be the family I'd been wanting. The person who could fill the void left by my grandma. Of course, my parents gave me dire warnings, but I ignored them all. Part of the reason I stayed so long is because I didn't want them to be right." Mya looks miserable. "How stupid is that?"

"Hey, don't do that. You're not stupid at all. Sometimes it's hard for us to recognize the lessons that life is trying to teach us. But, when we do, we're much better for it." My fingers stroke along her arm. I understand how she feels more than she could know. How many times had I felt that nudge that Nikki wasn't right for me after we'd gotten married? Each time, I ignored it and doubled down on the decision we'd made until life forced me to face the truth.

"Not an easy lesson to learn, but I'm glad I did. Jamal and I grew apart. He didn't like that I became more confident and more successful and less reliant upon him. He was passive aggressive, quitting his job so he could manipulate me into taking care of him. Like I owed him something and I guess a part of me felt like I did. He took care of me for years after my parents disowned me. But one day I woke up and I could no longer ignore the fact that we didn't fit anymore."

"Did you wake up this morning and realize you and I could fit?"

Mya's hand rests against my face, stroking my beard. The touch soothes and enthralls me as I lean closer toward her.

"I did," she says, then pauses. "But I'm scared that I could be rushing things again."

"Me too," I say. "I think we're different people than we were in those other relationships. We've learned and know some pitfalls to avoid. I don't want you to be afraid to try a relationship with me."

"Why do I feel like this is inevitable?"

"Because it is," I say, then caress her face in my hands. "This is absolutely inevitable."

My mouth finds her sweet lips.

My hands cup the back of her head as her arms clamp around my neck. There's no sense of urgency. Our mouths dance in unison, patiently exploring and enjoying the decadent feel of each other. The glorious sensations are exciting and new, yet familiar and right.

I can't imagine why I waited so long to kiss Mya.

It's a mistake I don't plan to make again.

CHAPTER 25

R *ONAN*

~

The Lasso County Carnival isn't my first choice for my first date with Mya. Not my second or third either, but finding a place that wasn't haunted by memories of Nikki had proven to be harder than I expected. But not as hard as waiting two days before I could be alone with Mya. The day after our epic kiss, I'd already promised the boys we would go to Lake Conroe and fish with Santos. They woke up early, excited about the outing. I didn't have the heart to cancel, even though it's what I wanted to do.

I wanted to spend time with Mya.

I needed to be near her. A need I can't explain or understand. It just is. After locking up my heart and refusing to entertain the idea of dating anyone, Mya came along with a key that fit perfectly. Now that she's unlocked these feelings, it's impossible for me to ignore them.

Impossible for me to deny how much I want a relationship with her.

The outing was fun, but didn't stop me from wondering what Mya was doing without me. The next day, I saw her briefly as I was leaving for work. All the time apart vanished from my mind as she gave me a blistering kiss.

"Be careful," Mya whispered between kisses. "You owe me the best date of my life tomorrow."

"You know how to raise the bar, don't you?" I said, eager to meet her expectations.

"Trust me, you're up to the challenge," she said, then knocked me off my feet with that stunning smile.

I thought about our date the entire time I was at work, even going so far to get advice from the guys. Turns out they were useful in helping me settle on the carnival. As Wiley explained, it's casual with enough activities to keep a date interesting, but also provides ample opportunities for romance.

That was all I needed to hear.

I glance ahead at the empty grassy area, a little larger than a football field, crammed with rides, food, and games from the latest traveling carnival entertainment group passing through town.

I squeeze my SUV between a pair of F-250s and make my way through the makeshift parking lot. A couple passes me, the guy's arm wrapped around the girl's waist. He's in a button down and trousers while she wears a flowing dress. She giggles as he kisses her neck.

Tugging at the collar of my Rockets t-shirt, I panic and wonder if I'm dressed too casually. When did the carnival become a place to dress up? Even if you were on a date. Has it been so long that I've lost touch with what I should wear? The idea that Mya would look at me and think I look like crap starts my palms to sweating. I swipe my hands against my jeans and remind myself dating is like riding a bike. You might wobble a little at the start, but you'll quickly get your balance and take off. At least I hope.

I wasn't tempted to date anyone after Nikki left, and I wasn't lacking for offers. It's like the women of Kimbell had been waiting to pounce on me, ready to step in and be stepmother to my sons and become my second wife. But I wasn't ready for any of that.

As I raised my sons, the urge to commit to another relationship faded. Not that I didn't satisfy my basic needs. I just made sure it was crystal clear that I was only around for a casual fling until even that got old.

For the last year and a half, there's been no one. No woman who peaked my interested or set off a spark within me … until I saw Mya in Bell Park catching a sixty-pound dog in her arms.

The jaunty jingle of carnival music grows louder as I get closer to the entrance. A crowd looms around the ticket booth. For the third or fourth time, I double check that I have the passes to get inside and the single red rose I bought for Mya in the pocket of my shorts. Satisfied that both are in place, I check my watch. Mya insisted she'd meet me here instead of allowing me to pick her up. Still a good fifteen minutes before the time we agreed to meet. I meander over to the line for ride tickets and look at the prices.

"Is that Ronan?" A voice bellows from behind me.

I turn, then break out in a wide smile. "Timmy Quinn! It's been a while. How've you been?"

"Doing good, my man. Glad to see you out and about in an unofficial capacity," Timmy says, stopping next to me with his lady du jour.

"It's hard to remember to squeeze some fun in on my days off, but I'm trying. How's the P.I. business?"

"A little slow. Thought I'd get a call to help find Joe Little when the brewery burned, but you know how that turned out." Timmy kicks at a rock as he flicks a gaze upward to the sky. "I'm scraping by, though. No complaints. Where are your little tykes?"

"Spending time with their uncle for the evening."

Timmy's eyebrows raise to the top of his forehead. He glances around me as if I'm lying or hiding the boys. "You're here … alone?"

"Not exactly," I say, clearing my throat and eager to change the subject. "Who's your friend?"

The stick figure blonde beams from being acknowledged and extends a hand toward me. "I'm Dee Dee. Nice to meet you."

"Good to meet you, too," I say, giving her a friendly smile. I cringe as she flushes red and looks away. I don't miss Timmy's clenched jaw at her reaction to me. He's a nice guy, but not one women would swoon over. To salvage their night, I say, "I'm here on a date."

"You are?" A female voice says in a higher pitch than what I remember.

I squeeze my eyes shut and take a quick breath. I turn to see Tiffany staring at me. She's with her sister and her four nieces.

"Hey, Tiff," I say, then greet her sister and the kids.

"I didn't realize you were dating anyone." Hurt drips from her words. I feel like a jerk for her finding out this way.

"Well, I think it's about time he got off the wagon and started fishing again. There are plenty of women out there and being hung up on your ex for this long is not healthy," Timmy says.

A growl rumbles from my mouth. "I'm not hung up on Nikki. I've been over her for years."

"If you say so," Timmy shrugs, then tugs Dee Dee forward. "Hope you have a good time tonight, man. It was good seeing you."

I give them a wave, then turn my attention back to Tiffany, who has her arms crossed as she waits for my answer. Her sister and the kids have disappeared in the ticket line, leaving us alone.

"Guess I'm good enough for a quickie, but not a date," Tiffany says, referencing the one time we were together over a year ago.

No matter how many times I try to explain that she caught me at a moment of weakness, she's made it clear she was hoping we could be more.

"Tiff, we've talked about this," I say, rubbing a finger against my throbbing temple.

"Yeah, I know. What happened between us was a mistake," Tiff says and her eyes convey all the hurt she feels. Coming to this carnival is turning out to be a bad idea. Maybe the worst.

"I'm sorry—"

"Of course, I know. I've heard this all before. Just wish it would sink into my heart and I'd stop …" Tiff shakes her head. "Bye, Ronan."

I drop my head and stare at the crushed gravel. Not the conversations I want to have right before Mya arrives. My mood has plummeted from excitement to dread. Who else am I going to bump into tonight? Maybe it isn't too late to change the venue. I slip my hand in my pocket and pull out my cell phone. I'm about to dial Mya's number when I see her walking toward me.

My hand falls to my side, and I swear it's like I forget to breathe.

I watch her heading straight for me. Her hips swaying sensually as she crosses the grassy terrain. She's wearing a black tank top with criss crossing straps that show off the sculpted muscles of her tattooed arms. Brother, does this woman have some guns. Her legs seem to stretch for miles as she wears a pair of neon pink shorts. To round it off, she's in her signature black Army boots.

As she stops in front of me, I let out a low whistle.

"Worth the wait, handsome?"

"Absolutely," I say, then step closer to wrap my arms around her in a tight hug. Her head fits beneath my chin, like we are two puzzle pieces meant to be connected. "Hope you like carnivals."

"They're kinda my favorite," she says and her eyes light up brighter than Declan and Finnegan when I've brought home a new toy. "How'd you know?"

"Got lucky, I guess," I say, and give her a wink. Reaching into my pocket, I pull out the rose and hand it to her.

"Ronan, this is so sweet," she says, pressing it to her nose.

"Or cheesy, depending on how you look at it."

Mya laughs. "Not cheesy at all. Classically thoughtful and I adore it. Red roses are my favorite. I love all the typical romantic things, like boxes of chocolate and flowers and—"

"Moonlight serenades?" I ask.

"Do you sing?" Mya's face brightens as her eyes grow wide.

"No. It was a joke." I chuckle under my breath. "Who would have thought tough as nails, Mya was a softy on the inside."

"I could say the same thing about you, Ronan. You're all fierce and hard, but so thoughtful and caring, too."

"Guess we have that in common."

"Among other things." Mya twirls the rose between her fingers. "What should we do first? Rides or games?"

"Ladies choice."

"Rides! I want to get on all of them." Mya loops an arm through mine.

Her touch sends heat blazing across my skin and I hope I'm not blushing like Dee Dee did earlier.

"There's nothing like the feel of your stomach dropping from a carnival ride. I'm a bit of an adrenaline junkie. My grandma used to take me to amusement parks every summer. I'd get on the biggest and tallest rides and love it. I wasn't scared one bit."

"The only thing I'm scared of is not fitting in one of these things," I say, laughing under my breath. We inch closer to the attendant in the line to buy ride tickets.

Mya takes a step back and rakes her eyes over me from head to toe. The one action elicits a reaction from me that isn't appropriate for an area teeming with children. I force myself to think of grandmothers and babies to calm myself down.

"What are you like, six-four?"

"Six-five, two-seventy."

Mya fans herself. "Whoa! That's a lot of gorgeous ginger man!"

I burst into laughter.

"You might not fit in all the rides, but that's okay. I'll skip those for you."

We reach the front of the line and I lean over to talk to the attendant. "How many tickets do we need to ride every ride here?"

"Ronan, we don't have to do that!" Mya protests, clinging to my arm.

"I'm trying to impress you on our first date."

"Trust me." Mya gives me the prettiest smile in the world. "You already have."

The attendant beams at us, then says, "Well, there's twenty rides and the cost is between five and ten tickets."

"So two hundred tickets would more than cover us?" I whip out my credit card and hand it to the attendant.

"Ronan, you do not need to buy two hundred tickets. Get fifty and we can work it out." Mya pleads as she bounces next to me with excitement. "That's so indulgent and unnecessary."

The straight strands of her jet black hair catch in the wind and whip across her face. I take a moment to smooth them behind her ears. My fingers lingering on her soft skin as I stare into those gorgeous dark brown pools.

"You want to ride every ride, that's what we're going to do." I lean down and kiss her sweet lips.

The attendant hands me four books of fifty tickets. I thank her, then slip my arm around Mya, leading her toward the chaos that is the Lasso County carnival. A giant Ferris wheel turns in the distance as kids jockey for position in line for the see-sawing swinging pirate ship and mutton petting zoo near the entrance. Rides form the outer boundary of the carnival while the food trailers and games dominate the center.

Three hours later, we've ridden every ride once and Mya's favorites —the Tilt-a-whirl, Slingshot and Starship—three times each with our excess tickets. Surprisingly, I had little trouble fitting into the rides, even though a few of them I wanted to use that as an excuse.

"No more tickets," Mya says, looking disappointed.

My stomach is aching for food as I carry a giant four-foot tall stuffed unicorn on my back that I won for her in that crazy water balloon carnival game. It took me twelve tries, but I finally beat out a group of teenagers who'd been dominating the spot for thirty minutes.

"What's next? Should we get more tickets?"

"You're not starving?" I ask, my body about to revolt if I don't eat.

She shrugs, then says, "I could eat. I know the best spot to grab some food, too. Come on, let's go!"

CHAPTER 26

R *ONAN*

~

"THE FOOD SMELLS SO GOOD," MYA SAYS, OBLIVIOUS TO HOW captivated I am by her. Intense aromas float in the air—giant turkey legs, corn dogs, roasted corn and funnel cakes. My stomach rumbles. I could eat all of the above and still not be satisfied.

Her hand rests securely in mine as if this is our hundredth date and not our very first. We weave through the crowd of mothers holding cranky toddlers while pushing strollers, teenagers giggling and laughing in groups, and families trying to decide what to ride next. I stop to speak to a couple dozen more friends and introduce Mya. None of them can hide their shock at seeing me out on a date after all these years. I'm sure this will be the talk of town by morning, but none of that matters to me.

All that matters is how good it feels to be with someone who gets me like Mya does. I want to pinch myself to be sure this is real, but I'll wait until after the night is over. Because if it isn't, the last thing I want to do is wake up.

Mya stops at one booth and points up to the painted trailer. She looks so alive and relaxed and down-right beautiful that I don't pay attention to what kind of food is offered.

"Voila!" Mya giggles. "Have you ever had fried gumbo?"

"I'm more of a turkey leg, roasted corn kind of guy," I say, staring at the small, round fried bundles. I'd need ten or more of those to stop these hunger pangs.

"They are so good," Mya says, swaying back and forth.

A smile plays at the corners of my lips as I watch her. An intense urge to kiss her overwhelms me and I don't bother holding back. The unicorn slips from my hand and I step into her space and grip her face in my hands.

"You're so beautiful," I say.

"Shut up and kiss me," Mya says.

Before the words are out of her mouth, my lips are pressed against hers. Softly at first as I let the sensations ripple through me. Mya's arms slip around my neck and I pull her in close. Her hands caress the nape of my neck as our kiss deepens. It doesn't take long for us to find the perfect rhythm, our mouths exploring and enjoying each other.

"Are you going to order or stand there lip locking?" A wise crack comes from the trailer.

Mya pulls away from me, laughing.

I turn to see Bobby Lee Senior grinning at me like a Cheshire Cat.

"What'll it be, O'Reilly?"

I glance at Mya, then up at the menu. "How about one of each?" I say.

"Yes!" Mya squeals, then peppers my face with more kisses.

"That's one lady you got there and I dare say an upgrade from the one you had before," Bobby Lee Senior says, tipping his head toward Mya.

"You don't have to tell me that. I already know." I slip my arm around Mya and hold her close to me. A need for her bubbles within me that is as enthralling as it is frightening.

"So, I'm your lady now?" Mya whispers in my ear.

"Okay, that might be a little premature, but can't say I don't like the sound of it," I admit, then search her eyes for a reaction. What I see reflected back is the only answer I need. Those gorgeous brown eyes dance with excitement.

"I like the sound of it too and not because you're so hot. You got me sweating behind my knees," Mya says, then swipes at her legs.

"You're crazy, you know that?" I rub a hand behind her damp legs, slow and sensually.

"Keep touching me like that, Ronan, and there's going to be a fire you'll have to put out," Mya teases.

I suck in a deep breath, then give her another decadent kiss.

"Order up!" Bobby Lee Senior says.

Grabbing the tray over flowing with food, I follow Mya to an area filled with picnic tables. A small round table cluttered with discarded bottles and empty paper plates opens up as another couple finishes devouring a large brisket BBQ pizza. I clear the trash from the table and we sit down with our spoils.

"So, what's all this?" I ask.

Mya says, "These are the fried gumbo with dipping sauce." She points at one paper container, then to another. "This is the fried Alfredo with Texas toast and this is the fried Frito pie, I think." She lifts one and takes a bite. She nods as gooey cheese drips down her chin. I love that she's not self conscious in the slightest. Her down-to-earth honesty is refreshing. The polar opposite of Nikki. I swipe a finger against her skin, then lick the cheese.

"And this one?" I ask.

"Fried red velvet cupcake. So much better than funnel cake."

"You've lost your mind." I shake my head in mock disappointment. "And here I thought you were perfect. The flaws are coming out."

"Sounds like a challenge and you know how much I love those," Mya says. "Shall we make another bet?"

"No, my track record isn't too good with you and bets," I say, thinking back on the weight lifting fiasco.

"This is your chance to even the score," Mya says, wiggling her eyebrows at me. "I'll be right back."

She returns with a funnel cake covered in a mound of white powder sugar. "First dinner, then we'll have a dessert tasting contest."

"What are the stakes this time?"

"Let's see. If you win and the funnel cake tastes better than my beloved red velvet cake, then you'll get another date with me."

"And if I lose, what do you get?"

"Another date with you." Mya scrunches her nose in the cutest way, then stuffs a piece of fried gumbo in her mouth.

"That's the kind of bet I'll take any day," I say, tasting the fried gumbo. "Hey, this is good."

"Told you," Mya says.

"So, should we talk about the elephant in the room?" I ask.

"The massive elephant stalking us through the carnival, you mean," Mya laughs, then points behind me. I turn to see one of the carnival workers dressed in a Dumbo costume greeting and enthralling the kids in the area.

"Do not tell Finnegan and Declan about this. They'll be so mad at me for not bringing them along," I say, then add, "But I thought we needed not just a first date, but some time to … talk."

"And you're right," Mya says. She breaks off a piece of fried Alfredo and dunks it into the creamy white sauce, then takes a bite. She groans with ecstasy as she chews. "But first, you gotta try this."

Dunking another piece, she raises up and feeds me. Her hands linger long enough against my lips for me to kiss them.

"That's delicious," I murmur.

Mya sits back down and rests her elbows on the table.

"Have you decided what your next move will be?" I focus on devouring the rest of the fried Frito Pie. The end of the month is next week, and I don't know what Mya's plans are. If she'll be sticking around Kimbell for longer to give us a chance to see more of each other.

Or if this is our first … and last … date.

I almost lose my appetite thinking about that possibility.

Still, from what I know about Mya, there's no way she would've agreed to this date if she was planning to leave soon. She's too straightforward to not make that clear before accepting.

"All this time, I was supposed to be figuring out how to salvage my personal training career. I should've been networking and reaching out to old friends in the industry so I could strike out on my own," Mya says, her voice strained. "I didn't do any of that. I'm no closer to having a new job or a plan than I was the day I arrived in Kimbell."

I force myself to hide my smile and keep a passive look plastered on my face. "And I was supposed to be interviewing nannies to replace you after you've left town … for good."

"How's that going for you?"

"Haven't interviewed a single one."

Mock shock crosses Mya's face and I smile.

"Part of me hoped that you'd stick around a little longer," I say, fixing my eyes on her. "But not because you're an amazing nanny."

Mya laughs. "Because we both know that I'm not. Don't get me wrong, I'm doing a decent job, but it's not what you'd get from a real nanny, for sure."

"You're still the boys' favorite, and that counts for a lot. You're kinda becoming my favorite, too."

"Especially since I'm the first woman you've dated since your ex left," Mya said, wagging a finger at me. "I heard all the rumbling about it as we went from ride to ride. We are officially the talk of the town."

"Sorry about that," I say, even though I'm not in the slightest.

"You want me to stay so we can figure out if there is something special between us?"

I hesitate and glance away. The full moon shines brightly in the cloudless sky, casting long shadows across the carnival. Am I doing the right thing? We only met a few weeks ago. How can I be so sure I want to spend more time with Mya? How can I be sure I'm ready for this?

"It must seem crazy." I scratch my beard and lean back from the table. "We haven't known each other for long."

"But is that why you want me to stay?"

I nod my head. "You know it is."

"Then that's enough for me."

"What do you want, Mya?"

"The same as you. No one has to tell me how impulsive I can be. I know that. I've lived it. Got the t-shirt and the coffee mug. I tried to resist these feelings for you, Ronan, and it didn't work," Mya admits without a hint of remorse.

"What about your plans to get your life back on track and start personal training again? What are you going to do about that?"

"I have some ideas, but I need a couple more months to flesh them out. I was distracted by an irresistible ginger man and his adorable twin boys."

"Why am I not surprised that we're on the same page? Seems like we have this innate ability to be in sync with each other," I say, letting everything I've been thinking and feeling out. With Mya, I don't worry about opening up to her because she's so open about who she is and, more importantly, what she wants.

"There's one little problem with our plan," she says.

"What's that?"

"I don't have any money to cover another month of bills on the house. Uncle Tony would let me stay longer rent free, but it doesn't feel right. I know he wants to sell the house and get rid of that mortgage payment. I need to move out so he can do that."

"Or—"

"I'm not taking money from you, Ronan!" Mya says, then swipes a piece of Texas toast from my plate.

"Hear me out? Please. I'm not offering to give you money. But there's no denying that my sons would love to have you stay on as their nanny a couple more months or however long you'd need."

"Not a good idea. I don't want them to think this is going to be a permanent job for me. The longer I'm their nanny, the harder it will be for them and you to replace me."

I extend my pinky toward her. "Pinky swear that I'll find another nanny before the two months are over. I'll do a couple of trial runs so that the boys can get used to someone new. You'll have plenty of time to explore new work opportunities … maybe right here in Kimbell."

Mya shakes her head. "You heard Wheeler a couple of weeks ago. I've been black balled."

"From the gyms, yes. But didn't you tell me your focus is on women who don't have the confidence to step foot in a big gym. I know Erin, our receptionist at the station, feels that way. She would love to have private classes that will get her in shape without feeling inadequate. There are plenty of other women like that right here in Lasso County. You need a little more time to find them."

Mya's eyes narrow as she processes my suggestion. Maybe she hadn't been thinking about her next step, but I'd put in some time on the topic for her. Anything to keep her around longer.

"That's a good idea," Mya says, polishing off her last fried gumbo ball. "Wonder why I didn't think of it."

"Could be those adorable twins distracting you."

"Or that man they call Daddy."

I laugh.

"So, you're offering to pay me for two more months of nanny services."

"And you're accepting my offer," I say, wiggling my pinky at her.

A bright smile spreads across her face as she links her pinky with mine.

"Glad that's settled," I say, stuffing the fried Alfredo ball into my mouth.

"That is not how you settle a deal," Mya says, walking over to me.

"How do you propose we do that?" I ask, leaning back to allow her to sit in my lap.

"With a kiss." Mya says, then gives me one that rocks my world to the moon and back.

CHAPTER 27

THE PARKING LOT IS DARK AND DESERTED AT THIS HOUR OF
the night. Throngs of families and teenagers that had crowded the
carnival are long gone. Only a few cars remain, all a far distance from
where I parked my Honda.

Could this night have been any more perfect?

Maybe I have little to compare it to since I spent the past six years
tied down to a guy I met when I was only nineteen. My high school
relationships were fleeting and superficial. Boys at that age don't know
how to date or make a girl truly feel like she's the most beautiful
woman in the world.

But a man?

That's an entirely different story, especially when that man is
Ronan O'Reilly. If this is what a relationship is going to be like with
him, then he's already shattered the glass ceiling of my previous

experiences. Raised the bar so high, I'm not sure any other man will top it.

The cool night air whips against my skin. Ronan's intoxicating scent—a heady mixture of cologne and testosterone—entices my senses.

He's close behind me.

Only inches separate us.

Fingertips caress my bare shoulders, moving deliberately to my neck. Soft kisses follow the trail of his touch. My skin flushes hot as goosebumps pepper my skin. A strange dichotomy I didn't think was possible, yet this is what Ronan does to me. Makes me feel in ways I never imagined.

I inhale as his muscular arms wrap around my waist, pulling me closer. I lean back against Ronan's chest, my head tilting toward him to feel the coarse hairs of his beard brushing against my face.

I turn around in his arms and stare into his blue eyes. They've turned a shade lighter in the darkness, almost translucent blue-gray.

"Stop looking at me like that," I say, feeling self-conscious.

"Why? You're beautiful," Ronan says, then presses a soft kiss against my nose. "If you think I'd ever get tired of looking at you, you're fooling yourself. I could stare at you all night and all day."

"Sounds like a pretty boring day, if you ask me." I try to lighten the mood, but my joke does nothing to diffuse the intensity wafting from Ronan.

"I like boring," he responds, giving me the cutest wink.

When this was nothing more than meaningless flirting, I could handle being around Ronan easily. Now that I'm getting to know him on a deeper level, seeing the layers of the complex and amazing man he is, I can barely keep my feelings under control.

"And I think I like you a bit too much," I say before I can stop myself.

"Well, I think I like that you like me too much. Means my plan is working."

"What plan is that, exactly?" I raise an eyebrow as my heartbeat kicks against my ribcage.

"The plan to make you—"

Beep. Beep. Beep. Beep.

My eyes fling open. The living room is dark and clouded in shadows as only a hint of the breaking dawn seeps through the blinds. I reach frantically for my cell phone and silence it, hoping I got to it in time. A quick glance to the corner of the room and I see Jellybean is asleep on his doggie pillow a couple of feet away from my air mattress, which has deflated during the night. Again.

I stretch to ease the kink out of my back and sit up.

Dragging a hand down my face, I blink as fragments of my dream dance in my head.

Last night's date at the carnival was cut short when Ronan's brother got called into the hospital for an emergency. Ronan had to leave to pick up his sons. There was no time for more talk or kisses as he hurried me to my car before driving off in his SUV.

A low groan escapes my lips, and I fall back onto the hard floor.

Leave it to my own twisted brain to torment me with my secret desires.

But I suppose they aren't a secret.

I knew the moment I set eyes on Ronan that there was a distinct and undeniable vibe between us. An attraction that can't be denied. What I didn't expect was to connect with him on an emotional and personal level, sharing similar interests and life experiences. When he talks about his past and his views, it's like he's reading my mind. Deciphering my heart. Connecting with my soul.

The whole thing makes me nervous about being around him again.

I laugh out loud.

Like that's going to stop me.

But I don't want to make the same mistakes I made in the past. I will not rush into a relationship with a man again. The next time I decide to be exclusive, I want to know for sure the lucky guy and I are compatible in more than one way.

Beep. Beep. Beep. Beep.

Glancing at my phone, I see the screen illuminated.

Well, that wasn't my alarm after all.

I access my texts. A smile spreads across my face as I see they are from Ronan. Four texts in a row.

Woke up thinking about you. Not mad at all about that.

Had a great time last night. Guess you know that already.

When can I see you again?

Call me when you wake up.

A thrilling jolt shoots through me as I sit up and cross my legs like a pretzel. I tap the phone with a black lacquered nail, then press it to my ear to hear the rings.

Two, three, four rings.

I fight disappointment and prepare to leave a message.

"Hey," Ronan's voice warms my heart. His voice is low and husky and the sexiest sound that could ever greet me in the morning. "Did I wake you?"

"As a matter of fact, you did," I say, then parrot his text. "But I'm not mad at all about that."

I swear I can hear him smile. "So my boys won't be home from their sleepover until this afternoon. Want to grab a workout this morning?"

"That sounds perfect. I need about fifteen minutes to get ready," I say, feeling giddy. "Where should I meet you?"

"I'll pick you up."

"No," I shake my head, glancing around the bare living room. Trash bags filled with everything I own are cluttered against one wall. A trail of clothes, some clean, some not so much, stretch from the living room to the laundry room. No way I want Ronan to see this. "You don't have to do that."

"It's no problem. See you in fifteen."

"Ronan—" The call ends.

I scramble from the floor and jump to my feet. There's no way I can get ready and make this place not look like a homeless woman has crashed in the living room. I stare at the trash bags and try to remember which one has my workout clothes.

Ten minutes later, I've washed up and I'm donning a camo sports bra, matching capri leggings and black sneakers. I grab a towel and drape it over my shoulder as I twist my bob styled hair into a short spiky ponytail. A quick peek at Jellybean and he's still knocked out. His food and water dish have enough to hold him until I get back. Grabbing my keys, I slip out the front door so Ronan won't have a reason to come inside—

"That was quicker than fifteen minutes."

I shriek and turn to see Ronan sitting on the worn, weather-beaten rocking chair in the corner of the porch. His ginger hair tumbles in loose waves over his forehead and his beard looks scraggy and unkempt.

In other words, he's breathtaking.

And it's the crack of dawn!

How in the world could a single father pull that off?

"Are you trying to give me a heart attack?" I ask, my hand flying to my chest. "How did you get here so fast?"

"I was in the neighborhood." He gives me a sheepish grin.

"Were you already here when you texted me?" My eyes narrow as I stalk over toward him.

"Well, ma'am, I'm going to plead the fifth on that one," Ronan stands to his full height and glory and smiles down at me. "You ready to go?"

I nod.

"Good, because I have a surprise for you." He extends his bent arm toward me. I loop my arm in his and follow him down the sidewalk to his SUV parked in front of the house.

"Did I mention I love surprises? Best thing ever," I say.

"What am I? Batting like a thousand now?"

"If not, you're very close to it. I hope you know what you're doing, Ronan O'Reilly."

He opens the door to the SUV and waits for me to get in.

"I do," he says, then leans in and gives me a soft kiss on the lips. "And I'm glad it's still working."

CHAPTER 28

"WHY ARE WE AT A HIGH SCHOOL?" I TURN IN MY SEAT TO face Ronan as he turns the engine off.

"You losing faith in me already?" He teases. I wait for him to come around and open my door, since it's not lost on me how chivalrous he is.

"I mean, when you said surprise, this isn't what I had in mind."

"What kind of surprise giver would I be if you could figure it all out?" Ronan drapes an arm over my shoulders. He steers me past the main dull brown brick building devoid of windows toward a corrugated steel cover walkway. Behind the main building is the track stadium and next to it is a warehouse.

Ronan stops at the double doors and fishes in his pocket. He pulls out a key and wiggles it at me, then uses it to open the padlock on the door. Pushing them wide open, he steps to the side and says, "Welcome to paradise."

My mouth drops open as I stare into the space. Soaring ceilings stretch high toward clouded, spider web covered windows. Dust bunnies float in the sun rays streaming inside. I feel like my heart is going to burst as I gaze at all the standard equipment, exercise stations and weights of a Crossfit focused gym. I'm stunned by his thoughtfulness as the familiar pull to dive into an intense workout washes over me.

"Ronan ..."

"Don't go getting all mushy. We only have an hour, ninety minutes tops, before the football team arrives for their workout," Ronan says, then cups my chin in his hands. "And I, for one, don't want you around a bunch of horny teenagers."

I laugh out loud and grab his hands in mine. "This is amazing. Thank you."

"Anytime. What's the plan?"

Workout ideas crowd my head as I inventory options from the varied machines in the massive room. One of my favorite workouts come to mind. It's a tough one and I'm not sure Ronan will be able to keep up. But I don't tell him that.

"Three sets of declining reps. Thirty. Twenty. Ten. And we'll begin with a classic clean and jerk."

We are pouring sweat after the first exercise. I collapse onto the mat and gulp from the bottle of water Ronan brought in his gym bag.

"Did you always know you wanted to be a personal trainer?" Ronan asks. His skin is flushed red from the exertion. I know this is stretching him from his typical slow paced weightlifting workouts. But he's already shown that he's more than capable of keeping up with me.

"Honestly, I never would've guessed this would be my life. My parents did everything in their power to persuade me this was a foolish career choice, but I didn't listen to them."

"Are you glad you didn't?"

"Yes, I am. I've touched lives in ways I never would've imagined by doing something that I'd do even if I wasn't getting paid. It's the best kind of job to have."

Ronan turns on his side and stares at me with a surprised look. "I feel the same about being a firefighter."

"Were you one of those kids who played with fire trucks and knew all along it's what you wanted to do?" I ask, imagining how adorable Ronan must've been when he was younger.

"Nope. I grew up wanting to be a football player until a hurricane hit Kimbell when I was thirteen."

"I remember that hurricane," I say, even though I was only seven or eight at that time. "No one expected for it to come this far in from the Gulf or squat over Texas for so many days."

"The poorer areas of Kimbell flooded bad. Four and five feet of water in houses. My family was trapped and my dad had a heart attack trying to make sure we didn't drown."

"That's horrible. Did he … survive?"

"Yeah, he did. He and my mom are doing great living in Belize after retiring. But that night, I watched the Kimbell fire fighters come to our house and rescue us. They got us to the hospital and the doctors at St. Elizabeth's saved my dad." Ronan's face is contemplative, as if he's reliving the memories real time. "It's funny to think back on that time because it's the exact moment I knew I was going to be a fire fighter. It's also the exact moment my brother knew he was going to be a doctor."

"Is your brother older or younger?"

"A twin, like my boys. But older by minutes."

"And they say it doesn't run in families."

Ronan laughs. "It doesn't."

"Does he look like you?"

"In a way. He's the smaller, preppier version of me."

"So, he's not six foot five and two hundred seventy pounds?"

"You remember that, huh?" Ronan looks pleased. "No, he's six-one and two twenty. Fit but not big like me. No beard. If you saw him, though, you'd know he was my brother."

"I see. He's smoking hot, too."

Ronan's scowl sends me into a fit of laughter.

"Come on. That's enough rest. Box jump burpees are next," I say, pushing off the ground. Ronan raises an eyebrow. "Start with a burpee. Jump onto the box." I point to a pair of two-foot-tall wooden boxes. "Jump down and do another burpee and repeat for all the sets."

"You're joking."

"It's easy." I say, tugging on his massive muscular arm. All conversation ceases as we work through the sets of the second exercise. We both collapse onto the box and gulp water until our breathing returns to normal.

"That was intense," Ronan says, then rests a finger on the most important tattoo on my left arm. "Who's that?"

My heart warms at the drawing of my grandma etched in ink on my forearm. "That's Grandma Marguerite. The woman who raised me when my parents couldn't be bothered. My dad thought he'd bribe Grandma to do it by naming me after her. But Grandma thought her name was too old-fashioned for a young girl. She told my dad to name me Mya instead after Maya Angelou, who was born Marguerite Johnson. I think my mom spelled it differently to be difficult."

"That's a great story, though, and a wonderful person to be named after. I think my mom got my name from an Irish baby book because she thought it sounded cool."

"So, you're not Irish?"

"I'm sure a DNA test would confirm Irish blood somewhere far back in my lineage, but I'm one hundred percent Texan," Ronan says, exaggerating his accent.

"Me too. Texan to my bones. People always think I'm mixed, which I guess maybe a hundred years ago there was some intermingling with my black ancestors. But my parents are both black. My mom is fair skinned like me, but my dad is darker like Uncle Tony," I explain, then jump to my feet.

"What's next Crossfit guru?" Ronan asks, looking like he's ready to call it quits.

"Chin up and toes to bar lift combo," I say, then point to the pull up station. "We do a full chin up, clearing the bar, then drop back down and ab crunch until our toes tap the bar. Then repeat."

Ronan groans as he leads the way.

I don't mind when he bails out on the last set. I'm surprised he could keep up this much after finding out he'd never done a Crossfit workout before.

Tapping my toes to the bar for my last rep, I free fall to the ground and land in a squat. Ronan is resting on the mat, a salacious grin on his face.

"Did you enjoy the view?" I ask, throwing my sweaty towel at him.

"Very much so," He says and the look in his eyes blazes a trail over my body. He pats the space next to him. I flop onto the mat so close to him that our legs touch. His hands brush against my thigh, then course down to my knee, sending an electric current sizzling through me. I'm not sure how much more of this I can take.

"Ronan," I say, my voice shaking. "Can we, umm, take things … slow?"

He's quiet for a long moment, his hand still lingering on my leg. I feel him shift slightly, moving closer to me. I can't look at him or I might lose my resolve.

"It's not that I don't want to … I just … considering my past and how things bombed with my last relationship … I really, really like you and I want this to be … different. I want a chance for it to …" I stop my rambling and look at him. Where in the world did my normal self-confidence disappear to?

"I have no problem with that." Ronan strokes a finger along my face. His expression is amused and relaxed. Unfazed and unconcerned by my suggestion.

Should that worry me?

Ronan says, "Given both of our track records, it's best that we don't rush into being intimate. I'm loving every minute of getting to know you, Mya. It's a step I've skipped in my past relationships. I don't want to make that mistake with you."

No, it shouldn't worry me at all.

"Because you are interested in this, maybe turning serious in the future?" I ask, wanting to put all the cards on the table.

"You are the only woman who has made me want to be in a relationship since Nikki left." Ronan's gaze grows more intense. "Part of me thought I wasn't capable of having these feelings for anyone again. Then you abandon your dog and show up in Bell Park—"

"I did not abandon Jellybean. I had to get my arm stitched up at the hospital and he escaped the car!" I wave my forearm in his face to show him the scar visible within the ink of my Texas flag tattoo.

"And you take my breath away. All I wanted was a chance to get to know you better and by some crazy twisted luck, I've gotten it. I won't do anything to waste this time we have together." Ronan's eyes dance with excitement. "I want to see where this leads, Mya."

"Me too."

"There's just one thing I need."

I pause, waiting for him to continue.

"You know my boys are pretty attached to you. If they think for one minute that you and I are getting close, it's going to be much harder for them to not put pressure on us to speed up things."

"And they are very persuasive."

"And manipulative. We don't need that kind of pressure."

"So, we keep this a secret."

"Only from my boys," Ronan clarifies. "The rest of Kimbell needs to be on alert that you're not available to date anyone but me." He says, growing more serious as he points at his chest.

"I like the sound of that," I say, grabbing his hands and pulling both of us up from the floor. "Now let's finish up this work out before the horny high school football players arrive."

"What's next?"

"Handstand push-ups," I do a little shimmy dance around him. "Followed by rope climbs."

Ronan shakes his head. "Ladies first."

CHAPTER 29

M^{YA}

~

TEN DATES AND TWO WEEKS LATER, I'M SUFFICIENTLY
motivated to revamp my career as a personal trainer right here in the
quaint town of Kimbell. I use the term date loosely, though, since
Ronan and I have only been without the boys for four of the ten times
we've hung out.

Whenever Ronan isn't working, he and I mostly hang out at his
house after the boys have gone to sleep. We follow that up with some
fun outing on his full day off before he starts his shift the next day.
Bowling, bumper cars, picking strawberries and apples, hay rides and
haunted houses, we've covered a lot of ground.

But none more so than the strings growing between us, attaching
us in ways neither of us wants to remove. When the boys are around,
we're careful to keep any public displays of affection to a minimum.
Our conversations, though, continue to explore the depths of our pasts

and experiences and all the marvelous things that make him, him and me, me.

Would I have ever guessed that he's deathly afraid of needles, so he has no tattoos and has to be cajoled by his doctor brother to go in for regular check-ups? Or that he once played checkers with his sons for eight hours straight until they figured out the point of the game?

The man has endless patience and a heart of pure gold. I see it every time he's with his sons, navigating their latest antics without blowing a gasket. He rarely raises his voice at them. He has this uncanny knack of encouraging them to see and admit their own deplorable behavior before it goes too far. Not that it stops Finnegan and Declan from coming up with a different prank to test the limits of their dad. It's a little game they all enjoy playing.

And now I'm firmly in the middle of it.

I glance down at the two little boys skipping along the sidewalk next to me. Today, they insisted on dressing alike. When they emerged from their room, they had on black t-shirts and jean shorts. Outfits identical to what I'm wearing. We look like a cute family.

Except I'm not part of the family.

I have to remind myself that to Finnegan and Declan, I'm their cool nanny who they like a lot. A whole lot. And that's enough for me.

For now.

"Miss Mya, there's your flyer," Declan says, running up to a light pole. He jumps high, slapping a hand on the bright neon paper taped to the metal. A couple weeks ago, the boys helped me put them up all around Kimbell to advertise a Saturday morning, all female fitness class I was offering at the high school football stadium.

Ronan had opened my eyes to possibilities I hadn't considered when he reminded me about women who didn't feel comfortable coming to a gym. There was a plethora of gyms that catered only to women. Created sanctuaries where women could gather to work out and make social connections that helped motivate and hold them accountable to their workout goals.

That was the foundation of my Saturday work-out sessions. I took my fitness approach that women are strong enough to take on the hardest of fitness workouts, even coming off the couch, and combined that with a "pay-what-you-like" pricing plan. Last weekend's turn out had blown me away, thanks to a bit of word-of-mouth advertising by Ronan and my good friend, Jasmine.

Over forty women showed up, ranging from teenagers to seniors. After the hour long workout was complete, I checked the pay jar and had earned over a thousand dollars. More than enough money to cover next month's rent on Uncle Tony's house without having to continue to be the twin's nanny, but the thought of quitting never crossed my mind. A couple of ladies signed up for one-on-one training sessions, including Erin, the receptionist at the fire station.

As much as I love personal training, I also love being with Finnegan and Declan. I'm not deluding myself. I know I don't have some secret burning desire to be a full-time caregiver to random children. There's no way I'm abandoning my career to take on nanny duties for families. But for Ronan's twins, I'm doing everything I can to make both work.

The thought of not seeing them four days every week when Ronan is at the fire station turns my stomach sour. Even though I know this arrangement is supposed to end in a month, a big part of me hopes Ronan and I have progressed enough in our relationship to tell the boys about us. Then I won't have to miss out on spending time with them or stop being in their lives. The more I'm with them, the more I want to be there for all the future milestones. But I know better to mention any of this to Ronan. He's committed to protecting his sons from any future abandonment, real or perceived, and I trust him to do the right thing.

"Miss Mya, why did you make your flyers pink when you never wear anything pink?" Finnegan asks, staring up at me with a serious expression.

"Because that color pops. It gets people's attention and makes them want to find out what it says," I explain as we catch up with Declan. I grab Declan's hand and we continue our walk toward the Lasso County Public Library.

"You wear a lot of black, Miss Mya," Declan says. "You have black shirts with long sleeves, black shirts with short sleeves."

"Black shirts with no sleeves and some black shirts with really skinny strings that cover your shoulders," Finnegan adds.

"And black shorts and black boots," Declan says.

I giggle under my breath. "Well, for the two of you, I will buy something pink and wear it the next time I come over. How about that?"

Finnegan suggests, "Why don't you wear something green? That's Declan's favorite color."

"It's yours, too!" Declan says.

We take the steps up to the doors.

"I can do green," I say, and the boys look satisfied. We enter the cool air-condition of the library. The boys drag me over to the children's section, where a series of chairs are arranged in a semi-circle for story time. All of their friends from the daycare are already milling about, looking at books on the shelves while others are seated. Declan races Finnegan to the front and they plop down a few feet from where Odalis, the librarian, will sit to read this week's story: Larry Llama Loves Lakes.

The boys made me check it out last week and I've been reading it to them before bed. It's a clever story about enjoying activities on the lake, all while recognizing the dangers and knowing how to be safe around water.

Satisfied that the boys' obsession with Larry Llama books would have them rooted to that spot for the next thirty minutes, I make my way to the business section and peruse for books on starting a new business. I'm building a good clientele in Kimbell, but I don't know the first thing about setting up a company, doing the accounting or evaluating what kind of insurance I might need since the exercises I take the class through could cause injuries.

Jasmine has already offered to connect me with a few of her friends, Lance Bassett, a lawyer, and Kennedy Tarkington, an accountant. I want to be ready for each of those discussions and not embarrass myself. I grab a few books that look beginner friendly and make my way to a table where I can monitor the boys. Like I thought, they are riveted by the story, yelling out parts they have already memorized along with the librarian. She takes it all in stride, encouraging the participation of them and the other kids.

My mind is swirling with concepts of LLCs, S Corps, accrual versus cash methods, insurance liability limits, and premiums when I hear Declan and Finnegan screaming my name. I jolt up from the chair as they trip all over themselves, heading toward me.

I hold a finger up to my lips. "This is a library, and what do we do when we are at a library?"

"We whisper," the boys say in unison, lowering their voices.

I close the books on the table, then ask, "What's going on?"

"There's a scavenger hunt next month and we need to sign up," Declan says. I notice Finnegan's eyes grow wide as saucers as he looks at anything and everything but me.

"Here's the paper," Declan continues, shoving a single sheet into my hands. "You put our names on there and then you put your name on it too and then we turn it in to the Liberrian."

"Librarian," I correct.

"That's what I said," Declan says, frowning at me.

"No, it isn't," Finnegan whispers, then reaches into his pocket. He pulls out a pencil, then stretches it in my direction.

It doesn't take a rocket scientist to know these two are trying to pull one over on me. I straighten the paper in my hands, then read the header out loud. "Sign up now for the Kimbell, Texas Annual Mother … Son … Scavenger Hunt."

My hands tremble as the words sink in.

"Yes, sign us up," Declan says, nodding his head.

I ease down in my chair and motion for the boys to sit down, too. I place the paper on the table, not sure what to say. If I'm honest with myself, I'm honored and overjoyed that they would ask me to be the stand-in for their mom at this activity. Everything I feel for those precious little boys, they feel for me. It's an amazing feeling.

But then there's Ronan to consider.

What would he think about this? Would he be happy that I'm participating with his sons? Or see it as a sign that I'm moving too fast? Maybe trying to use his kids to manipulate him into a long-term relationship, which is not what's happening here.

"This scavenger hunt is for little boys to do with their moms," I say.

"We know," Declan says, growing impatient.

"We don't have a mommy. We talked about it and we thought if we had a mommy, we would want her to look like you and act like you," Finnegan explains, as if it's the most logical rationale in the world.

"So that's why we are asking you to do it with us. Please!" Declan says.

"We really want to do the scavenger hunt," Finnegan adds, adopting adorable puppy-dog eyes. "You can be our pretend mommy—"

"You don't need a pretend mommy." Georgia's voice is stern and laced with irritation booming from behind me.

I cringe. This situation has gone from bad to def-con five. I swivel around in the chair and give her a big smile.

Instead of smiling back like she usually would, she greets me with an icy, suspicious stare. Could she know Ronan and I are dating? Who am I kidding? Almost the whole town knows. I'm sure she's noticed I've been spending less and less time at Uncle Tony's house over the past two weeks. Now she overheard her grandsons asking me to be their pretend mommy.

I stifle an internal scream.

"Finnegan, Declan," Georgia says, easing between the boys. She wraps her arms around them and gives each a kiss on the head. "You have a mommy. She just doesn't live here."

"We know," Declan snaps. "She lives in London." His words are full of snark.

Finnegan fidgets in his chair and looks away.

"If you need someone to do the scavenger hunt with you, I'm happy to," Georgia says, staring daggers at me. "Wouldn't it be fun to make it a grandmother and grandson activity? Plus, I'm sure Mya will be too busy next month."

Finnegan's head jerks up, and he looks at me. The fear and anxiety I see in his slate-blue eyes rip at my heart. "Are you going away, Miss Mya?"

"No, of course not, honey," I say.

"Good," Declan says. "So, you and Granny can do the scavenger hunt with us!"

Finnegan's face lights up. "Yes! That's going to be so fun!"

Declan pushes the paper and pencil back toward me. "You have to write on that so we can turn it in."

I hesitate, my hand hovering over the pencil and the paper.

Georgia's chest heaves and I swear I can almost see the smoke shooting from her ears.

"How about I check with your daddy and make sure he's okay with this scavenger hunt idea? If he says it's okay, we'll fill it out tonight and turn it in tomorrow," I say, looking at Declan and then Finnegan.

The boys exchange looks and do that telepathic thing they do, reading each other's faces, then say in unison, "Okay."

"What are you doing at the library, Granny? I didn't know you read books," Finnegan says.

"I'm here to see you and your brother. I wanted to take you to lunch," Georgia says.

My eyes narrow as I look at her.

"That's interesting," I say as unease snakes along my skin. "Ronan didn't mention that you'd be taking the boys to lunch."

That's not something he would forget to tell me. Whenever the boys have play dates or outings with other kids, he leaves detailed instructions and phone numbers for me on a notepad and follows it up with a text.

"They are my grandsons. I should be able to treat them to a meal when my schedule frees up—"

An alarm blares through the library as bright white lights flash.

Declan and Finnegan press their hands to their ears and look at me.

An automated voice booms through the intercom: "Attention! Attention! An emergency has been reported. Walk to the nearest exit. Attention! Attention!"

CHAPTER 30

R*ONAN*

~

"No visible smoke or fire," Darren says as he pulls
the fire truck to a stop in front of the main lobby doors of the Lasso
County Library. Nate opens the door and I follow him out, crossing in
front of the truck as we make our way up the steps of the single-story
building.

A crowd is gathered on the front lawn. A myriad of adults and
children gawking for a glimpse of what emergency sent them rushing
out of the library.

I call back to Wiley. "Hey, get these people across the street.
They're too close."

"Got it," Wiley says, then heads over to the largest group of
children.

My eyes scan the crowd, and my breath catches as I see Finnegan and Declan clinging to Mya's legs. She's stroking their backs and saying something to them as they look up at her with bright eyes. Concern is etched on her face, her eyes trained on me and my crew passing by.

"Your boys are here," Nate says as he sprints past me to open the door.

"Yeah, I see that." I take one more quick glance back and almost have to do a double-take.

Is that Georgia reaching down to lift Finnegan into her arms?

What is she doing here with Mya and my kids?

My jaw clenches as I jerk my attention away. The only thing that matters is that they are all safe and outside. I'll deal with the rest later. I step into the foyer and greet the librarian, Odalis Cruz.

"Any idea what triggered the alarm?" I ask.

She shakes her head. "I went through the building to make sure everyone got out. I didn't see any smoke or smell anything."

I nod at her. "We'll check everything out and let you know. Go on outside and join the others across the street."

I bark orders to Luke, Darren and Nate, sending them off to follow our protocols for checking the interior and exterior of the building. Wiley bursts through the doors a minute later.

"Where's the alarm operational panel in this place?" I ask. Wiley is the technology guru on our crew, responsible for helping us gain information from the alarm monitoring systems.

"It's around this corner," Wiley says, then turns to look at me. "Did you see Georgia out there with your kids?"

My ears burn with irritation, and I swallow past the lump in my throat. "Yeah, I did."

"Take it you knew nothing about that?"

"Nothing at all. I'll get to the bottom of everything once we finish up here," I say.

"You better." Wiley opens the panel and cycles through the settings, then walks over to the safety map of the building on the wall. "Alarm was triggered from this section." He points to a large open space near the back of the building lined with wide ceiling to floor windows that overlook the forest.

I cycle through my memories and recognize what could be the culprit. "That's where the computer stations are. Could be an electrical blaze."

"Let's go check it out," Wiley says.

I radio the information to Luke, Darren and Nate, then lead Wiley through the empty building to the computer area. There's no sign of any smoke and I'm thinking it's a false alarm. I say, "A computer could've overheated and triggered an alarm."

"We reviewed the permit for the system. It is a higher sensitivity system because of the risk of blaze with all the books," Wiley agrees as he slips his helmet from his head. "A significant increase in temperature in a small area near the sensor could've done it."

I unhook my TIC from my belt and canvas the space, looking for an infrared sign of a blaze and come up empty. Wiley starts down one row to check each computer.

"All clear on the perimeter outside and inside," Nate says, as Luke and Darren follow him over.

"You think one of these computers shot off some sparks?" Darren asks, moving to the opposite end from Wiley.

We each take a row, going station by station, looking for any signs of a fire. This is one time when I don't mind a false alarm. The idea of a fire in the library in the middle of the day, when it's packed with children, is enough to fray any parent's nerves.

"Found it," Luke yells.

I rush toward him, followed by the others, and stare down at a white computer cord plugged into an outlet that looks blackened and burned out.

"Is it still hot?" I ask.

"No sign of any fire. Probably put itself out as quickly as it sparked," Nate says.

Wiley and Darren drop on their knees and give it a closer look.

"This doesn't look fresh. Could've happened weeks or months ago," Wiley says.

Another glance at the spot and I see his point.

"I'll tell Odalis to have an electrician come out and check the outlets and wiring, but I think our work here is done." I turn toward Wiley. "Can you get the alarm reset?"

He salutes and takes off for the front of the building. Darren and Luke follow him to reload our equipment and perform final inventory checks before we leave the scene.

Luke ambles up to me. "How about I tell Odalis our findings? You can go outside and figure out what Georgia's trying to pull now."

Normally, I wouldn't think of handling personal business while working. This time, I'm going to make an exception. "Yeah, I'll do that."

Minutes later, I'm walking out into the bright sunshine of midday. The crowds have dispersed, with only the library employees and a handful of patrons still milling around across the street. Declan and Finnegan are playing some kind of game where they have to jump and try to slap Mya's hands. I watch as she keeps lifting her palms higher and higher, challenging the boys to push past what they may think their limits are.

I smile, then feel my smile wane.

Did Mya orchestrate this meet-up of Georgia and my kids? I know Georgia was kind to Mya when she came to town. Plus, they're neighbors. In the past month of Mya taking care of the boys, I hadn't needed to tell her about my history with Georgia or why it's important to limit their interactions with Nikki's mother.

Georgia stands a few feet behind Mya and glares at me as I step up on the curb.

"Daddy! Daddy!" The chorus of my sons lifts my mood, distracting me.

"Hey buddies," I say, then squat down and hug them.

"Did you find the fire, Daddy?" Declan asks.

"No, it was a false alarm."

"I'm glad, Daddy," Finnegan says, looking adorably relieved. "I don't want to be stuck in a fire."

"I don't want you to be either," I say, squeezing his nose until he squeals with laughter. I turn to Declan. "Or you." I squeeze his nose, but Declan is quicker and able to wiggle from my grasp.

I stand up and look at Mya.

My mouth opens, but words don't come out. She's so beautiful, standing in front of me with a cute furrow in her brows.

"You okay?" I ask.

She nods. "That was enough excitement for the day, even if there wasn't a fire. What do you think triggered it?"

"A surge from an electrical outlet to one of the computers, probably." I stiffen as I detect Georgia approaching in my periphery. My hands grip Declan and Finnegan's shoulders protectively, shifting away from their granny.

I turn to her and ask, "What are you doing here with my sons? And don't give me some crap about it being a coincidence."

Georgia rolls her eyes. "I have every right to spend time with my grandsons."

"You don't get to decide when you see *my* sons!" I growl.

Finnegan gasps and wiggles from my grasp and runs to Mya.

A look of disdain clouds Georgia's face as she watches him.

"How many times are we going to have this same old argument? None of this is about what's best for you, Ronan," Georgia pokes a finger at my chest. "It's about what's best for those sweet little boys. Knowing that they have more family than you and Connor and *your* parents is what's right. They need to know and feel that they are loved by so many people, including their mother."

"Miss Mya …" Declan's voice is low and strained.

"Don't you bring up Nikki to me right now! I have no problem with you spending time with my sons, but you can't ambush them and try to see them without telling me," I say, taking another step toward her. Georgia doesn't flinch, but she should. If she knew the thoughts going through my mind right now, she wouldn't be so brave. "You keep pulling stunts like this and I'll make sure you never see them again. Do you hear me?"

"Ronan!"

Mya's voice cracks through my anger, diffusing all my frustration, pain, and fury. I turn to see her reassuring my sons as they look scared out of their minds.

I exhale a deep breath, willing myself to calm down.

"I'm sure you and Granny can work out those details later, right?" Her eyes pleading with me to calm down in front of my sons. The sight of them clinging to Mya for reassurance and comfort pierces the hardness triggered in my heart by seeing Georgia. A calm oozes through me as I watch the positive influence she has on them.

I force a smile on my face, then squat down to eye level with the boys.

"Miss Mya is right. Granny and I will talk about all of this later and figure out when y'all can hang out with her. How does that sound?"

"Good," Declan whispers as Finnegan nods. Neither of them look convinced. They look more like they want to flee this scene as fast as they can and never look back. I hate I lost my temper in front of them. "So, what do y'all have planned for the rest of the day?"

"I'm tired," Finnegan says, then walks over to me and gives me a big hug. "Be careful, Daddy. I hope you only have fake fires for the rest of the day."

"Thanks, son," I say and squeeze him tight.

"I should get back so they can take a nap," Mya says, then adds. "See you in the morning?" I hear her words, but I know what she's asking.

Are you okay? Do you need me?

And the answer is yes. And yes.

"Yep, see y'all in the morning." I glance at Declan, who looks irritated. "You, good Dec?"

He smiles brightly at me—a pure, genuine smile brimming with love. He says, "Of course, Daddy!" Like I'm making a big deal out of nothing.

But it isn't nothing.

I make a promise to myself that I'll never let them get caught between me and Georgia ever again.

"Say bye to Daddy," Mya says.

The boys wave and say bye, then walk down the sidewalk.

"This isn't over by a long shot," Georgia hisses from behind me.

I rise to my full height and turn to stare daggers at her.

"If you think I'm going to let you erase my daughter from those boys' lives and replace her with Mya, you're crazy. I will never let that happen." Georgia huffs, then storms off in the opposite direction.

"Nikki has no place in their lives to replace," I call out after her.

She flips a hand at me and disappears around the corner.

CHAPTER 31

YA

~

THE NEXT MORNING, I STAND BEHIND FINNEGAN AND
Declan as they brush their teeth and make funny faces in the mirror,
feeling on edge. Frothy toothpaste drips down Declan's chin and
Finnegan sticks his tongue out to scrub it with his toothbrush. I'm
grateful the boys aren't picking up on my mood. Ever since the false
alarm at the library, I haven't been able to shake the guilt snaking
through me.

If I'm being honest, I can't blame Georgia for being upset with me.
I thought about calling to apologize, but what could I actually say?
Would I lie and pretend like I don't want to be a mother-figure to her
grandsons? Like I haven't fallen for Ronan and want to make him
forget he ever knew Nikki? How can I convince her I'm not trying to
stake a space in the O'Reilly family when I know it isn't true?

No part of me wants the boys to forget their mom, but the truth is, she isn't around. She's not here to see them humming songs as they brush their teeth in the morning. She has no clue that they don't like cereal and prefer scrambled eggs and bacon for breakfast. Nikki's not around to be proud of how well they take care of Jellybean, making sure he's fed and walked whenever I come over. I'm here to see these things with Ronan. Not her.

That's why her children are bonding with me.

It's not my fault or even a bad thing, so why do I feel like I've committed some reprehensible crime?

"Alright, that's enough. Rinse out your mouths so you can get changed. Your daddy will be home soon," I say, reaching over to tickle them.

The boys giggle and squirm, then finish up at the sink.

"I still wish you were going to the park with us today," Finnegan says.

"Me too, but I have some business to take care of," I say. While the boys were napping yesterday, I made appointments to meet with the lawyer and accountant Jasmine recommended. If I'm going to start my personal training business here in Kimbell, I want to make sure I do everything right. No cutting corners. The sign-ups for my Saturday class tomorrow have increased by fifty percent. Word of mouth has led to increased interest. I've gotten a few inquiries from guys and I'm contemplating setting up a later session for both men and women to join.

"The pink flyer business?" Declan asks.

"Yes, that's the one. If things go well, I'll be helping people in Lasso County get in shape and feel good about themselves," I say, reaching between them to turn off the faucet.

Declan snatches the toothbrush from Finnegan's hand, then places both of them in the container next to the sink. Finnegan frowns at his brother but doesn't complain.

"You make us feel good about ourselves, so I know you can make everybody feel that way," Finnegan says, giving me that killer smile so like his father's.

"Thank you," I wink at him, then push the boys out the bathroom door. "Go get dressed and then we'll eat breakfast."

"Okay!" Declan says, then challenges Finnegan to a race down the hallway to their bedroom.

I shake my head, then turn toward the living room where my phone is ringing. I reach it before it goes to voicemail and answer.

"Mya, it's Candy. How are you?"

Well, isn't this interesting? Candy Erikson calling me today of all days. I wonder if she heard about Paige firing me after getting pregnant by Jamal and called to extend her condolences.

"Not too bad considering," I say, not bothering to ignore that she's likely heard all the gossip about me.

"I'm sorry Jamal cheated on you. He always seemed like such a great guy. I never would've guessed he'd do that. We all thought y'all would be headed down the aisle soon."

I'm quiet. There's no way I was marrying Jamal. I had been biding my time to plan my exit, but no need to tell Candy this.

"Things aren't always what they seem," I say, then ask. "What's going on? I'm surprised to hear from you."

Candy says, "Construction has wrapped up on my gym and we'll be opening in a matter of weeks. I have more people signing up for memberships than I could've dreamed."

"That's what happens when you get prime real estate near the university," I say, still not sure what any of this has to do with me. I'm sure she got the call from Paige trashing my reputation like everyone else.

"True. So, Jamal called me …"

"He did?"

"He said that Paige has been making it hard for you to find work after she fired you. He still loves you despite the mistakes he made and wants what's best for you."

I roll my eyes but remain quiet.

"You know Paige and I have been colleagues for a long time. Normally, I respect her as a businesswoman, but this time she's gone too far. But her loss might be my gain," Candy says, bubbling with excitement.

"How so?"

"I want to offer you a position as head personal trainer at Iron Woman Gym of Austin. A trainer of your caliber and talent shouldn't be on the sidelines. I need you, Mya. What do you say?"

"I say I'm shocked," I swallow past the lump in my throat as Candy fills me in on the highlights of the high-profile members she's secured, the employment benefits and the salary that is far beyond anything I made working for Paige. "Candy, you're giving me an offer I can't refuse, aren't you?"

"That was the plan," Candy says.

"Can I take a week to think about it?" I ask, unable to deny the excitement coursing through me from the opportunity. As much as I want to say yes, this would mean moving back to Austin. Moving away from Ronan. I don't want to do that, but I'm also not sure where the relationship with Ronan is going. Should I make another sacrifice for a relationship? Or will I live to regret it like I did my time with Jamal?

"Of course. Take as much time as you need. The offer has no expiration."

"Thanks," I say, dropping my cell phone on the couch.

"Miss Mya! Miss Mya!" The twins scream my name as they come racing into the living room. I look down at them dressed in mix-matched clothes and wonder what were they thinking when they decided what to wear.

Declan shakes the paper from the library at me. "Here. Don't forget to ask Daddy—"

"Don't forget to ask Daddy what?" Ronan asks.

I freeze and snatch the paper from Declan, then try to stop my heart from pounding in my chest. Every time Ronan came home from work, I got the same feeling—belonging. I belong here with Ronan and his sons, and they belong with me. This is the family I dreamed of, but I'm not sure that I'll actually get.

Turning around slowly, I suck in a deep breath as his handsomeness sends a jolt through my body. I hide the paper behind my back and fight the urge to give him a kiss. Ronan's eyes drift to my lips and I know he feels the same thing I'm feeling. We've kept to our plans of withholding our relationship from his sons, even though I'd hoped we could tell them by now.

Declan and Finnegan rush past me and leap into Ronan's arms. He hugs them tight, then tucks them under his arms and carries them to the kitchen table.

"Sit down and eat your breakfast," Ronan says, kissing each boy on the head. "We have a big day ahead of us at the park and you'll need your energy."

The boys turn their attention on the food I cooked as Ronan walks back over to me.

"What's that you're hiding behind your back?" Ronan asks, a playful hint in his eyes.

"The reason that my neighbor hates me now," I say, then slowly hand the paper to Ronan. We step further away from the dining table into the living room, dodging Jellybean as he trots to the table to accept scraps of food from the boys.

Ronan sits on the couch as he reads the document, then looks up at me.

"Yesterday, your sons asked me to be their pretend mommy and participate in the scavenger hunt with them," I explain. Ronan's expression doesn't change as he listens to me. "Georgia overheard, and she wasn't pleased. She probably thinks I'm trying to make the boys forget about Nikki."

"My sons don't know Nikki. She's a woman in photos and on videos who has never, not once, lifted a finger to meet them," Ronan says, his voice low and strained. His jaw clenches and I can see him fighting back a wave of anger.

"What's with you and Georgia? Why are you so opposed to her spending time with her grandsons?"

Ronan drags a hand down his face. "Trust me, Georgia isn't the nice woman she pretends to be. I don't want to drag you into this anymore than you already are.”

His words sting. I want him to share with me. The good and the bad. I hate he feels he can’t confide in me about his past with Georgia. He has to know that no matter what, I’ll always be on his side. Right?

Turning the paper toward me, Ronan asks, “How do you feel about this? Really? Is it … too much?”

“No,” I blurt. “I was touched and honored that they felt comfortable enough to ask me. I don’t see this as trying to take Nikki’s place. She’s not here, and I’m happy to step in and help. I love those little guys.”

A smile spreads across Ronan’s face. “I know you do.”

“But I’m also not trying to put more strain on your relationship with Georgia or Nikki. What happened between y’all yesterday—”

“Was a mistake. I never should’ve lost my temper like that. I’m glad you were there to smooth things over with Finn and Dec. It means more to me than you realize,” Ronan says. He pats a hand on the couch next to him.

Taking the cue, I sit, careful to keep some distance between us.

“Did you notice the date of the scavenger hunt? It’s a month from now.”

“And you’re wondering if I’ll be in Kimbell to participate with your sons?”

“I’m wondering if you’ll be around to be with … me,” Ronan says. “It’s only been three weeks that we’ve been …” he looks back at the twins. They are oblivious to our conversation, prattling on and on about which Larry Llama book they like the best. Ronan continues, “I shouldn’t feel this way after three weeks of dating, but I do. I don’t want you to leave Kimbell, but I also don’t want you sticking around if it’s because you feel bad for my boys. I want to be the main reason you want to stay. Is that selfish?”

I slip my hand over his, gripping it within mine. “You are the number one reason I want to stay in Kimbell. Those little boys of yours are the cherry on top,” I say, the words gushing from my mouth. All thoughts of taking Candy's job offer disappear from my mind and I'm completely sold on staying.

"Is that so?" Ronan asks, lifting my hand to kiss it gently.

My eyes grow wide. "Stop that. I still think it's too soon for Finn and Dec to find out about us. Shouldn't we wait a little longer?"

"No," Ronan shakes his head. "I think we've waited long enough."

CHAPTER 32

R *ONAN*

~

"AT THIS RATE, TIFFANY WILL HAVE TO KICK ALL THE OTHER kids out of daycare. She can't run a business with just those two little girls," Connor says, laughing under his breath.

We cut through Bell Park and head down the sidewalk toward the fire station. The park is unusually busy for a Saturday with more families than normal, taking advantage of this warm October morning. Kids are racing through the playground, squealing and playing while the parents sit on park benches, swapping the latest gossip.

"Who was the culprit this time?" I ask, feeling a bit vindicated by my brother's news. The glue incident my sons took part in paled compared to the latest prank pulled on the little girls. Three hours trapped in a toy chest while the rest of the kids pretended not to know where they were had left them traumatized.

"Too many kids to count. Apparently, the girls are bullies and the rest of the kids locked them in the chest because they were tired of being pushed around by them," Connor explained. "After I got them hydrated and calmed down from being 'buried alive', I had a little conversation with Tiff."

"Did she admit she overreacted to my kids' prank?"

"Reluctantly. She can't take the risk that you'll file a complaint about inconsistencies in her policies for the two incidents. I have a feeling she'll be reaching out to you to allow the boys back at daycare."

"Good thing because these nanny interviews have been pretty bad," I say, rubbing a hand through my hair. "I promised Mya I'd have a replacement lined up by the end of this month. Sending the boys back to Tiff's daycare would be the better option."

Connor scoffs. "Of course, because you promised Mya."

"Don't start with me."

"You brought her up, so now she's fair game."

"What is it with you and Mya? Why are you so opposed to my relationship with her?" I stop, facing off with my brother. Connor's irritation is clear and I'm over his constant negativity toward her. It triggers every instinct in me to protect Mya. I won't let anyone hurt her, not even my brother.

"I'm not opposed to your relationship." Connor sighs. "It may not seem like it, but I want you to be happy. I get Mya does that for you. But you're also falling into all the old patterns, rushing things with her. One minute you're taking things slow, the next you want to introduce her as your girlfriend to your sons and let her play mommy to them for the annual scavenger hunt. Seriously, Ronan? You've only been dating for a month."

"Sometimes a month is all it takes." I insist. It's been a week since I suggested telling the boys about our relationship, but we decided to hold off a little longer. Mya was swamped working out the details for her new business with Lance and Kennedy and we couldn't find the right time.

"I've heard that before. Remember when you tried to convince me you knew Nikki was the love of your life after only two weeks? I warned you then not to rush things, but you didn't listen to me."

"Stop comparing what I have with Mya to my marriage to Nikki. They aren't close to being the same. Mya shouldn't be penalized because I made a bad mistake back then."

"I'm not concerned about Mya. I'm concerned about you!" Connor says, giving me a shove. "You need to take your time and make sure you know Mya, all parts of her. That doesn't happen in a month. It takes time. If this thing between the two of you is as special as you claim, then waiting a few months won't matter. So, my question to you is why are you in such a hurry? You worried she won't stick around? That her feelings aren't as strong as yours?"

"I know how Mya feels about me. She's putting roots down in Kimbell to be with me, starting with her personal training business and her plans to buy her great-uncle's house," I say, wanting Connor to understand how different things are for me and Mya. It burns that he's too busy with his dire warnings to be happy that I've found someone that I deeply care about. Someone who makes me want to love again, which I didn't think would ever happen.

"Businesses fail and plans change. If she's in this for the long haul, make her prove it. I don't want my nephews getting attached to her if, at the first sign of an issue, she bolts. You need to tread carefully and not set your sons up to be abandoned again. Things are good now, but what happens when y'all hit a rough patch? Will she fight for the relationship or skip town like Nikki?"

"Are you done?"

"For now," Connor says, then pulls me into a rough half hug. "I want the best for you. Remember that while you're pissed at me for the rest of the day."

I groan under my breath as Connor crosses the street toward Gwen's Country Cafe. I wish I could heed my brother's concerns, but Mya makes me feel too much.

That makes me want everything with her.

Now.

I've never been a patient man, especially not when love is involved. And I'm definitely falling in love with Mya. I haven't said anything because I don't want to spook her and because, deep down, I know Connor is right.

I thought I loved Nikki, and all that ended after two years.

I need to take my time with Mya.

It's the only way I'll know for sure that things will be different this time.

That my bad luck in love has changed for good.

Pulling on the door of the fire station, I wave to Erin, the receptionist, then take the stairs to the second floor where I hear Wiley and Luke engaged in a heated discussion on the World Series game last night. I'm in no mood to participate.

I stalk into the dining area and grab a bottle of water before sitting in my usual spot at the table. My thoughts are a jumbled mess as I fight to suppress what my heart wants to follow what my head knows is best.

"Trouble in paradise?" Wiley pipes up, turning toward me. His blue eyes growing darker, concern etched on his face.

"What's that supposed to mean?" I bark back, in no mood to share what happened with them.

"Alright," Luke says, abandoning his spoonful of cereal. He pushes the bowl toward the center of the table. "Santos is nowhere to be found, and you got some stuff you need to get off your chest. I'm sure we aren't top on your list to confide in, but we're all you got at the moment."

"I think I should be at the top of your list, though," Wiley says, stirring his watery bowl of oatmeal. "Think about it. You and I hang out as much as you and Santos, if not more. Connor is blood, but y'all fight about every time you have to spend more than an hour with each other, so I'm rising as the closest friend you have."

I chuckle under my breath and relax a bit. Wiley isn't wrong. And neither is Luke. If I don't talk about this to someone, anyone, my head is going to explode.

"First, is this about Mya?" Luke asks, treading carefully into the subject.

"Of course it is," Wiley responds before I do. "Ronan's been floating into this fire station on cloud nine for the past month since they started dating. Now, all of a sudden, he's brooding and pissed off. This has 'woman' written all over it."

"Yeah, but that woman could be Nikki," Luke says.

I raise a hand, shaking my head. "Please, don't conjure her up. I'm dealing with enough right now and thinking about adding my ex to the mix would push me over the edge."

"Told you," Wiley taunts Luke. "I was right. What happened?"

"Connor thinks I'm moving too fast with Mya. That I'm going to make the same mistake I did with Nikki," I say, feeling increasingly miserable as the words pour out. "Falling for a woman that I really didn't know."

"Trust me, I was around when you and Nikki were together. You know a thousand times more about Mya than you knew about Nikki," Wiley says.

"True," Luke agrees, then points his spoon at me. "But what's the risk in slowing down a bit?"

I shrug, because I don't have an answer to that question. I'm not sure I can trust my feelings about Mya. Every part of me thinks she fits perfectly with my family, with me and my boys. It's like she's that puzzle piece we were always missing and now that she's connected to us, I don't see a reason to hold back. To waste time when I know she's the woman I want. She's the mother my boys have dreamed of.

But what if my brother is right and I'm wrong about her?

"There's no risk at all," Wiley pipes up. "Mya is a keeper. She's not going anywhere and you aren't either. Go fast or go slow. I don't think it matters. So what do you want to do?"

A knock on the kitchen door saves me from responding. I look up to see Mrs. Williamson. Her thick red hair, normally slicked back in the familiar severe bun, has wayward tendrils flowing freely as she barges into the room. A sheen of sweat covers her freckled face.

"Ronan, it's been too long, especially since you were conspicuously absent from the Founder's Day activities," Mrs. Williamson says, dabbing at her forehead with a handkerchief. She motions toward Luke, then points a finger at the refrigerator. "Get me a cool drink, would you, dear?"

Luke does as he's told and grabs a bottle of water from the fridge and hands it to her. Mrs. Williamson takes long, loud gulps before fixing her eyes back on me.

"I can't imagine why you would've missed out on celebrating the anniversary of our wonderful town and the day when our founding mother, Kimberly Bell, settled here over one hundred years ago," she says, swiping at a rogue droplet of sweat coursing down her witch-like nose. "I know your shift wasn't working that day since both Luke and Wiley were in attendance." She turns to give each of them a broad smile as she grabs Darren's chair and sits between us. "But at least Mya had the decency to bring your boys. They got a proper education on the history of our glorious town."

"Yes, they told me. They were pretty exhausted after spending one day at the festivities. I kept them home so they could rest the next day. I'm sure you understand," I say.

"Of course. You know Kimberly Bell had twins of her own. Little girls, not boys, but that doesn't matter. She was left all alone to raise them as a single parent after her husband died unexpectedly, not unlike yourself, except your wife abandoned you to become a pop star." She winces. "I'm certain our founding mother would have compassion for your plight, as I do."

"So, what brings you to the fire station, Mrs. Williamson?" I ask, ignoring her comment.

"It's a serious matter that concerns you and Mya," she continues.

My mouth goes dry, wondering what the woman could know about Mya and me. I had left the house abruptly this morning and hadn't checked with Mya like I normally would've in the past couple of hours while at work.

"I was at Mya's workout this morning," Mrs. Williamson starts.

"Mya canceled the workout today. She's taking care of my sons since I'm on shift," I interrupt, growing irritated.

Mrs. Williamson frowns. "Oh, she didn't cancel it. We were all there sweating like pigs trying to do that tough workout. Your boys were there as well. After the class, Mya and I were talking. We only took our eyes off of the children playing for a moment, but that was long enough."

"Long enough ... for what?" I push up from my chair, sending it toppling over with a loud crash. I force my heart rate to remain steady as I wait for what the woman would say next. Mrs. Williamson picks up on my alarm and shrinks under my glare.

"Well, we ... umm ... the children were huddled around the old fountain in front of the high school track shouting 'jump, jump, jump'," she says, standing up to act out the scene. "Declan had climbed to the top of the cowboy statue and was sitting on the top. We tried to get him to climb back down ..."

My heart stops in my chest. I barely register Wiley and Luke standing in the periphery, ready to act as soon as we get some intelligible information out of Mrs. Williamson.

"And?" I say, my voice a hard, cold growl.

"He jumped. By the time we rushed over, we saw Declan lying in the water with blood gushing from his head—"

My body goes rigid as the room spins. A vision of my fearless son, Declan, floating lifeless in blood-soaked water of the fountain slams into my head. He was more like Connor than me—bullheaded and strong, decisive and resilient. The perfect yin to Finnegan's yang. Just like Connor was for me.

I stumble back, bumping into the table.

Wiley is at my side, gripping my shoulder.

"How could Mya take her eyes off him?" I ask to no one in particular as the sound of my heartbeat speeding a mile a minute thunders in my ears. "He's a four-year-old little boy."

Bile rises in my throat, and I think I'm going to be sick.

"Where is he? Where's my son?" I scream at Mrs. Williamson.

She stands and takes a few steps away from me as she answers, "We were fortunate that Ace Lallo was changing light bulbs around the track. Mya grabbed Declan and Finnegan and jumped into his golf cart. Ace is taking them to the hospital, and I came here right away to let you know."

"I ... need ... to ... go," I say, brushing past her as worry drowns me.

Wiley says, "I'll drive you."

As we rush out of the kitchen, I hear Luke say, "You know, Mrs. Williamson, you should've led with that."

CHAPTER 33

M^{YA}

IT'S BEEN A LONG TIME SINCE I'VE CRIED. A DECADE AGO, when I stood over my grandma's grave at the cemetery. I grieved. Hard. Until there were no more tears left.

So, it's no surprise to me that my eyes are as dry as a desert as I stand in the middle of the waiting area of the emergency room, gripping Finnegan's hand. The nurses had to rip Declan's limp body from my arms as I ran inside screaming for help.

My tank top is stained red with blood.

Declan's blood.

The gash on the side of his head wouldn't stop bleeding.

"Declan! Do not jump!" I screamed as I ran toward him. "Climb down now!"

He looked at me, spooked by the fear he heard in my voice.

We locked gazes, and I knew he'd be okay.

He'd climb down from the cowboy statue and rush toward me, face full of remorse for scaring the crap out of me.

But that's not what happened.

His leg dangled, reaching for the shoulder of the statue, and slipped.

Arms flailing, I saw the terror on his face as he lost control of his body, free falling.

His head hit the outstretched hand of the statue and then his body went limp, crashing into the fountain below.

I heard Finnegan's anguished scream as he jumped into the water to help his brother.

It doesn't matter I was there within seconds. Performing CPR, I found a pulse and determined he had swallowed no water from the seconds he'd been submerged underwater. Thanks to Finnegan's quick action.

But he was still.

Not moving.

And there was so much blood.

"Miss Mya," Finnegan's voice pierces the fog of my mind.

"Yes, sweetie," I say, unable to look at him. Guilt courses through me like a freight train. I was supposed to protect him and his brother. Make sure they didn't get hurt. It's my fault Declan is in the hospital unconscious. I let my own selfish needs distract me from the most important thing I was given to do today—care for two of the most precious little boys that I've grown to love like my own.

"Declan's going to want some cookies when he wakes up," Finnegan says. I admire his determined resolve to believe that his brother will be fine. But it does nothing to bolster my own. The only thought creeping around the edges of my mind is how can I face Ronan after letting his son get a horrible head injury? What if Declan is never the same after this? How can I explain how I let this happen?

"Yes, he is," I say, knowing that I have to be strong for Finnegan. I reach down and lift him onto my hip. He's way too big for that, but I can tell by the way he holds onto me he appreciates it. I need to hold him as much as he needs to be held. "What kind do you think we should get him?"

"Chocolate chip, silly! It's his favorite," Finnegan says, then leans his head against my neck.

"How could I have forgotten?" I say, rocking him. "We'll go to the gift shop and buy some as soon as the doctor comes back with news on your brother."

"Miss Mya," Finnegan says.

"Yes."

"How long do you think Declan is going to be asleep?"

"Not long, honey. He'll miss you too much to stay asleep for very long."

Finnegan raises and graces me with the most gorgeous smile. "Good. I miss him too. I want to go home."

"And we will as soon as ..." My voice trails off as Jasmine approaches me. She walks briskly and efficiently with an unreadable expression on her face. I can't tell if she's about to give me the best news or wreck my life to pieces.

I open my mouth to ask how Declan is, but no words come out. I frown and try to force myself to breathe.

Jasmine reaches for Finnegan and strokes his back, then gives me a small smile.

"Hey Finnegan," Jasmine says, smiling brighter for him.

"Hi, Dr. Jones," Finnegan responds.

"How would you like to go say hi to your granny while you're here?"

"Granny is here?" Finnegan's eyes light up.

"She is. Do you remember Nurse Avril?" Jasmine asks as a woman a couple inches short of five feet tall appears out of nowhere.

Finnegan nods his head, but his arms remain wrapped around my shoulders. I look down at her and my heart clenches at the pity I see in her eyes. I don't want to let go of Finnegan, but I need to. He should be with Georgia right now.

"Nurse Avril can take you to see your granny," I say, trying to encourage him. His grip tightens around me.

"I don't want to leave you. Tell Granny to come here," Finnegan says.

"Miss Georgia asked me to get you. She wants to see you, Finnegan," Avril says.

"Can you do that, Finn? Go see Granny?" I ask him as I slide a hand under his arm to loosen his grip. He looks torn as his eyes search mine. I give him a reassuring smile. "I'll be right here when you get back."

"Pinky swear?" Finnegan thrusts his hand toward mine. I loop our pinkies and tug on his tightly. That was enough.

Minutes later, Avril disappears with Finnegan behind a closed door, accessible only to hospital personnel.

"Georgia's pretty upset," Jasmine says as we walk through the near empty waiting room to a couch near the window. "I thought she might rip your head off if she came to get Finnegan herself, so I suggested Avril do it for her."

"She has a right to be."

"Don't start that. Kids have accidents all the time. There's no way you could watch them every second," Jasmine says.

"How bad is it?" I whisper, bracing myself for the cold, hard truth. Jasmine won't sugarcoat things, even though this is one time when I wish she would.

Her hand grips mine. I'm surprised by the softness in her eyes. "It was touch and go. He has a four-inch gash on his head that we got stitched up. There was intercranial swelling, but it responded well to treatment and it's under control now."

"But he's still not awake."

"No."

"Is that normal?"

"Too hard to say what's normal for head injuries, especially in children," Jasmine says.

"Ronan's going to kill me."

"No, he isn't."

"Yes, he is. He's going to hate me and then he's going to kill me," I say.

"Girl, are you crazy?" Jasmine rolls her eyes at me and I feel foolish. "I'm sorry, but you are going to be the last thing on Ronan's mind for a change." Jasmine wraps an arm around my shoulders and gives me a squeeze. "He's only going to be focused on Declan. And after that, it'll be Finnegan. That's it."

"Of course, you're right. I'm not important right now. The only thing that matters is Declan getting better."

"And the best thing you can do is fade to the background until all of this works itself out. When Declan wakes up and we've cleared his brain scans, then you and Ronan can deal with processing what happened and what it means for your relationship—"

"Jas!" A booming baritone feels the space.

I glance up and see a face that looks so familiar, yet different from what I expected. In all the weeks that Ronan and I have been together, I've never met his brother. They are far from identical, yet the similarities in their features leave no doubt they are brothers. Where Ronan is towering and athletic, Dr. Connor O'Reilly has the slender build of a surfer and could rock the runway in Ralph Lauren. The same strong jaw and blazing red hair on a thinner face and sans beard. The same almost translucent slate-blue eyes that are staring daggers at me. If looks could kill, I wouldn't survive Connor's glare.

"Declan is awake," Connor says, raking a hand through his short curls. "You need to come check him out."

Jasmine gives me another squeeze, then hurries out of the waiting area. Connor lingers near the entrance, his arms crossed over his chest. His anger is palpable, causing the air to thicken with tension.

I step forward, ready to face the music.

Connor frowns, a look of disgust on his face. He shakes his head and turns his back to me. He walks out of the waiting room toward the nurses' station.

"Connor, wait," I call out.

He stops and glances over his shoulder.

I cross the room and face him. "I'm really—"

"Sorry? Is that what you're going to say?" Connor asks. "You think that means anything to me right now? My nephew was unconscious for almost an hour and we didn't know *if*," he pauses, letting the word linger, "*if* he was going to wake up. My brother is a wreck and you think someone cares about your remorse?"

"Ronan is here?" I ask.

"Yeah, Wiley brought him about thirty minutes ago. They came through the ambulance entrance, which is for the best," Connor says, his words dripping with anger. "The last thing my brother needs is to see you."

His words are like daggers, leaving me riddled and with a pain like I've never felt before. Ever.

"For some reason, my brother thought it was a good idea to trust you with his children. They are his reason for living. After everything those little boys have been through, the last thing they need is a lost, clueless and careless part-time babysitter neglecting her duties and letting them get seriously injured. You should be ashamed of yourself!"

"That's enough." Ronan's words echo in the hallway.

I don't look at him. I can hear the tension and strain in his words. The unshed tears and worry that must've dogged him from the minute he found out Declan was at the hospital. I know I should've been the one to call him. To tell him myself what happened, but I couldn't bring myself to do it.

"You're not going to defend her after what she did?" Connor challenges.

"Not another word, Connor. I swear, I can't deal with this right now," Ronan says.

I glance up and see the anguish and pain settled into the lines of his face. His fists clench at his sides as he stands off with his brother. Connor sends another glare my way, then says, "I'll go get Finnegan."

Ronan nods as Connor walks away.

"I'm so glad Declan is awake," I say.

Ronan nods again. He's not making eye contact with me.

"Is there anything you need?" I ask, feeling out of place. I don't belong here. Not anymore.

"No," Ronan says, and when his eyes lock onto mine, it's like he's looking at a stranger. His voice is distant as he says, "You should go home."

I don't protest or resist. Turning around to grab my purse from the couch, I loop it over my shoulder and face the entrance to the waiting area.

Ronan is gone.

CHAPTER 34

RONAN

~

DDECLAN'S LIGHT BLUE EYES STARE BACK AT ME, FULL OF
sparkle and mischief. It's a sight I wasn't sure I'd see again. The
horrible tragedies I'd witnessed as a firefighter had flooded through my
mind as he lay lifeless in the hospital bed. Declan could've died or
been paralyzed or brain damaged.

Yet none of those horrible fates had occurred.

Declan smiles at me as he plays with a toy car the nurse left
behind. It is a tool for them to assess whether there's any damage to
his motor skills after verifying that he had a full range of motion to all
his limbs.

"Am I in trouble?" Declan asks with a contrite smile.

I rub a hand over his soft buzz cut, poking through the top of his
bandaged head. "No, little fella. I think you've suffered enough from
your actions. What have you learned after today?"

"No climbing on the Kimbell Cowboy statue," he says with a bright smile. I give him a high-five.

"How's your head feeling?"

"Hurts ... a little." His voice is small and I get the feeling he's putting up a brave front for me. When they told me he was awake, I burst into the room and couldn't stop the flood of tears as I gripped him in my arms. I know I scared the crap out of him, but I couldn't help it.

"Want me to call the nurse? She can give you something for the pain."

He shakes his head, then winces.

"Be careful. You can't move your head around like that until the stitches heal."

"Sorry, Daddy." He frowns as he raises a hand to rub on the bandage wrapped around his skull. I'll have to keep an eye on him or that bandage will be on the floor before morning.

"You feel up for some visitors?"

"Finnegan!" He screams, bouncing on the bed. "Can he come inside and stay with me?"

"Of course he can." I say, pleased to see Declan acting more and more like his normal self. "I'll go get him."

I exit the hospital room and motion for the nurse to sit with my son until I get back. I make my way past the nurses' station to a small sitting area where Georgia and Finnegan have been waiting.

Georgia stands up as soon as I enter, smoothing the wrinkles in her scrubs. "How is he?"

"Pretty much back to normal. His head hurts a bit, which is to be expected, I suppose. But he wants to see his brother." I glance down at Finnegan curled up on a chair, sleeping soundly. It's been a long day for both boys.

"I don't think that's a good idea," Georgia says, resting a hand on my arm. "Finnegan has been agitated for hours and I finally got him to go to sleep. It's better if you let me take him home and he visits

Declan in the morning. If he sees Declan all wrapped up in bandages, it could traumatize him."

I scoff and jerk my arm away from her touch. "If I want medical advice about what's best for my son, I'll ask my brother."

Georgia's eyes grow cold. "It's not medical advice. As a parent, I'd think you'd want to do what's best for both of your sons."

"Again, you're the last person I'd come to for parenting advice. Why don't you give some of that to your daughter instead of me?" I brush past her to sit next to Finnegan.

"I'm not the enemy here, and neither is Nikki. She's worried sick about Declan."

"Is she?" I ask, unable to hide the sarcasm dripping from my tone. "She lost the right to be upset about anything that happens to my sons the minute she abandoned them."

"You know she regrets that." Georgia paces in front of me. "She wants to give her sons a good life. As soon as she's established her music career, she will make time for them."

I laugh out loud. "Make time for her own kids. Do you hear yourself? You know, every move Nikki has made has been with only one person in mind—Nikki. If she cared about what happened to Declan and Finnegan, she wouldn't have left."

"When are you going to stop holding a grudge against my daughter and do what's best for your sons?"

"What would that be? Tell me, Georgia. What am I not doing that's in the best interest of my sons?"

"Let's talk about Mya," Georgia points a finger at me.

Memories of Mya standing in the waiting room flood my mind. The worried, scared look in her dark brown eyes searching mine for any news on Declan's condition. Instead of asking her to stay by my side as I fight through one of the most difficult moments I've ever had as a parent, I pushed her away. As angry and disappointed as I am with Mya, I'd still give anything to have her standing here with me instead of Georgia. I rub the back of my neck, trying to force the knots away as I glare up at Nikki's mom.

"Don't get me wrong. I like her. She's a sweet girl who hit a rough patch, and I was happy to help Tony out by getting her settled in town," Georgia says, pulling a chair to sit across from me. The condescending admonishment in her tone makes my skin crawl. "Despite what you may think, she can't replace my daughter in the twins' lives. She is not their mother! She's not a nanny! That's how this whole tragic incident happened. Mya wasn't paying attention and your son ended up with brain swelling and a gash in his head!"

"My son is fine, and he's ready to see his brother." I rub a hand on Finnegan's back, trying to wake him.

"It doesn't change the fact that you should have hired a qualified nanny weeks ago. Hiring Mya because the boys like playing with her dog and think she's cool and fun is irresponsible. Keeping her around because you wanted to date her is even more foolish."

"Are you finished?" I ask. Finnegan stirs in the chair.

"No, I'm just getting started. It's about time that you allow the boys to see their mother—"

"Their mother doesn't want to see them."

"Nikki doesn't want to see … you. If she could be with the boys without you around to make her feel like the worst person on the planet, she would jump at the chance."

"The minute your daughter walked out on her nine-month-old sons, she lost the right to have any say in what can or can't happen for them. I get to set the terms of any visitation, which I will remind you has not been requested by your daughter."

"If you could put aside your anger at Nikki leaving you and focus on what's best for the boys, you would see having their mother in their lives is worth it."

He wouldn't argue with Georgia on the point. The boys had benefitted from Mya taking that role over the past month. Not their biological mother.

"Think about allowing me to take the boys to London to see Nikki. It would be good for them."

"I can't believe you're using my son's injury to push your own agenda. The answer is and will forever be hell no. If Nikki wants to see her sons, she knows how to reach me."

I lift a hand under Finnegan and lift him into my arms.

"Daddy, where's Declan? Is he awake now?" Finnegan rubs the sleep out of his eyes and yawns.

"He is, and he wants to see you," I say, ignoring Georgia as I walk out of the sitting area and down the hall.

"It's about time." A bright smile beams across Finnegan's face. "I've been waiting forever."

CHAPTER 35

THE SOUND OF MY CELL PHONE RINGING PIERCES THE silence and I jump. I reach for the phone, unsure if I want to answer it or stay in my ignorant bliss. A state where I can imagine that today never happened.

I could pretend I canceled the workout session instead of trying to do two jobs at the same time. I could've stayed in with Declan and Finnegan, playing with Jellybean in the backyard without a care in the world until Ronan got home.

I glance at the screen and see Ronan's name illuminated.

Fumbling the phone, I swipe at the screen trying to answer the call.

"Hello, hello, hello," I say, hoping that I answered in time.

"Hey," Ronan's voice is low and heavy. "Declan's scans came back fine. No damage from the swelling."

"Thank God." I collapse onto the air mattress, my body trembling with relief. "I appreciate you calling to let me know. I can't tell you how—"

"The boys would like to see you," Ronan interrupts.

"They would?"

"Declan's about to have a fit wondering where you are and Finnegan thinks you went out to get Declan's chocolate chip cookies. He's convinced you'll be back right away."

I remember the last conversation Finnegan and I had before he left to be with his Granny. He thought Declan would wake up and want cookies, and I promised to get them.

Ronan clears his throat. "Would you mind … coming back to the hospital?"

I can't imagine how hard this is for him. Deep down, I know I'm the last person he wants to be in the same room with, yet he's making an exception and sacrificing his wants for his sons.

"Are you sure? I don't want to make things awkward for Connor or Georgia or … you."

Ronan exhales as silence stretches between us. I almost think the line has disconnected when I hear him speak. His words are low and pained.

"I need you, Mya," His voice gravelly and full of emotion as he says each word with painful carefulness.

My breath catches in my throat. Fleeting hope flutters in my chest, but I force the feeling away. I'm a realist, after all. He needs me for his sons' sake. After everything that happened today under my watch, the least I can do is not let him down now. "I'm on my way."

"Thank you."

He sounds relieved and … pleased?

I add, "And I'll bring cookies."

"The little monsters will expect nothing less."

I stuff the phone into my pocket and then dash around the room like a mad woman trying to get everything Jellybean might need while I'm gone.

Jellybean trots into the living room, confused by the change in my solemn behavior to these new manic, frantic movements. I rush through the house, grabbing dog food and his water dish. After dumping the food in a bowl, I fill the dish with water and place them in the corner of the living room. I leave the patio door open a crack in case he gets anxious and wants to go outside, then pull his favorite doggie pillow in front of the television.

He watches me with keen interest, tail wagging. I pat my knee and beckon for him.

"I have to go out."

Jellybean slumps, not pleased with this news.

"I'm not sure how long I'll be gone. But I need you to be good while I'm away," I say, scratching the back of his ears. Jellybean moves to the side to check if I've left enough food. Seemingly satisfied, he walks away and curls up on the pillow next to the television. I change the channel to one of his favorite stations, then grab my keys and head out the door.

Thirty minutes later, I have a death grip on a bag of freshly made chocolate chip cookies from Elevation Cupcake Shop as I head down the hallway to Declan's hospital room. He's been moved from the E.R. to the pediatrics floor. Connor greeted me with a reluctant smile and pointed me in the direction. I'm lucky he didn't tell me once again what a horrible person he thinks I am. I guess there's enough time for that after I visit with the boys.

Stopping in the doorway, I raise a hand to knock, but my hand doesn't make it to the door. The scene in front of me is like something out of a postcard.

Ronan sits like a giant in the middle of the bed, clearly sized for children, with Declan wrapped in one arm and Finnegan in the other. His strong, toned legs are crossed, toes wiggling as he reads from Larry Llama Loves Lasagna, the boys' favorite book.

I pause to listen.

"Larry Llama gathers all his friends from far and wide to sit with him at the table," Ronan says, then waits for Finnegan to turn the page. "His friends are excited and hungry to taste the lasagna. Larry Llama says—"

"Just you wait. It's going to be great." I say, finishing the lines of the book I have memorized.

Finnegan squeals and jumps from the bed and runs toward me. I scoop him up in my arms as he hugs me tight.

"Where have you been?" Declan asks, a smile spreading across his adorable face.

I wiggle the bag of cookies toward him. "Kinda thought having some chocolate chip cookies would make you feel better after hitting your head."

Declan nods and wiggles his hands toward me.

I approach the bed, my heart rate kicking up the closer I get to Ronan. His eyes never leave mine. The softness I see in his gaze touches my soul.

Easing Finnegan back down on the bed, I give the bag to Declan. He reaches inside, grabbing a cookie in each hand, then pushes the bag toward Finnegan.

"How are you feeling?" I ask Declan as I run a hand over his hair. The side of his face has a pale purple bruise, and a bandage is wrapped around half of his head. I wince, remembering the blood pouring from his head as I clutched him to my chest, willing him to be okay.

"I'm fine," Declan says, chomping down on the cookie. "My head hurts a little if I move it too much. Daddy says I need to sit still, but that's hard."

"I know that's going to be hard for you. But I'm so glad you're okay. I was worried."

"I wasn't." Finnegan says, picking the chocolate chips from the cookie and popping them in his mouth. "As soon as I saw Declan fall, I knew you'd make sure he was okay, Miss Mya. That's why I screamed for you."

"Thank you, Miss Mya, for saving me," Declan says, an earnest look in his eyes.

"You don't have to thank me, Declan," I say, then swallow past the lump in my throat. "I'm the one who owes you a big apology."

"Why?" Declan asks, frowning.

"Because I was supposed to be watching you and making sure you were safe. I should have been there to stop you from climbing on the cowboy statue so you wouldn't have gotten hurt. I'm sorry I wasn't there to take care of you," I say, then shoot a quick glance at Ronan.

Declan chews his cookie, mouth agape, as he contemplates what I've said. After a minute of processing, he shakes his head. "No, it was my fault. I knew I shouldn't climb up there, but Bobby Lee Junior said I couldn't get to the top. I knew I could, but then I fell and hurt myself. I won't do it again."

"I'll make sure he won't," Finnegan adds.

There's a knock on the door. I turn to see Connor standing in the doorway.

"Ready for me to tag in?" Connor asks. He's holding an arm full of Lego blocks.

"Uncle Connor!" The boys squeal with glee.

Ronan eases off the bed, then looks at me. I take his cue and follow him toward the door.

"Remember what I said," Connor says, extending an arm to stop Ronan as he tries to pass by. "Don't head down that same road. Choose a different path for your sons' sake and your own."

Ronan gives Connor a scowl that would've turned any other man to dust. Just not one cut from the rugged, hard stone he's made of. Connor's stare is intense and unyielding. The tension building between the two men causes goosebumps to pepper my skin. Somewhere deep down, I know this standoff between them is because of me and that's something I never wanted.

Connor's hand falls to his side. Ronan shoulder checks him as he pushes into the hall. I glance at Connor as I pass by, but he looks past me as if I don't exist.

"Who wants to build a castle with some Lego's?" Connor asks the boys. The sounds of "me" bounce off the walls and tickle my ears as I enter the near empty hallway.

Ronan is waiting for me, leaning against the wall. His stormy blue eyes guarded as he watches me. I know what I need to say to him, but for once, I hold back. This beautiful man looks like he had the worst day of his life. The weight of worrying about his son has his shoulders slumped and his face ragged and drawn.

"You up for a walk outside?" He asks, although it sounds more like a command than a request.

"Sure," I whisper and follow him to the elevator.

CHAPTER 36

M*YA*

~

THE BREEZE HAS A HINT OF CHILL AS TEXAS EMBRACES fall. I should have grabbed a cardigan before heading back over to the hospital, but in hindsight, I didn't think I'd stay this long. I thought Ronan would've excused me after the boys got their cookies and chatted with me a bit. I never thought he'd want to speak to me again.

We meander through the hospital lawn and onto the pathway that leads to Bell Park in silence. Ronan let me apologize to Declan, but he hasn't let me apologize to him. Maybe it's because he doesn't want to think about forgiving me. Maybe he can't forgive me.

I keep up with Ronan's long, determined strides until we reach the gazebo. It's lit up with a string of lights and on any other night, I would think this was romantic.

Ronan takes the steps two at a time, then eases down on the bench seating that lines the interior of the octagonal structure. I sit next to him, but keep a body's length distance so I can face him. He fidgets with his firefighter badge, twisting it between his fingers as if he was executing some fancy magic card trick.

"What happened today?" Ronan asks, without looking at me.

My nerves kick in and I exhale a shaky breath. I know Ronan deserves answers. Hadn't I practiced what I would say to him from the moment I left the hospital earlier? But now that the time has come to explain myself, explain how I allowed his son to end up in the hospital, I can't seem to find the words.

"I made a mistake—"

He scoffs. "That's putting it mildly, don't you think? Why didn't you tell me you were holding your class this morning?" Ronan's voice hardens as his eyes lock onto mine.

"I had every intention of canceling the class, but then I was busy all week getting the legal paperwork and accounting set up for my new company and I forgot," I admit, feeling worse. "Then when I realized ladies were showing up at the track already, I made the call on the fly to take the boys to the stadium and do the class, anyway."

"But you can't make calls on the fly when you have two little boys at your side," Ronan erupts, pounding the bench with his fist. "You're not a parent. You don't get it."

His words are like razor blades slicing through my heart.

"Quite a few of the women who come are moms. They've been bringing their kids to the stadium to hang out while they are in my class. I thought the boys would have fun playing with the other kids."

"How many of those other kids haven't started kindergarten yet? What are their ages?"

I blink, registering the point Ronan is making. None of the other kids are as young as Declan and Finnegan. I left his four-year-old sons alone to play with kids who were twice their age and older. My stomach lurches at the realization of what a massive risk I took. One that had devastating consequences.

"Answer me!" Ronan demands, his fists clenching in his lap.

"None of them," I say, staring into his cold eyes.

"That's what I figured," Ronan shakes his head, disappointment, and anger cascading across his face. "You don't know all the things to watch out for or how to juggle multiple priorities when you have kids around. You think taking care of them for a couple days a week for about a month is enough to make that kind of judgment call? Or maybe you should've run it by me first. I could have told you what an asinine idea it was."

I flinch. "I'm so sorry." My words sound trite, but it's the only response I can give. "If I could go back in time and do things over, I would." I cover my face in my hands.

"I wish you could. You don't know how much I want that, right now," Ronan says, his words full of emotion. "I want this whole day to be a nightmare that I can wake up from. But there's no waking up from this."

A subtle shift happens between us.

The man who stole my heart when I was least expecting it is now looking at me like I'm a stranger.

All the strings that had bound us loosen. They snap and break under the tremendous strain of the result of one poor decision. A decision I never should've made.

We are drifting apart and there's nothing I can do to stop it.

I don't deserve to have this man in my life or his wonderful kids.

I know it.

And now Ronan does, too.

He clears his throat. "Raising my sons is the hardest thing I've ever had to do. I've had to make every single decision on my own, not sure if I was doing the right thing or the wrong thing. Hoping that I wouldn't choose something that would scar them for life. Praying that I was surrounding them with people who would care for them as if they were their own."

"Yes, I made the wrong choice. I own that. But I love Finn and Dec. They mean the world to me. I didn't set out to do anything to hurt your sons."

"I know that," Ronan says. For the first time, his voice softens a fraction. "They love you, too. That's why all of this is so hard. To see this … different side of you I never expected was there."

"Different side of me?" I grip the edge of the bench, feeling faint.

"You didn't think of my boys at all today. You were only thinking about yourself and your career. Getting a deeper foothold in the community with your fitness class at the expense of my son's safety." Ronan pushes up from the bench and stalks across the wooden planks of the gazebo to the other side. It's as if he can't stand to be close to me. "I trusted you with the two people I love most in this world."

I know what he's thinking. I'm no different from Nikki.

"And I let you down." I stand up and cross my arms over my chest. Ronan isn't wrong. I thought I was some kind of superwoman. Like juggling two jobs at the same time was going to be a walk in the park, instead of my epic down fall. The reason I've lost all three of them. "I'm grateful we could get Declan to the hospital in time and that he's okay. But even with that, I know you won't ever trust me with them again."

"I can't." His voice is low and pained.

I rub my arms as goosebumps pepper my skin. In my heart, I had those same feelings. Those same concerns. But deep down, I know what I felt was a fraction of the fear Ronan had. There's no way I felt the depths of his anxiety and concern. I couldn't. He's their father.

And I'm … not their mother.

I'm not family.

I go rigid and my heart sinks.

I knew this was coming. Why do I feel blindsided? Sadness pools in my gut and anchors there, threatening to pull me under.

Ronan drags a hand down his face. "Declan's accident has spread all over town. Tiff reached out to me. She's going to let the boys come back to her daycare."

I'm stunned by the immediate sense of loss and loneliness I feel, although I know Ronan is doing the right thing.

"I know the boys liked it there. They were always telling me stories about things that happened with Miss Tiffany."

"And I'll be taking the rest of the week off, maybe longer, depending on how long they want to keep Declan in the hospital," Ronan says, then moves closer to me. "Look, I know this is hard on you, too. Part of the reason you stayed in Kimbell is because of me. I'll pay you for the last two weeks of the month to cover the expenses of the house."

"You don't need to do that." I swallow past the lump in my throat. "I got a job offer from the owner of Iron Woman Gym in Austin."

"A job in … Austin?" Ronan's slate-blue eyes turn to ice. "When did that happen?"

"Does it matter?" I shrug and look away. "It's a manager position, which is good for me, I suppose. It's a new gym opening in a couple of weeks. I have enough cash from the Saturday fitness classes to hold me until I move back home."

Ronan shoves his hands in his pockets. The muscles in his jaw tic as the tension between us thickens.

"You won't leave without saying bye to my boys?" Ronan asks.

"Of course, not. I'll text you before I move so we can make arrangements." I choke the words out.

"Good," Ronan says, then rushes out of the gazebo, leaving me all alone.

CHAPTER 37

R*ONAN*

~

The paper cup is warm in my hands as steam wafts from the black coffee. I've grown used to the taste after spending three days and nights living in Declan's hospital room. My son's recovery from the traumatic brain injury turned out to be short-lived. The next day, he had a series of seizures and convulsions that the doctors all claim are typical side-effects and go away over time. Even Connor's experience in these situations was little comfort for me.

Surprisingly, I drew strength from my other son, Finnegan.

He witnessed the seizures, and I thought the sight of seeing his brother shaking in the hospital bed would freak him out.

It didn't.

He was so strong, talking to Declan the whole time. He encouraged his brother and told him to fight to get better so they could play again.

The sight of Finn refusing to leave Dec's side overwhelmed me with love and pride. If my four-year-old son can be strong for his brother, then I surely could do the same.

And through all of that, I missed Mya like I'd lost the biggest part of myself. As I faced each day with Declan still suffering from his injuries, I wanted her strength and her toughness by my side. I wanted her to squeeze my hand and tell me everything was going to be alright, even if neither of us was sure that it would be.

She was leaving Kimbell in a few weeks, and that truth gutted me.

I couldn't fathom what my life would be like when she was gone. Some kind of way, I'd convinced myself she'd still be around. She'd still check in on my sons and I'd get to see her around town.

She wouldn't vanish from my life completely.

I glance up as Santos places a plate filled with kolaches in front of me, then sits down on the white plastic chair. The hospital cafeteria is packed with doctors, nurses and family members of patients. Some stand in line to pay for food, while others gaze out toward the open area for an empty table.

"When did the doctors say you can take Declan home?" Santos asks.

I grab a kolache, turning it in my hand. I don't have much of an appetite. I haven't for days now, choosing only to eat when Connor or Santos forces me to.

"They haven't." I take a bite of the kolache, surprised that the hospital did a really good job on them. "Connor says since it's been two days since he had a seizure and his headaches have all gone away, it should be in the next day or two."

"I'm sure they are ready to get home," Santos says, devouring a kolache and grabbing a second.

"Those two are treating being in the hospital like some kind of twisted vacation. They have the nurses wrapped around their little fingers. Each night someone has sneaked in a treat for them, something off the official hospital food menu." I chuckle under my breath. I'm almost afraid to see what those two will do to the ladies when they get older. I'm glad I have a good ten years or more before I have to deal with that.

"Other than the bandage around his head, I never would've guessed Declan had gone through all of that. He seems like his normal self."

"That's what's so weird. It was like that the day he was brought to the hospital. He was unconscious for hours, then he woke up and he was like normal. Twelve hours later, he's having seizures. It blindsided me. I don't know if he's back to his normal self for good now, or if something is lurking around the corner tomorrow."

"You gotta think positive. That's why he's still here, so the doctors can make sure he is out of the woods before releasing him," Santos says, trying to reassure me.

Coming from him, it helps.

Santos continues, "With two medical professionals in the family, you have ample support either way. Connor and Georgia will help keep an eye out for any signs of trouble, but I don't think there'll be any. Declan has turned the corner. I know it."

"From your lips ..." I say, then point a finger at the sky.

"I'm kinda surprised I haven't run into Mya since I've been here," Santos says, fixing me with a pointed glare.

I knew this conversation was coming. But I hoped I could avoid it for a while longer. I reach down and grab my coffee, taking a sip to buy some time before responding. "She's moving back to Austin." Not what I planned to blurt out, but there it was. On cue, a chill sinks into my bones and I feel physically ill. The same thing has happened every time I remember my last conversation with her.

Santos raises an eyebrow. "Start talking."

I rub my temples and stare at the table, not sure where to begin. Over the next hour, I take Santos through everything that happened. From the moment I found out from Mrs. Williamson that Declan had been injured to when I walked away from Mya, leaving her at the gazebo in Bell Park.

"That's it?"

I frown and lean back in my chair. "Brother, isn't that enough?"

"I'm waiting for the part where you told Mya that you didn't blame her for Declan's accident. That you understand how hard it is to keep up with two four-year-olds as precocious as my little nephews and for her not to beat herself up over it," Santos says, his honey eyes searching mine. "You told her that, didn't you?"

I rake a hand through my beard. "No. I didn't. I was angry. My son had spent the whole day in the E.R. unconscious. I wasn't in a forgiving mood."

Santos shakes his head. "So, you defend Mya behind her back. You rip Connor and Georgia a new one for blaming Mya for Declan's accident. Put them in their place. But you withhold your true feelings from the one person who needed to hear it the most."

I groan and stuff another kolache in my mouth.

"Let me ask you this." Santos cocks his head to the side. "What if it had been me instead? Do you know how many times I've agreed to watch the boys, then multi-tasked and did something else at the same time?"

"You always tell me, though."

"Doesn't matter. I did it. Declan could've been hurt on my watch. If that had happened, would we no longer be friends now?"

"Of course not."

"Then why are you so hard on the women in your life when they make mistakes? Why does Mya get extra punishment and pushed out of your life for slipping up one time?" Santos badgers me. "You did the same thing with Nikki."

"No, I didn't. Nikki left me and the boys because being a singer was more important than being with her family."

"You didn't go after her."

I freeze. His words slam into me. Crush me.

"You loved her and you didn't fight for her. You didn't show her that maybe there was a way that y'all could make things work. For her to be a mother and not give up her career," Santos says. "You punished her instead for leaving. Instead of reaching out to her, you wallowed in your own heartbreak and disappointment."

"I didn't go after her because it wouldn't have mattered. It wouldn't have changed anything. She was never going to come back to me and the boys." My mind races as the content of the Dear John letter Nikki left for me resurfaces. The things it didn't say. The gaps I filled in without ever making her say the words. Had I been wrong this whole time?

"You don't know that. You'll never know if that is true or not because you didn't try. I'm watching you make the same mistake with Mya, just in a different way," Santos says, leaning across the table. "You think I'd be as happy as I am now if I hadn't been forgiven for all the lies I told? Nobody is perfect, Ronan."

"Mya was. She was open and honest and I didn't have to guess around her. I knew what she thought and felt because she trusted me enough to tell me the truth. We didn't keep things from each other. But she fooled me. At the end of the day, re-establishing her career was more important than taking care of my sons."

"Why can't she do both? Everything y'all shared doesn't change because she made one bad decision," Santos says. "Do you realize you love her? Or are you too busy being pissed off at her for reminding you of Nikki in one moment to allow yourself to acknowledge it?"

My mouth gapes open. "I ..." I pause, not sure how to respond to Santos. "What I feel for Mya ... it's complicated. More importantly, it's irrelevant. She got a job in Austin and she's taking it. If Declan hadn't gotten hurt, I don't know when she would've sprung that little surprise on me. She was leaving, Santos. Whatever we shared wasn't enough to make her stick around."

Santos raises from his chair and grips my shoulders, shaking me. "Are you this daft? I thought you were a smart dude."

"What?"

"There's no way Mya was planning to leave Kimbell. Her Saturday fitness classes are blowing up. There's so much buzz around town about them, she doesn't need to leave for a better job," Santos says. "She's leaving because you made her feel like you wanted her gone. So, my question is this: do you want Mya gone? Do you want her out of your life?"

"I don't know!" I snap, agitated by the question. Irritated that everything Santos says is ringing true.

"Well, you better figure it out soon before you lose another woman you love."

CHAPTER 38

R*ONAN*

~

"GOOD NEWS?" GEORGIA ASKS AS SHE LEANS AGAINST THE counter of the nurses' station next to me.

"Got the all clear to take Declan home, double-checked and co-signed by Connor."

I turn to Georgia and smile, knowing she'll be as relieved as I am. She looks taken aback, then returns my smile with a huge grin of her own. Before I realize what's happening, Georgia has flung her arms around me. I feel the dampness from her tears on my neck.

"I'm so glad he's okay. That he's going to go home," Georgia says, then pulls away. A sheepish look crosses her face as she wipes at her tears. "We were so worried."

I don't have to ask who makes up the "we." I know who she's referring to. The same person who's been on my mind a lot since my conversation with Santos this morning. It's not lost on me that if things had taken a turn for the worse, Nikki never would have gotten a chance to meet Declan. She wouldn't have had a chance to get to know him. More importantly, my son wouldn't have had a chance to get to know his mother or to love her.

"You know, I was thinking," I say, then pause as Nurse Danielle hands me a clipboard filled with papers to sign for Declan's release. "It would be cool if you could take the boys with you to London the next time you go to visit Nikki. They'd love to meet her."

"Are you serious?" Georgia asks, her voice squeaking as she grips my arm.

I take a slow breath. "It's time. This whole situation has been a wake-up call. I don't want my boys to grow up not knowing their mother. If that means I need to step aside and let you make that happen, then that's what I'll do."

"Ronan, you don't know how much this is going to mean to Nikki. I'm sure she'll want them to come right away. Well, as soon as the doctors say it's okay for Declan to fly."

"That's fine," I say, ignoring the tension in my muscles. "We can do the paperwork to get passports, so whenever she can make time for them, they'll be ready to go." I look away, regretting that comment and the sarcasm dripping from my words. I take another deep breath and try again. "I mean, it's better for them to go this year. They'll start kindergarten next year and it won't be so easy to arrange a visit then."

Georgia contemplates my rationale and nods. "I understand. I'll get some dates from her and get back to you. You're doing the right thing, Ronan."

"I know." I say. It's about time I do the right thing. For my sons and for myself.

"Need any help getting the boys settled at home?"

I sign the last of the forms, then glance over at her. "No, I got it. But you could swing by after your shift and check on them."

Her face lights up with surprise. "I'm off now, but I can give you a few hours to get them home and resting before I come over," she says as if she expects for me to rescind the offer if she hesitates. "I have a few errands to run anyway, and I need to get my television from Tony's house."

My heart sinks. Mya had borrowed a T.V. from Georgia on her first day in Kimbell. If Georgia was going to pick it up, that could only mean one thing. I squeeze the bridge of my nose and fight back the flood of regret washing over me. I thought I'd talk to Mya again before she left, but seems like that door has been shut for good.

After our last conversation, I'm not surprised she decided not to tell me before she left town. Coming to say goodbye to my boys would be hard enough without having to cross paths with me again. It was easier to avoid the whole thing. I hate she chose that route, even if I understand why she did.

"Hope you're not running into any problems with the place being empty."

"Is that your way of trying to find out if Mya has left for Austin?" Georgia gives me a shrewd look. "She hasn't."

Busted. I rub my beard and exhale. "She's still in Kimbell?"

"Yes, she's still at the house … for now. We don't talk much anymore, for obvious reasons. But she texted me about dropping off my television today when I get home from work. I told her she could throw that old air mattress in the trash. I'm guessing she's planning to leave soon, though."

There's still a chance to talk to Mya, but I'm not sure what to say or if I should say anything. I don't know if it's fair of me to give her hope when I can't say for certain that we have a future. A relationship between us is not only about the two of us. I have my boys and they warrant more careful consideration before I decide what to do.

"I know the boys would be very disappointed if they don't get to see her before she moves back. That's why I was wondering."

"They have gotten attached to her, haven't they?" Georgia says, I pick up on the hint of worry in her tone. A concern that the boys look at Mya as more than a nanny. As a mother.

"Yeah, they have." I say.

I don't realize how attached they are until the two of them are pouting in the backseat of my SUV. We're only a few minutes from home when they demand to see Mya. I haven't told them she's moving away, and they expect for her to continue to take care of them the next time I go to work. I thought breaking the news to them so soon after Declan was released from the hospital would be too much.

The meltdown they are having in the back of the car proves I was right.

"I don't want to go home! I want to see Mya!" Declan yells.

"Why can't we go see her? We haven't seen her in so long," Finnegan adds.

Tears well in both their eyes and I know I'm over a barrel. I've got to at least try or the boys won't let this drop. I pull into my driveway and put the car in park. Turning in my seat, I look back at them.

"I will text Mya and see if she's available. But you both need to be okay if she's not able to see you today," I say, but neither one of them seems to grasp that concept.

"Text her, please!" Declan says.

I grab my cell phone and type.

Declan was released from the hospital today. He's asking to see you.

I wait for several minutes for a response, but none comes.

"Daddy, text takes too long. Call her," Finnegan says, fidgeting with the seatbelt.

Despite my better judgment, I press the call button and put the phone to my ear. I let it ring until I get her voicemail, then hang up.

"She's not answering. I'm sure as soon as she gets the text, she'll call and let me know when we can visit her," I say, unbuckling my seatbelt.

"Can we go to her house?" Declan asks.

"She probably isn't home, Dec." I say, growing exasperated by their insistence.

"But maybe she is at home and she's outside playing with Jellybean, and she can't hear her phone ringing and she's going to be so upset she missed our call," Finnegan tries.

I buckle my seatbelt. "We'll go over there. But if she's not home, we are going to wait for her to call us back. Is that clear? No more driving around trying to find her, okay?"

"Okay," Finnegan says.

I glance at Declan and give him a stern look. He squirms, then says, "Okay."

It only takes fifteen minutes to get to Sterlingshire. I turn down the street and pull the SUV to a stop along the curb. Water is rushing out of the garage and the front door flooding into a pool on the street.

"What in the world?" I mutter under my breath. I let the windows down, then turn to the boys.

"Why is there so much water, Daddy?" Declan asks, craning his neck to see out the front window.

"Where is Mya?" Finnegan asks, a hint of worry in his voice.

"Let me go check things out and I'll be right back."

As I open the car door, Mya emerges from the side of the house soaking wet and looking defeated. I rush toward her.

"Mya! Mya!" I call out.

"Ronan?" Mya runs her hands over her drenched hair as shock spreads across her face. "What are you doing?"

"What happened? Did a pipe burst?"

"I think so, but I can't tell where. The entire house is flooded. I can't figure out how to turn the water off." Mya looks dazed. Her face is pale, and she's trembling. "How am I going to explain this to Uncle Tony?" Her beautiful brown eyes search mine. "Why do I keep making horrible mistakes?"

I grab her hands and squeeze them. "Hey, I'm going to help you. Everything is going to be okay." I push my keys into her hands. "There are some beach towels in the back of the SUV. You can dry off with those and then say hi to a couple of handsome little devils who couldn't wait to see you."

"Declan was released from the hospital?"

"He was, and the first person he wanted to see was you."

Mya closes her eyes for a long moment, fighting her emotions.

When she opens them again, I say, "Go to him. I'll get the water turned off."

She follows my instructions and heads toward the SUV. I run to the side of the house and find the main water shut-off valve. Turning the rust covered red latch takes a lot more strength than I expected, but eventually I get it to budge and the river flowing from the house turns into a trickle.

As I walk back to the truck, I see Mya hugging my boys tight. All three of them beaming with bright smiles. I walk up behind Mya and rest my hand on her back.

She turns to look up at me.

"Get in. You're staying with us."

CHAPTER 39

M^{YA}

"You auditioning for the role of a hobo?" Ronan quips as he drops the last of my soaking wet trash bags filled with all my clothes and other belongings.

"Wow, way to kick a girl when she's down." I chuckle under my breath, surprised I can after the day I had. Grabbing another handful of water-soaked clothes, I wring them tight, sending a spattering of water flinging onto the grass.

"Can't believe you never hung them up. That alone would have kept them dry, even with no furniture in Tony's house." Ronan takes a quick glance at me, a playful glint in his eyes.

"Really, Ronan? I told you when I left Round Rock, I wasn't thinking clearly. Keeping clothes hangers and trying to take the furniture, which I paid for most of, was the last thing on my mind."

"Sleeping on an air mattress for weeks, though? No wonder you loved staying at my place." Ronan grabs a handful of clothes and twists them between his powerful hands. Water rushes from the cloth, pelting the driveway.

"That's not why I loved staying over," I say, then clamp my mouth shut. He's being so generous to me. I don't want to be ungrateful by harping on what I've lost. "Anyway, I wasn't supposed to be here for long," I remind him. I pick up an armful of damp clothes and head back into the garage.

"Right ..." Ronan says, turning to follow me.

I dump the clothes with the others in the washing machine, then wait for Ronan to toss the clothes he's holding inside. Reaching for the washing powder, I shake too much into the opening and slam the lid closed. Twisting the knobs, I fumble with the settings, then press the start button. As the machine roars to life, I turn to stare up at Ronan.

Those gorgeous slate-blue eyes peer down at me with an expression I've seen so many times before. From the days before Declan's accident when we were together. When we were happy.

"What are we doing?" I ask.

He shrugs, then says, "Washing your wet clothes."

I throw my hands in the air, then press them against my hips. "Don't pretend you don't know what I mean." I take a shaky breath and lean back against the washing machine. "I get Declan wanted to see me after getting out of the hospital. I even understand this weird way you always seem to be there when I'm at my lowest. I appreciate it. I really do. But it changes nothing."

"Mya, I—"

"No, Ronan. We can come up with a way to explain to the boys why I won't be staying here."

"Where are you going to go?"

"Jasmine will let me sleep on her couch." I say, thinking it's better to put as much distance between me and this ginger man as possible. I'm months, if not years, away from getting over how I destroyed our relationship. Spending more time with him and Finn and Dec would be a disaster for my heart.

"Why should you do that when I have a bed right here that you are more than welcome in?"

I can barely breathe from the intensity of his gaze. I wait for him to clarify or modify his statement, but he doesn't. We both know he's not talking about his guest bedroom, which has my mind reeling with confusion.

I shake my head and ease past him, trying to stop my hands from shaking.

Ronan reaches for me. His hand rests on my waist, then slides around me, stopping my forward progress.

"Are you ... ok?"

I hate the raw, unabashed concern I hear in his voice. "No, I'm about twenty seconds from falling apart." I push away from him and squat down to the garage floor. Now is not the time for a panic attack, although all I want to do is go screaming down the street like a banshee. "My life is an epic nightmare. I don't know what to do about it." I don't bother mentioning that him going from hating the sight of me to undressing me with his eyes has me reeling.

Ronan drops to his knees and cups my chin with his hand, lifting my face to look at him. "A pipe bursting isn't your fault, Mya. Your uncle already called the insurance company to come out and assess the damage. And like I've already told you, you *are* staying with me and my boys until ..." Ronan looks away. "You leave to start your new job."

He grabs my hands and lifts both of us to stand. Only a few inches separate us. The hint of his cologne, so familiar to me now, is soothing. I want nothing more than to walk into his arms and feel all the comfort he can give me.

Only problem is that his arms aren't open and welcoming me.

And after what happened with Declan, I don't deserve his kindness.

"Why are you doing this?" I ask, waving a hand at all my belongings lined against the wall of his garage. "I know you hate me for what I let happen to Declan—"

"I could never hate you." His words rush out, sending a jolt through my heart. I expect him to step away, but he comes closer. "I don't blame you for Declan's accident. It wasn't your fault. Kids push the envelope and try crazy things and sometimes they get hurt. My boys are on the more risk-taking end. The whole town knows that." He chuckles, a nervous and uneasy sound that surprises me. "I should've told you that at the gazebo instead of taking all my fear out on you."

"You weren't wrong for pointing out that I didn't think things through," I say, putting distance between us.

Ronan closes the distance as quickly as I created it.

"I was scared. I needed someone to blame. Some place to channel all that fear into anger so I wouldn't fall apart when my son needed me the most," Ronan says, then strokes his fingers through my hair. "But that wasn't fair to you. I made you feel worse than you were already feeling. Plus, I deprived my kids of your support. They were not shy about telling me how much they missed you and wanted to see you."

"I missed them, too." I say.

Ronan pauses, his eyebrow raised. He's waiting for me to say what we both know I can't. Telling him how much I've missed him is pointless.

"Then for my sons' sake, let me help you." Ronan rests his hands on my shoulders. "I wish you'd called me when the pipe burst," he says, caressing his hands down my arms. My body reacts to his touch, allowing it to ease my anxiety and despair. "I know why you didn't. But I want you to know that I will always help you. I'll be there for you if you need anything. So call me next time, no matter what. No matter … where you are."

My skin flushes hot, and I push against his chest. Hard. "Stop it!"

Ronan's eyes grow wide, a frown crinkles between his eyebrows.

"I can't deal with this. I can't stay here," I say, stalking toward the piles of garbage bags still filled with my belongings. I pick up one of the soaking bags, then turn around and realize that I left my car back at Uncle Tony's house. I can't leave without Ronan taking me back. I drop the bag and cover my face in my hands.

Ronan grabs my hands and pulls them away. "I'm not letting you deal with this alone."

"Why are you being so nice to me?"

Ronan takes a deep breath. "Look, I know when Declan got hurt, it caused distance between me and you. It put a strain on our relationship—"

"It *ended* our relationship." I say, snatching my hands from his. "We are not dating anymore. We aren't talking anymore. I'm moving away so you don't have to see me—"

"Mya, that's not what I want." Ronan blurts out. He seems as shocked to have said it as I am to hear it.

We stare at each other for minutes that feel like hours, chests heaving with pent up frustration and passion. Before I realize what's happening, Ronan's lips are on mine, crushing me with a salacious kiss that takes my breath away. I stretch my arms around his neck, running my hands through his thick locks as his arms cling to me. Our bodies press together.

In all my life, I've never experienced a kiss that comes close to this. It's raw and uninhibited, natural and possessive. Our mouths move in sync with each other, finding that perfect cadence and rhythm that seduces me into depths of the amazing gift it is to be cared for by this wonderful man.

Ronan lifts me from the ground, turning us in slow circles as the kiss deepens. His beard tickles my face as his kisses trail from my mouth to my neck, giving me a moment to gasp for air. When his lips find mine again, it's pure perfection, caressing with a delicate tenderness that makes me glad he's holding me up. If he wasn't, I'd be a puddle of goo at his feet by now.

After several minutes, Ronan lowers me back to the floor, tearing his lips away. His eyes are downcast.

Ronan says, "I'm sorry, I shouldn't have ..."

"Why not?"

"Because I don't want to hurt you." The look on Ronan's face says it all. "If it was just me, Mya. I wouldn't hesitate to be with you. I wouldn't worry about the future or what could go wrong because it would only be my heart that would get broken."

I stuff my hands in my pockets. I will not fall apart in front of Ronan. Not when he's fighting his own feelings as hard as I'm fighting mine.

"But it's not just me. I have to think about my sons. Every decision I make, I have to consider what impact it will have on them," Ronan rubs his forehead, then eases down on a metal chair resting near the side of the garage.

I don't follow him.

The space will help me absorb the blow he's about to deliver.

"I know that, Ronan. You think that changes anything for me? Don't you know how I feel about you and your sons?"

"Yeah, I think so," Ronan says. "I'm just not sure I'm ready to share my entire life with someone else. It's a big step for me. Huge. One that I can't make lightly." He stands and walks back over to me. "You are the only woman who has made me want this since Nikki left. Made me want to open up a space in my life and my sons' lives to make room for you."

I blink away the tears as his words pierce my heart.

"You, Mya," Ronan says, trailing a finger down my face. "But I'm not sure that I'm ready to do that. My hesitation is not fair to you."

"So what? You need more time to figure that out?" I ask. The last sliver of hope I have is waning.

"I can't ask you to wait. I won't ask you to put your life and your future on hold while I'm trying to figure all this out," Ronan explains. "It's like Declan getting hurt shined a light on my actions and my tendencies. I look back on the things I've done and I'm filled with regret. I don't want to have regrets anymore. I want to take the time to be sure before I make life-changing decisions again."

"Life changing? Who knew I was that special?" A shaky laugh escapes my lips. I'm putting on a brave face when inside, I'm dying.

Ronan's face grows more serious. "You are that special to me. What I want for us isn't casual, Mya. I care about you more than I realized."

"But that doesn't matter because you don't trust yourself to be in a relationship again, do you? Somewhere in the back of your mind, you think I'm going to walk out and abandon you and your sons like Nikki did," I say, with no hint of anger or disappointment in my voice. In a strange way, I not only understand what Ronan is doing, but I also agree with it.

"I'm sorry, Mya."

"Don't be." I give Ronan a sad smile. "You're doing the right thing."

Stepping away from him, I grab another pile of wet clothes and walk out onto the grass to twist the excess water from them. Behind me, I hear the door that leads from the garage to the house open and close. When I look back, Ronan is gone.

CHAPTER 40

YA

~

"No."

I pause and glance down at my cell phone, not sure I heard her correctly.

"Jasmine," I say, sitting up. Jellybean shifts from his spot, laying on my feet at the end of the bed and yawns. "Did you say no?"

"N-O. No." She repeats, a little louder this time.

After everything I told her about the day from hell I had yesterday, I can't believe she's turning me down.

"It would only be for a couple of weeks. I promise you won't know I'm there." Desperation sinks in and I'm almost at the point of begging.

"Come on, you know there's no way I'm letting you stay at my apartment," Jasmine chides. "First off, you have a dog. I don't do animals. I don't let animals in my house. What would you do with Jellybean?"

I'm quiet, realizing she has a point. I hadn't thought about how my dog factored into this equation. I reach down and rub his head, then scratch behind his ears as he looks up at me with curious amber eyes.

"Second, I'm still mad at you for moving away. You're the first good friend I've made in years, and now you're abandoning me," Jasmine says.

"Same here," I say, knowing that leaving Kimbell means more than putting distance between me and Ronan. I'm leaving a bunch of new friends I've made in such a short time. I understand why my grandma loved coming back to this little town. The people.

Jasmine adds, "While those are two good reasons, they're not why I won't let you stay with me."

"And what is that reason?" Bracing myself for the cold, hard truth.

"You and Ronan need this time together so y'all can come to your senses and realize that you're perfect for each other."

My mouth drops open. "Did you miss everything I told you about what happened in his garage last night?" I ask, jerking the covers off and standing. Jellybean lets out a yelp of surprise and stumbles, but manages not to topple onto the floor. "He's not sure he wants to commit to a relationship right now!"

"He already has. I think he wanted you to tell him he's wrong."

"What if I'm not sure that he is?" I pace across the plush carpet of the guest bedroom. My eyes linger on the closet door, ajar with most of my clothes hanging inside. Ronan's gift to me while I introduced his sons to The Muppet Movie, one of my all-time favorites. They loved it like I thought they would. We spent a couple hours past their bedtime ordering custom Muppets for each of them to be delivered before Christmas. Even though I won't be around to see them enjoy their gifts. "Jas, what if I'm not stepmom material?"

"Who decides that?" Jasmine counters. "All I know is that every move Ronan's made has ingratiated you deeper and deeper into his life. You fit in perfectly with him and his sons. You don't need some magic fairy to come down and whisper in your ear that you're ready for something that you already have."

"What if I try and he still pushes me away? That will break my heart."

"Because you love him, don't you? You love him and his crazy, bad kids."

"Maybe." I hedge. But the question breaks the dam that I've been using to hold back all my feelings for Ronan. As surely as I'm breathing, I know that I'm in love with him. It's so much stronger than the superficial love I shared with Jamal. I know Ronan in a way I never knew any man before. We started a relationship intent on not making the mistakes of our pasts. Hoping that it would lead to a more profound and honest love.

It worked.

At least for me, it did.

Ronan's still not sure, and that truth crushes me.

"Then you owe it to yourself to make him break your heart. Don't do it for him."

Her words stir something deep within my soul.

"If you're lucky, he might surprise you," Jasmine says. "I gotta go. Do not leave town without seeing me."

"I won't. I promise," I say, slumping down on the bed. "Thanks, Jasmine."

"Whatever. Girl, bye."

I glance at the clock. It's almost nine. Declan and Finnegan are probably enjoying breakfast with their dad. I hesitate, wondering if I should join them or let them have this time alone together.

My head says stay away until they've gone out for the day, but my heart wants to be close to them, even if this is one of the last moments I will have with them.

Rummaging through my closet, I find a green Polo t-shirt dress. Fifteen minutes later, I've showered, brushed my teeth and flat ironed my hair. I head down the hall and notice the eerie quiet.

Breakfast with the twins was typically a loud and raucous affair, filled with laughter and jokes and lots of swapping of stories, either about Ronan's more tame adventures as a fire fighter or others made up by the three of them. Breakfast was always a time I looked forward to spending with them for that very reason. I loved how they didn't hesitate to let me in on their inside jokes and morning stories.

But none of that was happening today.

I can't help but wonder why.

Turning the corner, I see Ronan sitting at the table opposite Declan and Finnegan. The boys are quiet, pushing cereal around their bowls but not eating much. I can't see Ronan's face, but his body is hunched and tense.

"Good morning, fellas," I say, injecting an extra ounce of cheer into my voice. The boys look up, then scramble from their chairs. They race toward me and I drop low to absorb their hugs. I bury my head against their skin, inhaling their fresh scent of soap.

"Miss Mya, you look so pretty," Declan says, stepping back to look at me. I raise back up and do a little twirl for them.

"Your dress is green today. Not black!" Finnegan beams.

"Your favorite color," I say, then glance up to see Ronan's eyes locked onto me. Am I dreaming, or does he look as happy and excited to see me as his sons? But behind his now relaxed expression is a hint of relief clouding his gorgeous blue eyes.

"You want breakfast?" Ronan asks, standing to his full height and muscular glory. He's wearing a UTSA t-shirt and basketball shorts that show off his ripped and toned arms and legs. "It's just cereal, but I could make you a bowl."

I shake my head, taking in the muddled mess of three bowls of soggy, barely eaten cereal sitting on the table. "I'll pass. What are y'all doing today?"

An uncomfortable quiet settles between father and sons. The boys are avoiding looking at Ronan and he exhales deeply.

Finnegan looks up at me and asks, "Can we play in the pool?"

"I don't think Declan should swim yet, since he just got out of the hospital." I'm surprised Finnegan asked me when his father is here.

That normally doesn't happen. What happened at breakfast between them? And how can I fix this? Seeing how awkward they are with each other breaks my heart.

Declan says, "Shoot."

"But maybe if you dangle your feet in the water and play with your remote-controlled boats, you could get some pool time. What do you think about that?" I glance up at Ronan and he gives me a quick nod of approval.

"That would be fun," Finnegan says, then turns to Declan. "Right, Dec?"

Declan nods, but he still looks disappointed. "You'll come with us, Miss Mya?"

"Of course," I say, glad to see my answer lifted Declan's spirits. "Go get changed into your swim trunks and I'll grab the toys."

Once they've disappeared down the hallway, I walk over to Ronan.

"What's going on?"

He drags a hand down his face, then slumps back down into the chair. "They aren't too happy with me right now."

"Anything you want to talk about?"

Ronan hesitates, face tensing, then relaxing. "Nothing worth mentioning. But it's good you're here to give them a little time away from me to cool down. Thanks for agreeing to watch them at the pool."

"You're not coming outside?"

"No, I think it's better for them if I stay inside. If you need to go out or want a break, come get me."

"Okay," I say, turning away from him. I head toward the living room patio doors leading to the pool, then stop. I pivot back toward him. "I don't know what happened this morning, but remember that they love you unconditionally. That won't ever change."

Ronan frowns, then bites his lower lip. "Yeah."

Don't get involved, Mya. Support Finnegan and Declan and leave Ronan to figure out the rest. Soon, I won't be around to witness these little riffs between father and sons. I'm sure everything will blow over by dinner.

In the meantime, I gather the remote control speed boats, placing them into the pool. I check that the batteries in the controllers are charged, then place them on the deck chair closest to the stairs leading into the pool.

Minutes later, Finnegan and Declan come outside with mopey expressions. Instead of sitting in the water, they make a beeline for me and crowd onto the deck chair where I'm sitting.

I open my arms and allow them to cuddle against me, giving them a tight hug.

"What's going on with you and your dad?" I ask, not wasting any time. I can't stand to see the tension between the three of them, especially not so close to when Declan was released from the hospital.

Finnegan shrugs, then flips on his back to look up at a flock of birds flying across the cloudless sky.

Declan clears his throat. "We gotta get passports. Daddy is going to make us go to London and meet … her." His words drip with annoyance.

London. Her.

"You're going to meet your mother? When?"

"We don't know." Finnegan says. "Granny is going to talk to her and find out. Then we have to fly all the way over there. It's across a big, old ocean. She's so far away."

"And we don't want to go. We don't want to meet her anymore," Declan says, fidgeting with the string on his swim trunks.

"But meeting your mom is a good thing. Don't you want to get to know her? Have her sing to you in person like you heard her singing to you when you were babies," I say, trying to help. "I'm sure she heard about your accident, Declan, and wants to make sure the two of you are okay."

"This is all my fault. We were going fine without her. Then I go and crack my head open and now she wants to meet us," Declan complains, crossing his arms over his chest.

"What if she doesn't like us?" Finnegan asks.

"That's impossible." I laugh and the boys can't help but smile. "Name one person in this town that doesn't like you."

"Mrs. Lewis," Declan says.

"And Mr. Barnes," Finnegan adds.

I can't help but laugh harder. "Okay, well, you put glue in the shampoo bottles and caused their little girls to lose a lot of hair. But other than those two, who else doesn't adore you?"

Finnegan raises up and looks at Declan. Their faces take on several expressions as they do their twin thing. Then, finally, they both shrug and lean back against me.

"My point exactly. She's going to take one look at the two of you and love you instantly. Everybody does."

"Even you, Miss Mya?" Declan asks, turning to look up at me. His slate-blue eyes, so much like his father's, search mine and demand an answer.

"Yes, Declan. Even me. I love you and Finnegan like crazy. I can't help but love y'all," I say.

Declan's grin spreads wide across his face. "We love you, too, Miss Mya,"

"Yeah, we do," Finnegan adds. "But what if we don't love … her? What if she's not a good mommy?"

"We'd rather have you as a mommy. Not her." Declan says, pouting.

I'm touched that the boys feel the same as I do. Any doubts I had about being step mom material have vanished. There's nothing more that I want than to have a permanent place in these boys' lives. But I know Nikki deserves a chance to be their mom, too.

"That's not fair. You don't know her yet. When you first met me, you didn't know if you'd like me or not. You liked my dog, but I could've been mean or boring," I explain, tickling them. They squirm and giggle in my grasp. "But the more time we spent together, the more we realized how much y'all like me and how much I like you. Doesn't your mom deserve that same chance?"

"If we like her, does that mean we have to stop liking you?" Finnegan asks.

"Nope. You can have your mom and me, too. I will always be there for y'all, no matter what. You don't have to worry about losing me." I say, my chest tightening at the thought of moving away from Kimbell. Distance won't change anything, but at four-years-old, it may take them a while to understand that.

"Well, that makes me feel better," Declan announces, then jumps off the chair and grabs the controller for the motorized boat.

"So, y'all are okay with going to meet your mom?"

Finnegan eases off the chair and grabs the other controller. "Guess so."

And I guess that's the best I can do.

CHAPTER 41

R ONAN

~

It hits me again and this time I can't deny it.

Finnegan and Declan stand in the middle of the dining room, clutching Mya's hand and looking to her to help comfort them after the nuclear bomb I dropped into their young lives. The look in Mya's eyes goes far beyond care and concern for two little kids. I see pure love there and it makes my heart swell.

No matter how much I rehearsed how to explain things in a way that my boys could understand, it was an epic disaster. The idea of meeting their mother for the first time sent them into a catatonic panic. I couldn't get them to look at me. Forget talking to me. Both boys lost their appetites as I tried to explain how important it is for mommies to know their sons and that their mommy wanted to meet them.

All the years I spent creating a stable and consistent foundation for my boys to grow up with cracked the minute I introduced Nikki into their lives. She is no longer the mythical woman that their granny talked about and that they saw on a few YouTube videos. She's about to become real and they didn't like it.

I can't help but believe that this is my fault. I never should've kept them away from their mother for this long. My insistence that Nikki come back to Kimbell to see them was stubborn and selfish. I'd convinced myself that since she left them here, she had to make amends by coming back here to see them. The truth was she left me here. I wanted her to have to face me in the place she walked away, abandoning me. It had nothing to do with Finnegan and Declan.

As I watched Declan laying unconscious in that hospital bed, I was wracked with guilt over my behavior. The thought that Nikki might not get a chance to meet him because of this war I'd waged with her seemed suddenly foolish. I knew I had to make amends.

I didn't expect for the boys to be so rattled and resistant to meeting their mom.

We'd been sitting in stony silence until Mya floated into the room and picked up the pieces. She stepped in to co-parent my sons like she's been doing for weeks. My silent partner in raising them. She's my rock and I can't believe I didn't realize how much I depended on her.

Somewhere along the road of our instant attraction and the deep connection we built from getting to know each other, we became a family. A real family. I don't know how, but it's here staring me in the face. There's no doubt in my mind that Mya belongs with us.

She belongs with me.

I listen as Mya works out a safe way for Declan and Finnegan to have play time in the pool, then watch as they go to their rooms to change into swim trunks.

As soon as they are out of sight, Mya rushes over to me. "What's going on?"

I drag a hand down my face, then slump back down into the chair. "They aren't too happy with me right now."

"Anything you want to talk about?"

I hesitate. There's so much I want to talk to Mya about, but the timing isn't right. I need her to help my kids now. Everything else I need to say to her can wait. "Nothing worth mentioning. But it's good you're here to give them a little time away from me to cool down. Thanks for agreeing to watch them at the pool."

"You're not coming outside?"

"No, I think it's better for them if I stay inside. If you need to go out or want a break, come get me, okay?"

"Okay," she says and turns away from me. She walks toward the living room patio doors leading to the pool. I take a moment to enjoy the view. Her green dress is the perfect contrast to her tawny brown skin. Seeing her in something other than black and camouflage gives her a lighter air. One I find irresistible. She stops and pivots back toward me.

Mya says, "I don't know what happened this morning, but remember that they love you unconditionally. That won't ever change."

I frown, then chew on my lower lip. "Yeah."

I close my eyes and try to figure out how to fix things for my boys and myself. The soft patter of footsteps tickles my ears. I look up to see Jellybean trotting toward me. He pants and looks at me, then out toward the glass patio doors at Mya.

"Come here, boy," I say.

Jellybean walks between my legs and stops, allowing me to pet him. "That's quite an owner you have there. Amazing woman."

Jellybean barks in agreement, and I laugh.

"Any ideas of how I convince her to stay?"

The dog wags his tail, then looks up at me with a blank expression in his amber eyes.

"I pushed her away and I have to figure out how to get her back on my own," I say, nodding. Jellybean tilts his head, then sits down between my feet.

Finnegan and Declan emerge from their rooms and don't give me a second glance as they walk out onto the patio and join Mya. I watch as they ignore the pool and instead cuddle up with her on one of the deck chairs.

Almost an hour passes as they sit there talking.

I can imagine what they are saying about how mean daddy is that he's making them fly to another country to meet their mommy. One day when they are much older, I believe in my heart they'll appreciate it. Just not today.

Finally, I see a grin break out on Declan's face and he's up, grabbing a controller to play with the motorized boats. Finnegan looks like the weight of the world has lifted from his shoulders and he races after his brother to play. My boys look like my boys again. Their demeanor completely changed.

And I have Mya to thank for all of this.

She's everything I want and everything I didn't know I needed.

My boys need her, too.

I know I haven't been a role model father and I don't need Mya to reach some imaginary bar of mothering to care for my sons. I just need her to love them and we can figure out the rest ... together. She clearly loves them and she's made it clear that she wants to be with me. Choosing Mya isn't a selfish move. It's what's best for me and the boys. They love her.

But I love her more.

My past with Nikki has haunted me for too long. Getting closure with my ex is hindering me from moving forward with Mya. But there are a lot of ways to get closure and it doesn't have to be facing off with the woman who left me and broke my heart.

Not when I've been blessed with a woman that erased all that pain and replaced it with pure pleasure and happiness.

And I know what I need to do to turn things around with Mya. To be free to let her know once and for all, she's the woman I want to spend the rest of my life with.

Reaching for my cell phone, I scroll through the contacts until I find the one I'm looking for.

After two rings, a receptionist answers the line.

"Law Office of Lance Bassett, how may I help you?"

"Hi, this is Ronan O'Reilly."

"Hey, Ronan. How's it going?"

"Good, good. I was wondering if I could get an appointment with Lance to discuss a legal matter. He knows the details."

"Of course, let me see when his next opening is …"

CHAPTER 42

YA

~

THE NEXT MORNING, I'M TRYING TO TEMPER MY excitement and force myself to recognize everything that happened with Ronan, the boys, and me yesterday doesn't change anything. Sure, I single-handedly got Finnegan and Declan to be neutral, if not a tad bit optimistic, about meeting their mother and forgiving their father for forcing them to do something they thought was unnecessary.

My reward for that was a wonderful afternoon with these three amazing guys on Lake Lasso. Ronan borrowed one of Nate Bell's boats and took us out for a lazy afternoon trip, where we fished and played games underneath the golden fall sun. The outing felt like all the times we'd spent together before Declan's accident. The times when Ronan and I were growing closer. I took tons of selfies of the four of us playing around and sent the photos to Ronan.

A huge part of me hopes maybe things don't have to end between

Ronan and me. He wants us to stay together. He's just not sure if I'm a good fit for his sons. The fact that he doubts that disappoints me more than I could ever tell him. Is he blind to how close I am with those little boys? How much I love them and they love me? How I'd do anything for them?

Sure, I'm not a mother. I don't know how I'd handle taking on that role in their lives, but I wouldn't be doing it alone. They say it takes a village to raise kids and I've witnessed that village in action with Declan and Finnegan—from Connor and Georgia to all the firefighters on Ronan's shift, plus the librarian and so many others. The boys want me to be part of that village, helping them to grow up to be strong, intelligent and kind men. Why is Ronan resisting?

My cell phone rings and I reach over on the nightstand to grab it. The area code is Austin, which sends my blood pressure through the roof. I answer the call.

"Hi, is this Mya Young?" A woman with a high soprano tone asks.

"Yes, it is."

"This is Katie. You called about renting the room in our house. We just had a roommate move out last weekend and want to get the room rented out so we can make our mortgage payment next month. Any chance you can move in this weekend?"

"Move this weekend?" I repeat, dread seeping through me. I wanted more time to take Jasmine's advice and change Ronan's mind. But maybe I shouldn't have to do that. If Ronan can't see how good what we have is, then why should I try to pressure him or change his mind? Maybe it's better that I leave. Save myself a future heartbreak of epic proportions.

"Yes, I know it's super short notice, but I figured it would help you out and us. What do you say?" Katie asks.

"Sure. I can move this weekend." I listen as Katie gives me some more detailed instructions about the house, the other roommates and my rent payment, which is dirt cheap compared to what I've been paying to stay at Uncle Tony's house. "Great, see y'all this weekend."

I drop the phone onto the bed.

"You're moving ... this weekend?"

I shriek and turn to see Ronan standing in my doorway. His face is devoid of an expression and voice is flat.

"Sorry, didn't mean to startle you," he says, leaning against the door frame.

I try to respond, but the sight of him is literally taking my breath away. No part of me wants to leave this gorgeous ginger man. But I also don't want to stick around and beg a guy to give a relationship with me a shot. I cringe at the thought and know that's not something I could do.

"Yes, my place is ready now and I can move in this weekend."

He nods and stares at me, trapping me with his intense blue gaze.

I fidget with my hands, not sure what else to say. Do I remind him he told me not to wait for him to figure things out? That the only reason I'm at his house is because a pipe burst at Uncle Tony's house. That he's the one pushing me away when we both want me to stay.

Anger wells within me. I clench my jaw, waiting for him to say something. Anything.

When he does, it's not at all what I expect.

"Before you leave, I think we should clear the air. Talk about everything. Tonight, maybe. Over dinner. Just the two of us." Ronan says, rambling a bit. "Would that be okay?"

A farewell dinner with the man I'm in love with.

Yeah, that won't be extreme torture at all.

But maybe Ronan is right. A chance to discuss everything and get closure on our brief, but intense, relationship could be what we both need. Didn't Jamal want that from me? I know Ronan needed it from Nikki and never got it.

"Sure, we can do that. Where should I meet you?"

"Here," he says, his voice low. "Georgia already picked up the boys to take them to get their passports and they'll be staying at her place tonight. I have a meeting at the fire station, then I'm headed over to Lake Lasso to take care of some errands. I should be back around five and can make dinner."

I ease down on the bed and grip the sheets. Ronan making me dinner right before we end things for good has tears pricking my eyes. I blink them away and say, "Sounds good. Do you need me to pick up something from the grocery store while you're out?"

"No, I'll take care of all of that," Ronan says, then backs out of the room. "See you tonight."

I nod in response, then collapse back on the bed once he's out of sight.

I spend the next few hours wallowing in my own pathetic misery and fighting off depression. Jellybean coaxes me to take him for a walk around lunch time and being out in the sunshine lifts my spirits, but only by little.

By the time I get back to Ronan's house, I'm of half mind to pack all my things and leave right now. But Ronan and his sons wouldn't be the only people disappointed if I skipped town. Jasmine would hunt me down and slap me for not visiting her before I leave. Plus, there's a whole other group of people I know and I want to say farewell to.

I push the thought from my mind and walk back into the house. My cell phone vibrates in my pocket and I can't help but hope that it's Katie telling me that the room isn't ready after all.

Glancing at the screen, I see Georgia's number instead. She and I have not spoken since Declan's accident. I know she's not pleased that Ronan invited me to stay with him after the pipe burst and flooded Uncle Tony's house. So why would she be calling me now?

Panic grips my heart and I hope nothing has happened to the boys.

I answer the phone.

"Mya, it's Georgia." Her tone is curt. "I'm at the passport office and I forgot to get the boys' birth certificates. Can you get them and bring them down to the Kimbell Courthouse building? This line has been so long and I'd rather not lose our place."

"I'd be happy to, but I have no clue where Ronan keeps those things."

Georgia lets out an annoyed sigh. "He keeps all the important papers for the boys in the chest of drawers in his bedroom. He already told me it was okay for me to go back and get it. I figured with you staying at his house, you could bring it instead."

I ignore her subtle dig and say, "Of course. I'll get them and bring them to you right away."

Maneuvering through the house, I stop and fill Jellybean's water bowl and leave him as he focuses all attention on drinking every drop. I walk toward Ronan's room and push the doors open. Memories slam into my mind of the first night I stayed over when I thought this was a guest bedroom.

You're in my bed, and you look real good there.

My face flushes with heat.

"Don't go there," I warn myself, then cross the room and pull at the top drawer. I'm relieved when I see it littered with papers and folders. Grabbing a couple of stacks, I sit in the chair and thumb through them. There are copies of home and life insurance policies for several years, property appraisals, and bills from Declan's most recent trip to the hospital.

Who knew Ronan was such a pack rat?

I keep flipping until my eyes scan the top of one document.

My blood runs cold and my hands tremble as I pull it from out of the folder.

In the Matter of the Marriage of Nicole Dart and Ronan O'Reilly
Original Petition for Divorce

My eyes are drawn to several yellow flags protruding from the page, all next to signature lines. Blank signature lines. Lines labeled with Ronan's name. But his signature is missing.

I flip the pages. Nikki has signed every spot designated for her, but Ronan didn't sign?

I drop the package of papers and look at the other contents of the folder. Letters from an attorney to Ronan dating back months all saying the same thing—following up on the signing of the divorce petition and filing with Lasso County. Each letter requesting that Ronan explain what else he needs to get him to sign the divorce papers so Nikki can end their marriage.

"Ronan isn't divorced," the words rush from my lips in a whisper.

I grab the last letter and look at the date.

It was sent after I got to Kimbell.

After Ronan and I started dating.

And he still didn't sign the divorce papers.

That's been the issue this whole time.

Ronan wants to be with me, but he can't …

He can't because he's still in love with Nikki.

I don't stop the hot, angry tears from coursing down my face.

He should've told me this a long time ago.

Why did he let me believe we could have a future if he was refusing to divorce his wife? Did he think I could help him get over her once and for all, then realized it was useless? Did he care that he used me? Got me to fall heads over heels in love with him when he could never be in love with me the same way?

Gripping the papers, I stand up and watch the other documents litter the floor.

Ronan wanted me to stick around to talk before I leave.

Well, I have something to say to him now.

And I'm not waiting for tonight.

CHAPTER 43

R ONAN

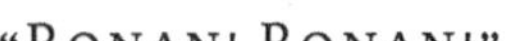

I hear the frantic cries of my name as I step up onto the sidewalk that leads to the Law Offices of Lance Bassett. I stop in my tracks, recognizing the voice. My heart lurches. I'm almost afraid to turn around. To see her coming because I know I'm not ready for this.

"Ronan, wait!" Her voice lingers in the air.

I inhale a deep breath and turn.

Nicole Dart O'Reilly is running toward me. Her long, dark, wavy hair blowing in the wind. She's a vision if I ever saw one, more gorgeous than I remember. Glamorous and sophisticated. Refined.

A face reflected at me when I look at my sons.

My heart pounds hard, trying to burst from my chest as she comes to a stop in front of me. I shake my head, my mind and my heart not able to fathom how she's standing here.

"What are you doing here?" I ask, my tone harsher than what I intended.

"It's good to see you, too, Ronan," Nikki says, her British accent stronger now than I remembered. The sound of my name on her tongue sends a shiver down my spine. How I used to love to hear her say it. Almost as if it was a melody. A favorite she loved to sing.

"I'm sorry, that was rude," I say, trying to shake off my shock.

"Always the gentlemen. Chivalry never dies in Kimbell, Texas, does it?"

"I suppose not. But I can absolutely say you're the last person I expected to see here," I admit. "When did you get back?"

"My flight landed in Houston this morning. I rented a car and drove straight here. I stopped by the fire station and they told me you were out here at Lake Lasso, so I took a chance that I'd be able to find you. It is still a pretty small town," Nikki says, brushing the wayward strands of her long hair from her face. "You look good."

I lick my lips. "So do you."

Nikki smiles. It's as if I'm transported back in time to the first day I met her. She was walking up and down the streets of the town center trying to find the antique shops. I swear she was the only person who could get lost in a town this small. I took one look at that beautiful face and knew I'd spend all day if necessary to help her get to where she was going.

"My mum and I have been trying to figure out the best time for the boys to fly to London. All the dates were too far away," Nikki explains. "I couldn't wait any longer. I needed to see Declan for myself. See that he was okay. It was horrible to think that my son could be hurt, could die, without ever knowing me. So, I got my assistant to book me the next flight to Houston and here I am."

"Your assistant, huh?" I say, chuckling under my breath. "Guess things are going well for you."

"Better than I dreamt." Nikki's face lights up. I've seen that look. It's the same one she gave me on the night I proposed to her. She didn't ask me if I was sure. She said yes, then started looking for flights to Vegas. We were married in a chapel on Fremont Street the next day.

Nikki says, "Why don't we go over there so we can talk in private?"

For the first time, I notice the townsfolk milling around, gawking at the sight of us. Nikki, being back in Kimbell, is going to have the gossip mongers blasting the news. The whole town will know she's back before the night is over.

"Good idea."

We walk side by side to a secluded area near Chesterton's Gym.

A flash of Mya's laughter assaults me. I grip the back of my neck as I remember her sitting in the middle of the lawn, surveying the spoils of the bet she won. Sixty dollars worth of pastries, snacks and sandwiches from the local coffee shop all spread out on the grass. Her gorgeous face slams into my mind, followed by a myriad of memories of her with me over the weeks we were dating. My heart yearns for her.

Battle lines are drawn across my heart.

A dangerous playing field where my feelings for Mya and my feelings for Nikki collide, crash, and burn.

Nikki stops under the wide branches of a towering pine tree and gazes out at the lake. "This place is stunning. I can't believe how much it's changed in the years I've been gone."

"It's not the only thing that's changed," I say, staring down at her. She looks up at me with those doe eyes and I fight to resist the pull of her.

"No, it's not. I thought maybe we could ask my mum to bring the boys here and we can have lunch at Thorn. I think it would be good if you are with them when they meet me for the first time."

"Probably for the best," I say, thinking back on Finnegan and Declan's reaction when I told them they'd be meeting their mother. If Mya hadn't been there to help them, I don't know if they would've become open to the idea.

"Great, I'll text her now." Nikki pulls out her phone and types. "She's going to freak when she finds out I'm here."

"I'm sure she'll be glad to see you."

Nikki nods. "Are you glad, Ronan?"

"What do you mean?"

"To see me."

I inhale a deep breath. "I don't know, Nikki. All of this is unexpected. I don't know how I feel yet."

"Or you don't know what you want to admit to feeling." She takes a step closer to me, resting a hand against my chest. "They say there's a thin line between love and hate. I can't help but believe there's a reason you haven't signed those divorce papers in over a year."

I grab her hand and remove it from my chest. "I never hated you. Was I angry? Absolutely. I didn't understand how you could walk off and leave me with no warning."

"No warning, Ronan?"

I throw up my hands. "I would never stand in your way of pursuing your career. But we had nine-month-old twins at home. I figured you could put that on the back burner for a little while until the boys were older."

"I had already put my dreams on the back burner when I fell in love with you. I sacrificed so much to be here with you and you stopped appreciating it. You convinced yourself that I was here because I wanted to be, but in reality, you were the only person who kept me here."

"Georgia was here, too."

"And I loved every minute of getting to know my mum. We have an amazing relationship now, but she didn't need me to move to Kimbell for that to continue. You were not going to leave this place, and I thought I could stay here for you."

"Then what? You realized your love for me wasn't enough. You needed to get away from here. Away from your sons."

"Don't do that! Don't make me out to be this horrible person," Nikki says, swiping at a tear rolling down her cheek. "When I wrote you that letter, I thought you'd come after me. I thought you loved me enough to make a sacrifice of your own, but you didn't."

"You thought I was going to travel thousands of miles to chase after you with my twin baby boys?" I scoff. Mya would never have played reckless games like this. She would have confronted me face-to-face, making it clear what she wanted and needed. With Mya, I never have to guess where she stands. A sinking feeling burrows into the pit of my stomach. As open as Mya has been with me, I haven't done the same for her. I haven't bared my soul and told her everything I was thinking and feeling. Instead, I pushed her away.

"You should have," Nikki says, adamant. "There was no reason that we had to stay in Kimbell. We could've lived in London."

"Nikki! And live off what? Your career wasn't bringing in much money back then," I say, glaring at her.

"Well, it is now. I don't want to argue about the past. That's something that neither one of us can change," Nikki says, smiling at me. "The future is a different story."

"I have no problem with you having a place in your sons' lives. I won't stand in the way of them visiting you in London," I say, trying to reassure her. I've let go of the anger and put my sons first.

"I want more than that." Nikki rests her hands against my waist, closing the distance between us. "I want you."

You are the only woman who has made me want this since Nikki left. Made me want to open up a space in my life and my sons' lives to make room for you. You, Mya.

My own words haunt me as I look at Nikki.

My thoughts are a jumbled, confused mess of wanting Mya and wanting what I lost with Nikki. How could I be this confused? Do I want them both? Do I love them both? Or am I losing my mind?

"We don't have to sign the divorce papers," Nikki says, tilting her head up toward mine. Her eyes linger on my lips. "My music career is everything I ever wanted, but it still feels empty because I don't have you to share it with. You are still my husband. I want it to stay that way."

"You do?" My voice is barely above a whisper.

"I love you, Ronan," Nikki says, then reaches up to pull my face toward her.

Our lips connect, and I remember the feel of her mouth on mine. The softness and decadence of her kisses. As our kiss deepens, there's no more confusion in my heart.

I know the woman that I want.

CHAPTER 44

R ONAN

~

Pinching the bridge of my nose, I glance over at
Finnegan and Declan as they stare at the kid sized brownie a la mode
sitting in front of them.

"Your granny told me brownies are one of your favorites," Nikki
says, trying again to get the boys to open up.

They've been unusually quiet all afternoon after meeting their
mother. The location doesn't help matters. Thorn isn't a kid friendly
restaurant. Still, Nikki insisted on having a celebration here instead of
choosing a more low-key place, like Gwen's Country Cafe, where the
boys would've been more comfortable.

Declan and Finnegan nod and give her a polite smile, then grab the
spoons from the side of the table. They look at me.

"Go ahead, eat up," I tell them.

The colored, towering glass bowl containing the decadent dessert is a bit intimidating to them. I can imagine they're afraid of breaking it, making them more anxious and uncomfortable. They both take a tentative bite and then glance at each other.

They visibly relax and dig into the dessert. I'm glad to see them enjoying something. The salad and chicken breasts were barely touched by them.

"Tell your mum how much you like brownies," Georgia encourages, ruffling Finnegan's hair.

Declan rolls his eyes and focuses on his dessert.

"We like brownies a lot, ma'am," Finnegan says.

The boys have resisted calling Nikki mom all night. They've alternated between the extremely polite "ma'am" and the more informal "Miss Nikki."

Nikki and Georgia can't hide their disappointment, but I'm not sure what they expected. Nikki is still a stranger to them. Maybe months or years in the future, they'll feel comfortable calling her mom. Just not today.

"I've thoroughly enjoyed spending the afternoon with both of you. You are marvelous little boys and I can't wait to get to know you better," Nikki says, trying to wow them with her dazzling smile.

The boys are quiet.

"Since I'm here for a few more days, I hope we can see each other again. Then maybe in a few months, you can come to London to visit me," Nikki says.

"We can't go to London," Declan blurts out. "We didn't get passports, so we can't go."

I glance at Georgia. "What happened at the passport office?"

Georgia huffs. "After I realized I didn't have the boys' birth certificates, I didn't want to lose our place in line. So, I called Mya and asked her to bring them to the courthouse instead."

"So why weren't you able to get the passports? Did she arrive too late?" I ask.

"She didn't come at all," Georgia says, her voice laced with agitation.

"Who is Mya? Is that the nanny?" Nikki asks.

I take a gulp of my beer.

"No," Finnegan shakes his head. "Well, she used to be our nanny, but now she's more like …"

"Daddy's girlfriend," Declan says.

Beer spews out of my mouth as Declan and Finnegan burst into laughter. The boys are nearly falling out of their chairs as my eyes grow wide. Georgia stares daggers at me. I don't turn to look at Nikki.

I say, "Hey, Miss Mya—"

"Lives with us," Finnegan says, with a huge grin. "We see her and Daddy kissing all the time when they think we're not looking."

"And Daddy makes dreamy eyes at her when she's not looking like this," Declan says, then acts out a sappy expression. Finnegan joins in, making matters worse.

Finnegan says, "She's the best. She takes us to the library and reads books to us."

"Larry Llama Loves Lasagna is our favorite. She reads that one to us almost every night," Declan pipes in, bouncing in his seat.

"And she takes us to the park and we play games and run and climb in the trees," Finnegan says.

"Oh, and she has the best dog. His name is Jellybean. Finnegan and I have to make sure he gets fed, and he drinks enough water. She says it will teach us responsibility," Declan adds.

"She has cool tattoos, too. I like the unicorn," Finnegan says.

"My favorite is the picture of her granny," Declan says, then turns to Georgia. "When I get older, I'm going to get a tattoo of you Granny on my arm."

Georgia gasps in horror. "You most certainly will not."

Declan frowns but doesn't respond.

The entire exchange is like a bad accident that I can't look away from. I'm not sure what to say, so I decide not to say anything.

"Well, that's wonderful that you have so much fun with Miss Mya," Nikki says, her voice shaking.

"Why don't you finish up that ice cream so I can get the two of you home? I promised that we'd watch Lion King before your bedtime, so we need to leave soon," Georgia says.

"Are you going to go to Georgia's house with the boys?" I ask Nikki.

She shakes her head. "No, I'm afraid I am very jet lagged and wouldn't be good company. I'll go back to my room at Crockett Manor and meet them tomorrow."

Declan and Finnegan exchange a look. I can't tell who is more relieved—Nikki or my sons.

The boys finish their dessert as an uncomfortable silence falls over the table. I swallow the last of my beer, but wish I had something stronger. The boys almost spring from their seats when Georgia tells them it's time to leave.

I get big hugs and kisses from both of them before they walk over to Nikki and shake her hand. I know this isn't how she wanted her first meeting with her sons to go, but it could've been worse.

We watch them leave, then sit back down at the table.

Nikki turns toward me. "The boys are enamored with Mya."

It's a statement laced with accusation.

I turn toward her. "She's become a big part of their life."

"And yours?"

"If you're asking if I'm in love with Mya, the answer is yes," I say, not bothering to skirt the issue.

"Then everything makes sense," Nikki says, dabbing at her eyes with her napkin.

"What makes sense?"

"Our kiss earlier. It felt more like the end of something than the beginning. Now I know why," Nikki says, then rests her hands on the table. "I suppose you'll want to finalize our divorce. That's why you were outside the attorney's office earlier."

"Lance Bassett reworked the petition to clarify items related to my sons."

"Our sons."

"I asked him to add in language to clarify that I have full custody, but you have access to unlimited visitation as long as we agree on the days and times," I say, then reach into my bag and pull out the document and hand it to her. "I didn't think you'd have a problem with that."

"I don't," Nikki says, then flips the pages. "You've already signed it."

I hand her a pen. "Once you sign, I can get this filed first thing tomorrow."

Nikki takes a deep breath, then signs all the pages. She hands them back to me.

"Thank you," I say.

"For giving up on the man I love?"

"For coming back to meet your sons. I know tonight was difficult, but I promise you it'll get better. Finn and Dec will warm up to you and you'll find your place in their lives. It's just going to take time," I say.

Nikki smiles at me. "I hope so."

I lean over and give her a hug.

For the first time, I feel nothing for Nikki.

Every space in my heart belongs to Mya.

And it's about time Mya knows it.

CHAPTER 45

R ONAN

~

"I'M NOT SURE I WANT TO GIVE YOU THIS," WILEY PEERS AT me with suspicion in his eyes. "Why do you need it?"

"Stop wasting my time and hand it over," I say, enjoying withholding information from my friend.

Wiley twirls the guitar in one hand, then frowns. "Look, the whole town knows that Nikki showed up out of the blue. People saw y'all at the lake and more people saw y'all at Thorn. You need to look me in the eye and tell me you haven't lost your mind and decided to get back together with her."

I reach for the guitar, but Wiley moves it quickly from my reach.

"Ronan, come on, man. What about Mya?" Wiley asks.

"I'm doing this for Mya," I say, then step closer and snatch the guitar from him, then hand him the rolled-up papers in my other hand.

Wiley unrolls them, his eyes scanning the document. He lets out a whoop and raises a hand for me to high-five.

"Does this mean what I think it does?"

"I'm in love with Mya and it's about time she knows that." I say, growing anxious. "After everything I've done, pushing her away and waffling over my feelings, I'm not sure she's going to give me another chance."

"But you have to try!" Wiley insists.

"Why do you think I'm here? She likes traditional gestures of love —the roses and candy and serenades. That's what I'm going to do for her tonight. I want her to know how much I love her and I'm willing to take things as fast or slow as she wants, as long as she takes me back."

"You know she will," Wiley says, with a big grin, and hands the divorce papers back to me. "Alright, I approve. Get out of here. Call me tomorrow and let me know how it goes."

I salute him, then jog back to my Denali and get inside.

I've already stopped by the grocery store and bought all the ingredients to make a delicious and healthy meal for Mya. Miso glazed sea bass with couscous and broccolini followed by a creme brûlée from Elevation Cupcakes for dessert.

Excitement races through my body as I drive back home.

The last conversation Mya and I had was a disaster. I regretted pushing her away the second after I did it, but I was struggling with my own fears and insecurities that she'd leave me and the boys like Nikki had. I was too stubborn and bullheaded to hear her when she said nothing would change her feelings for me or the boys.

She practically screamed from the rooftops that she wanted a life with us, and I was too daft to hear it. Now that I've come to my senses, I hope I can convince her to stay in Kimbell.

I grip the steering wheel tighter as I realize I want to marry Mya. I want her with me and the boys forever. Thinking about a future without her in our lives, in my life, feels like the worst kind of torture. How in the world did I think I was going to let her leave?

Finding out that my sons had picked up on our closeness and our connection made everything that much clearer. Mya knew my sons want her to be their mom, but despite that, she went above and beyond to help them understand why they needed to give their biological mother a fair chance. She didn't try to take Nikki's place, but helped Finn and Dec understand they could never have too much love. I'm so grateful she did that for my boys.

But when four-year-olds can tell that Mya and I were falling in love and they called me out about it at dinner, it's hard to keep denying it. Mya thawed the ice around my heart and helped me to love again. She changed my life and my sons. She means everything to me. Not making my feelings clear to Mya is the first of many mistakes I plan to rectify tonight.

I turn onto my street and drive a little too fast down the road until I reach the driveway. Slowing down, I notice that Mya's Honda isn't here. I'd texted her when I was leaving the restaurant, but she hasn't responded.

She's probably out doing some shopping for the move to Austin that I'm hoping won't happen. I put the SUV in park and grab all the bags, barreling into the house. It's past eight and going to take about thirty minutes to cook dinner. I didn't eat much at Thorn earlier, since my boys were struggling with meeting Nikki for the first time. Seeing them anxious and uncomfortable was enough to take away my appetite.

An hour later, dinner is ready. Soft light flickers from the candles on the table. The roses are in a vase I found in the garage and the chocolates are propped against the wall. The guitar rests against the couch. I take a step back and survey the room.

Not to brag, but I pulled off a pretty romantic scene in record time. I reach into my pocket and grab my cell phone, checking to see if Mya texted me back. My earlier texts are unanswered. I send another one.

Dinner is ready. Looking forward to seeing you and having our talk.

Falling back on the couch, I turn on ESPN and start watching the football game. Before I realize it, the game has ended and almost two hours have passed. I glance over at the table. The candles have burned down to half the size.

Where is Mya?

Unease settles in my chest. A hazard of being a firefighter. My thoughts fly to the worst scenarios. Had she broken down on the side of the road or gotten into an accident? No, if she had, I know she would've called me.

I push up from the couch and walk toward the front windows. Looking through the blinds, the street outside is empty. I turn around, expecting to trip over Jellybean's doggy pillow … but it's gone.

I turn to the right, where his toys and water bowl usually rest by the door. The space is empty.

My throat clenches as I stalk toward the hallway and speed up until I get to her bedroom. I fling the door open. My world comes to a crashing halt. The room is spotless. There's no sign that Mya was here. I glance at the open closet door. All of her clothes are gone.

I curse under my breath. My fists clench at my sides and I stand there in a daze.

She promised she would stick around until after I got back tonight. She was going to be here so we could talk. Why would she leave without saying anything?

I jog back into the living room and grab my cell phone. Dialing her number, the line rings once, then an automated voice comes on the line.

"The number you are trying to reach is not taking calls. Please hang up and try your call later."

The phone slips from my hand.

Mya blocked my number.

But why? Why now?

I rake a hand through my hair and stumble into my bedroom.

The top drawer of my chest, where I keep all important papers, is extended. I glance in the drawer and see the boys' birth certificates in one stack.

Georgia mentioned Mya was supposed to bring them to the

courthouse but never showed up. I look down and see the floor littered with papers.

"What the …" I reach down to pick them up.

Dread rushes through my body as I stare at the documents.

The divorce papers Nikki sent me over a year ago. The ones I never signed. The ones that prove to Mya that I'm still married to my sons' mother.

"You screwed this up, O'Reilly," I say, crushing the papers in my fists.

No wonder Mya left.

She thought I'd been lying to her all this time about my feelings while still being married to another woman. She didn't understand the real reason I wouldn't sign those papers. The boys needed to meet their mother. I'd hoped that not signing them would force her to come back to Kimbell, so that could happen. I never planned on staying married to Nikki, even if I wasn't sure I had residual feelings for the woman.

But Mya doesn't know any of that.

I have to find her. I have to explain that she has it all wrong. That she's the only woman I want. The only woman I love.

A quick call to Jasmine reveals she hasn't seen Mya, but maybe she was working out with Erin.

Erin answers my call after several rings.

"Hey Ronan, what's up?"

"Hey, I got home and Mya isn't here. Wondering if she's with you?" I ask, trying to keep the edge out of my tone.

"No, you didn't see her earlier this morning?" Erin asks.

"No," I say, hesitating. "Was I supposed to?"

"Well, she came by the fire station looking for you. It was right after the shift captains' meetings. You'd already left about fifteen minutes before she got there. I told her about you heading over to Lake Lasso to see Lance and probably to grab some lunch. She said she was heading that way."

My head throbs like a jackhammer is trying to crack my skull open.

"Yeah, we must have just missed each other," I say, not convinced that happened at all. If the timing works out, Mya got to Lake Lasso in time to see my reunion with Nikki.

I curse under my breath. Did she see Nikki kiss me? Is that why she left?

"Everything okay?" Erin asks, concerned.

"Yeah, it's fine. I'll wait for her to get back. Thanks, Erin."

Everything that could go wrong has absolutely gone wrong for me and Mya today. But I'm not giving up on her yet.

I access the internet on my phone and type quickly.

Iron Woman Gym of Austin

An address pops on the screen.

I don't know where Mya is spending the night, but I know where she's likely to be in the morning.

And I plan to be there when she gets there.

CHAPTER 46

M^{YA}

~

MY LEGS BURN LIKE THEY ARE ON FIRE FROM THE INSIDE out. Lactic acid build up weakens my intensity and fatigue claws at my body, but I press on and push myself to go faster and farther. My lungs wheeze from the exertion, but I don't care.

I need the physical pain to drown out and dull the pain in my heart.

The searing, blinding pain of seeing Ronan standing along the lakeside kissing Nikki … his wife.

It doesn't help that she's gorgeous. The woman looks like she could be a Kardashian cousin, minus the boobs and butt. Her petite and dainty body had been pressed against Ronan's as they kissed with reckless abandon, oblivious to anyone around watching.

I try to focus on the trail ahead, weaving along the pathways of Zilker Park as trees and fauna pass by in a blur. The leash tethering me to Jellybean lingers behind as my dog struggles to keep up.

I should slow down, but every time I do, the hurt of knowing I never had a chance with Ronan slams into me. I don't want to ache for a man who was torn between me and his wife. I'm not deluding myself. I know Ronan had real feelings for me. He couldn't fake the closeness that we shared, but there was always something holding him back. Like a fool, I worried he thought I wasn't mother material for his sons.

I was so wrong.

The real wedge between us is the love he still has for his wife.

I jerk at the leash and run faster. I'm too angry to cry. Too devastated to feel anything but rage at how I let myself end up in another failed relationship.

Falling for another man so quickly after leaving Jamal had never been part of my plans. But love doesn't know the rules. Love doesn't understand I was better off alone. Instead, love led me right across Ronan's path. Now I'm dealing with the biggest heartbreak of my life.

The leash yanks hard against my arm. I stumble, slowing down to glance back at Jellybean. Guilt floods me as I look down at him. His reddish coat is dripping with sweat. His tongue dangles out of his mouth as he pants heavily for air. I stop and drop to my knees in front of him. Grabbing my water bottle from my waist holder, I open the bottle and pour the liquid into his mouth. He drinks eagerly, his eyes thanking me for the reprieve.

"I'm sorry, boy. Guess I should've left you back at the hotel. No reason for me to take this out on you," I say, stroking a hand on his head. He eases closer and leans into my body. The offering of a hug he must know I need. I wrap my arms around him and hold him tight.

"What am I going to do?" I ask, staring into Jellybean's amber eyes. "How in the world am I going to stop loving Ronan?" I let out a heavy sigh.

Truth is, I don't have to know the answer to that right now.

I glance at my watch. It's a quarter til five in the morning and the sky is still dark. Iron Woman Gym opens at six and I need to be there before clients arrive. The best way I know how to manage the wreck that is my life is to lose myself in my work. Focus on helping others until I figure out how to help myself.

I'm not supposed to start for another two weeks, but I'm hoping Candy will let me start today. Anything to keep busy.

Thirty minutes later, I've showered and changed and dropped Jellybean off at a doggy daycare. Traffic hasn't started on Mopac heading north and I make it to the gym near the Dominion well before six. I park near the back of the parking lot, then walk across the almost deserted lot. A few cars are parked closer to the gym and the lights are on. Near the entrance, I see a huddled figure sitting on a bench outside. Some eager gym rat waiting for the place to open.

Stepping up on the curb, I stop as I notice a bouquet of wilted red roses laying on the bench next to the man. My eyes travel from the strong arm resting against them to the face of the man sitting there.

For a few seconds, my heart stops and I forget to breathe. I can't move and I can't think as I stare at Ronan's handsome face looking back at me. His eyes travel the length of my body as if he's trying to memorize every inch of me before settling on my face.

A box of chocolates rest on his lap. His relaxed disposition is gone. He's tense and rigid, sitting there all alone.

I swallow hard and try to understand what's happening.

It doesn't take long for the realization to sink in. Ronan wants closure. He wanted to talk to me last night. To tell me that despite the feelings he has for me, he still loves his wife. He's choosing to be with her instead of me. The candy and roses are to soften the blow, I suppose.

"Nice gesture, but those won't make this conversation any easier, handsome," I say, gaining control of my body again. I press forward, muscles crying out in pain as I close the gap between us.

"I didn't think so," Ronan says, a sad look in his eyes. "It was worth a try, though."

I shrug. "Flowers are pretty even if a bit wilted." I reach for one and press it against my nose. The heady fragrance catapults me back to our first date at the carnival. The rose he gave me then held so much promise. These just hold heartbreak.

"The candy melted," he says, sounding like it's the worse disaster in the world. "Sorry about that."

"It's okay," I say, then ease down next to him on the bench. The magnetic pull still exists between us. My heart rate quickens being this close to him. I want to leave, but I know we need to do this. We need to have this last conversation.

"I think I have something that will make this easier though," Ronan says, then hands me a rolled up batch of papers. I look at them, but don't budge. I can't imagine what he could give me. Maybe some drawing that Finnegan and Declan did?

My chest tightens at the thought of not seeing those precious little boys again. I'm going to miss them so much. I steal a glance at Ronan. His red hair shines under the waning moonlight. The shadows cast across his face, intensifying his gray-blue eyes and making him more irresistible. A slight smile plays on his lips. The lips I love to kiss.

I frown and grab the papers from his hands.

"What's this?" I ask, maneuvering the pages into a shaft of light cast from the gym windows.

"Read it." Ronan says, turning toward me.

I unroll the pages and scan the words. My hands tremble as I focus on the signature lines of the document. Flipping to the next page and the next. It's all the same. All lines signed. By both parties.

"My attorney, Lance Bassett, will file those today. It's uncontested with all terms agreed to. State requires a mandatory sixty day waiting period. After that, the divorce will be completed," Ronan explains, his eyes searching mine.

"I saw you kissing her at Lake Lasso," I say, shaking my head. "You still love her."

"No, I don't. That kiss was … goodbye. She's the mother of my sons, so she'll always be in my life, but I stopped loving her a long time ago."

"No, you've been married this whole time. All while we were

dating and getting close, you had a wife!" I say, my voice rising. "You had a wife, Ronan, and you didn't tell me. You let me …" I swipe at the tear falling from my eye. "You let me fall in love with you, knowing that you were still Nikki's husband. How do you think that makes me feel?"

Ronan grabs my hands, caressing them in his. I snatch my hands away.

"You shouldn't have done that," I say.

Ronan drags a hand down his face. "I was wrong. I should have told you the truth."

"Then why didn't you?"

"Because I couldn't fight this pull. I had to be with you, near you and to get to know you. It was out of my control the attraction that I felt for you on so many levels," Ronan says, then lays that gorgeous smile on me. "I knew my marriage was over and it wasn't worth bringing up."

"It was worth bringing up if you were still refusing to sign the divorce papers Nikki sent you over a year ago. How do you explain that? The attorneys sent you a letter after we started dating and you still wouldn't sign them," I say, feeling like the weight of the world is pressing down on me.

"I didn't sign them because I was angry at Nikki for leaving her sons. If she wanted a divorce, I wanted her to be forced to come back here to get it. So, she could face the kids she left behind," Ronan says, rubbing his neck. "It was selfish and foolish, but that's how I felt. Wasn't until I met you that I realized I didn't need to do that. My boys were okay whether they knew Nikki or not. They had so much love and support from our other family and friends … and then from you."

"You're not being honest with me right now. You opened up to me. You told me you weren't sure how you would feel if you saw Nikki again. You told me you weren't sure you were ready for a relationship with me. Now I know that was because of your feelings for Nikki."

Ronan reaches for me, pulling me closer. His hands rest on the sides of my face as he stares into my eyes.

"I'm not confused. When Nikki left me, she wanted me to chase after her, but I didn't. The thought never crossed my mind because our marriage didn't live up to the expectations that we had of each other from our two-week whirlwind romance," Ronan says, his fingers trailing a soft caress down to my neck.

Butterflies party in my stomach as his words break down the walls I erected to keep him out.

"When I came home last night and saw that you were gone, there's nothing that would've stopped me from coming after you. You and I have what I've always wanted. An open and pure and unconditional trust. A connection that can't be broken," Ronan gives me a wry smile. "There's no room in my heart to love Nikki. Not anymore."

Ronan grabs one of my hands and presses it against his heart. It's beating fast, matching the cadence of my own. Even in this moment, we can't help but be in perfect synchronicity with each other.

"Just say it," I demand, not able to take it anymore.

"I love you, Mya," Ronan says. "I am completely and utterly, head over heels, in love with you. I don't deserve a second chance after jerking you around after Declan's accident, but I'm going to ask for one, anyway. I will do whatever it takes to have you in my life … permanently."

A joy like I've never felt before floods through my body. I tremble with happiness as I slide my arms around Ronan's neck.

"Don't you want to know how I feel about you?" I tease as a giggle escapes my lips.

"I know how you feel. I can see it every time I'm close to you. You're too honest and open to hide it," Ronan says, then places a gentle kiss on my lips. The softness of his mouth against mine is like heaven. I lose myself in him, enthralled and enraptured by his touch. His kisses make the entire world fall away until there's nothing but me and him. I'm rocked back to reality when he pulls back and says. "But it would mean the world to me to hear you say it."

I bite my lower lip and run my fingers through his hair.

"Ronan O'Reilly, I love you," I whisper. "And I love those bad kiddos of yours, too."

His wide smile makes my heart soar.

"Now there's only one thing left for you to do," Ronan says, wrapping me in his arms.

"What's that?" I ask, feeling happier than I ever thought was possible.

"Quit this job you haven't started yet and come home with me, where you belong."

CHAPTER 47

RONAN

~

"Where'd you find these?" I ask, grabbing one of the coveted bottles of Elm Street Beer from Santos.

"Do you need to ask?" Wiley chuckles, then takes one of his own from Santos.

Santos's smile says it all. "Enjoy, fellas."

We pop the tops, then watch from within the large crowd lining the lake as the first annual Kimbell Mother and Son Scavenger Hunt is about to end.

I crane my neck to the left, looking around the corner to see if my boys are still in the lead. Planning for the event took on a seriousness I hadn't expected from those two, with us strategizing over two days on which items Finnegan would search for and which Declan would take the lead. I was careful to choose items that wouldn't be too taxing for

Declan, even though you would never guess that a month ago, he was unconscious in the hospital. Still, I don't want to take any chances so soon.

"I swear, love is in the air this year. Feel like I need to hold my breath to not get a whiff of what you two have been sniffing," Wiley teases, then takes a long pull on the beer.

"This from the man who has designed a dating app to speed up the finding of love?" Santos says, frowning.

"For others, not for myself," Wiley says, but I don't believe him. He worked for years on the A.I. for his app not just to make money. Despite his playboy, bachelor status, I know deep down he wants to find a woman who will capture his heart even if he doesn't want to admit it.

"Famous last words," I quip, then sip the beer.

A few women emerge from the water and grip their sons' hands as they scramble to find the next item on the list. The scavenger hunt included a list of twenty items in ten locations around town that had to be found. Half the list was provided in advance and the other half was kept a secret until you reached the area.

Lake Lasso is the last stop. Only two more items to grab, one being a turtle and the other a mystery item that I won't see until my kid finds it. I glance down at my tally sheet and the times to collect the items, then at the wooden leader board. The top reads "O'Reilly Family." They had a lead, but still could lose it if they took too long to find the mystery item.

"I don't have time to find love for myself," Wiley insists. "Not when I'm on the verge of my app going viral."

Santos raises an eyebrow. "How're you going to manage that?"

"Well, a freelance reporter friend of Ciara Thompson reached out to me. She pitched a story on A.I. dating apps to Good Morning America and they are interested. I'm one of three that she's considering as a feature for her story," Wiley explains.

"Are you serious? That's great news," I say, happy for my friend. The dating app had been an underground success throughout the small towns of the hill country and east Texas, and gaining ground in San Antonio and Austin.

"She'll be coming to Kimbell to interview me. If I can impress her, I'm halfway to massive success," Wiley says, nodding confidently.

"The lady doesn't stand a chance," Santos says.

I agree. Wiley isn't a favorite of the ladies for his smarts, even though he is an intelligent guy. Everywhere we go, women swoon all over his golden boy good looks and piercing aqua blue eyes.

"Whoa!" Wiley says, dropping his beer down to his side as he stares at the lake.

Santos grunts, then looks away.

I turn toward what has Wiley mesmerized and see Mya emerging from the lake, golf ball in hand, screaming, "We found it!" She looks like every male fantasy, racing out of the water. Her t-shirt and running shorts are wet, clinging to her amazing body.

Heat flushes my skin as I watch her speeding past us, holding Finnegan's hand.

"Now that is one good-looking—"

I slap Wiley in the back of the head. Hard.

"Ouch, dude! That hurt."

"She's mine, got that?" I say, glaring at him. I can't help but notice the attention Mya is getting from several other guys in the crowd, some single and others … not.

Since she agreed to come back to Kimbell, we've been taking our relationship slow. Mya rented a room at Crockett Manor for a couple of weeks until the renovations were finished at her uncle's house. After moving in, she resumed her minimalist living style, refusing to buy furniture. At least she moved her air mattress into a bedroom and hung her clothes in the closet. I can't help but be encouraged by her resistance to buying new things. Why should she bother if she'll eventually be moving in with me and my boys? I'm just anxious for that ultimate step to happen.

"Meant no disrespect, my man. None at all," Wiley says, then wisely looks away from Mya.

"Yes!!!" Declan screams, jumping up from his spot on the grass near the leader board where he's been holding the bag of all the items they'd collected over the day. He races toward Mya and Finnegan, then runs with them up to Odalis.

"Excuse me, fellas," I finish my beer and toss it in a nearby trash can. "It's time for me to join the winners' circle."

Santos and Wiley tip their heads to me and I maneuver through the crowd to Mya and my sons. No matter how many times I see them together like this, it never gets old. The picture of my perfect family standing in front of me. We are closer than ever. Mya has gotten the boys to open up to Nikki more and arranged for weekly phone calls between them and their biological mom.

"We won, Daddy!" Declan and Finnegan say in unison.

"Y'all did so good. I'm proud of you." I lean over and give them both high-five's then wrap them in a huge bear hug. I glance up at Mya and the love I see in her eyes takes my breath away.

Mya gives me a flirty, sizzling look. "Are you proud of me, too?"

My eyes travel down the length of her, then back to her face. "Most definitely." I raise up from the boys and pull Mya into my arms. She wraps her arms around my neck as I give her a kiss to show her just how proud I am. And that has nothing to do with the contest and everything to do with her agreeing to move back to Kimbell to be with me and my boys. I'll never forget the sacrifice she made so we could have this amazing love.

"Kissy face, kissy face," The boys sing as they dance around us.

Mya bursts into laughter. "Are they going to say that every time they see us kiss?"

I look down at my sons as they smile and giggle at us.

"Yep, I'm pretty sure it's going to be every time."

Mya shakes her head, then corrals the boys to get ready for the trophy ceremony. I watch as they receive identical gold-plated trophies and a gift certificate to Elevation Cupcake Shop. I applaud and whistle with the others in the crowd as they playfully bow and blow kisses.

As we walk back to the parking lot, I hold Mya's hand on my left and Declan's on my right. Finnegan holds Mya's left hand. The boys sing a made up song about being winners at the top of their lungs, eliciting more cheers and claps from the townsfolk still meandering in the area.

"Now, let's head back to my house to celebrate," I say, opening the back door for Finn and Dec.

"I'm exhausted and I have a jam-packed day of personal training tomorrow. Can I get a rain check and you drop me off at Uncle Tony's house?" Mya asks, leaning against the SUV.

I freeze, unable to come up with a good reason not to honor her request. She had spent almost eight hours traipsing across Lasso County with my sons. She deserves a night off. Just not tonight.

"No! Miss Mya, you have to come over," Finnegan says.

Declan looks at Finn with wide eyes, then turns to Mya. "It won't be the same if you're not there."

"Come on, guys. Can't you let me off the hook this one time?" Mya glances at me for back-up, but I can't give it.

I give her the same sad eyes she's getting from my kids.

"Not you, too, Ronan!" Mya says, resting a hand on my arm. I love the feel of her touch.

"I don't work tomorrow. You could always stay over and I take you back in the morning," I suggest. Come on, baby. Say yes.

Declan tugs on Mya's arm. "We have to celebrate tonight."

"Yes, tonight. It has to be tonight," Finnegan adds.

I cringe, then glance at Mya. "What do you say?"

"With three handsome men looking at me like y'all are, how could I say no?" Mya heads around the SUV to the passenger side.

I give my boys a wink and a round of high-fives.

Tonight is going to be one Mya won't forget.

CHAPTER 48

M^{YA}

I YAWN FOR THE HUNDREDTH TIME AND RECLINE THE SEAT
further. Ronan's hand rests on my thigh, his thumb brushing back and
forth against my skin. The sensation is soothing and intimate. His
touch is gentle and full of the love he has for me.

If I wasn't so exhausted, I'd pinch myself.

A month ago, I thought this life I'm living was a fantasy. A dream
that would never come true, yet here I am living it now. I turn my head
to see Ronan focused on the road. He looks tense as a quietness settles
in the car. I wonder what he's thinking.

In the back seat, Finnegan and Declan are exchanging looks with
each other. That strange way they have of communicating without
saying a word. They must be as tired as I am, but they look wired and
… excited.

Ronan pulls into the driveway but doesn't open the garage. Instead, he gets the boys out of the backseat, then comes around to open the door for me.

"Will you open the door for them?" Ronan asks stiffly as he tosses the keys toward me. "I need to get the rest of the stuff out of the back."

"Sure," I say, catching them in the air.

Finnegan and Declan trip over themselves to follow me to the door. I look down at them and see them giggling and exchanging conspiratorial looks. Ronan is only a few feet behind us, holding two backpacks stuffed full of the remnants of today's activities.

I put the key in the door and turn the knob.

"Oh my ... God," I say, frozen to the spot.

A banner hung across the living room reads, "Will you be part of our family?" Beneath the words are five drawn figures, two that look like Finnegan and Declan next to a dog the same color as mine. A towering fourth figure is definitely Ronan, and then a fifth in between them looks a lot like ... me.

Beneath the banner, sitting on the coffee table, were a dozen red roses and a box of chocolates. Jellybean barked and trotted into the middle of the room. A green bow is tied around his neck. He wags his tail and barks again.

I walk toward him, unable to take my eyes off the banner.

Turning around, I see Ronan standing in the middle holding his sons' hands.

"Go ahead," he whispers to them.

Finnegan clears his throat, then hops in front. "Miss Mya, we all love you so much. You are just like a mommy to me and Declan."

Declan looks up at Ronan. Ronan nods at him.

Declan hops to stand next to Finnegan and says, "Miss Nikki has two mommies. She has granny and her ... mum ... in London." He giggles. "Mum! That's so weird." He laughs again. "Miss Nikki says it's okay if we have two mommies."

"Miss Nikki is our mommy," Finnegan says, then smiles brightly. "And we want you to be our mommy, too!"

I suck in a breath as tears spring to my eyes.

Ronan steps forward, then sinks down on one knee. "Mya, I can't imagine spending my life without you. From the moment we met, I couldn't deny that you were special. Back then, I didn't know how special you are, but I do now. I love you with everything I am. You make me a better man and I want to spend every day in the future making you happy." Ronan reaches into his pocket and pulls out a black velvet box.

When he opens it, I gasp. A gorgeous emerald ring surrounded by diamonds rests in the center. Declan and Finnegan wiggle and hug each other.

"It's a green ring, Miss Mya," Finnegan says.

Declan adds, "Our favorite color."

Ronan gives them a look and they quiet down. When he looks back at me, I see the tears welling in his eyes. My heart is about to burst with happiness as he says, "I want nothing more than for you to be my wife. Will you marry me?"

I drop to my knees and rest my hands on the sides of his face. A tear escapes his eye and I kiss it away. I take my time and savor this moment, memorizing every part, then say, "Absolutely yes!"

Ronan grabs me and gives me a blistering kiss, his lips devouring mine as the boys hop and jump on top of us. When we come up for air, I turn to his sons and grab them.

"And yes, I would love to be your second mommy," I say, tickling them as they giggle and squirm in my arms. "I love you, Finnegan. I love you, Declan."

The boys yell, "We love you, Miss Mya!"

The words fill my heart with so much love. I think I'm about to burst.

"Now, aren't you happy you came home with us to celebrate?" Ronan asks.

"Best decision I made all day."

An hour later, after we ate all the chocolates and followed up with celebration banana splits, I watch from the doorway as Ronan carries the sleeping boys into their room. The emerald engagement ring sparkles in the light and fits perfectly on my finger. It's breathtaking, like the handsome, ginger man who gave it to me. Ronan tucks each boy into bed, kissing them on the head.

"I didn't think they'd ever get sleepy," I say, as he walks out of their room and closes the door behind him.

"Yeah, it's like they hit a wall and couldn't keep their eyes open. They'll be sleeping late tomorrow," Ronan says, then leans in to place a soft kiss on my lips. "You like the ring? It's untraditional."

"Perfect for our untraditional family, don't you think?" I say.

Ronan nods.

"Honestly, I love it. It's stunning." I wrap my arms around his waist and lean against his chest as he pulls me into a warm embrace. "And I love you. I feel so lucky right now."

Ronan's hand caresses my face, tilting my head to look up at him and says, "Trust me. I'm the lucky one."

Want more of Mya and Ronan? Get a bonus alternative scene delivered straight to your email inbox!
https://BookHip.com/QPDMZAS

Next up to find love in Kimbell, Texas is Ronan's friend Wiley Alexander. Wiley doesn't care about finding love, even though the dating app he created is singularly focused on using AI to help people find their soul mates. But a surprising gift falls in his lap when Zaire Kincaid becomes the key to everything he wants, professionally and ... in love.

Check out the next book in the Kimbell Texas Sweet Romances ...
FAKING LOVE!

ABOUT THE AUTHOR

Angel S. Vane never imagined she'd stumble into becoming an author. An avid fan of books her whole life combined with an active imagination were the right ingredients to embark on a single goal of completing one book.

Now she's written several books and has tapped into her love of Jane Austen novels by writing her own brand of satisfyingly sweet romances. Learn more at Angel's website.

ABOUT THE PUBLISHER

BONZAIMOON BOOKS

BonzaiMoon Books is a family-run, artisanal publishing company created in the summer of 2014. We publish works of fiction in various genres. Our passion and focus is working with authors who write the books you want to read, and giving those authors the opportunity to have more direct input in the publishing of their work.

For more information:
www.bonzaimoonbooks.com
info@bonzaimoonbooks.com

facebook.com/BonzaiMoonBooks